By the same author:

Miss Armistead Makes Her Choice

Miss Armistead Makes Her Choice

HEIDI ASHWORTH

Cover design by Laura J Miller
www.anauthorsart.com

ISBN-13: 978-0996104418
ISBN-10: 0996104410

*To my husband, the triumphant
participant of all three
love triangles I experienced
prior to our marriage.
Therein lies my inspiration.*

And to Sophie Andrews—she knows why.

Chapter One

England May 1815

It was fortuitous that Mr. Colin Lloyd-Jones chose to lift his gaze from the pavement at the very moment a matron emerged from her carriage to recklessly step out into his path. The London season had barely begun and Colin was already the injured party in one too many irrevocable tragedies; a collision with said matron should hardly improve his circumstances.

"I beg your pardon, Madame," he said as he thrust his walking stick in the path of his companion, a gorgeously attired young gentleman who, like Colin, was lost in the mental fog of a broken heart. In a graceless but noble action unacknowledged by the matron, the twosome came to an ungainly halt only to be peered at through a pair of thick spectacles in a manner most rude.

"I must confess," his companion bemoaned with a minor adjustment to his faultless cravat, "I have never felt quite so much like an exhibit at the Tower Menagerie."

Colin had his own thoughts on the subject. However, he was forced to delay his riposte so as to rescue the lady from a nasty fall as she caught her kid boot on the threshold to the milliner's shop. Once again, she failed to greet the gesture with even so much as a "good day."

"Bond is meant to be utterly void of the fair sex for the duration of late afternoon," Colin observed. "A man has a right to be availed of the opportunity to stroll down the street without women cluttering up the pavement," he added a bit crossly.

"To be sure, you are quite correct, *mon ami*," Sir Anthony Crenshaw, agreed. "But, pray, do not suggest we eschew Bond Street as thoroughly as we have agreed to obviate the balls and routs of the entire season. We shall be sadly ignorant as to how to place our bets at White's. How might we hope to know who is the loveliest debutante, or which among them shall prove most popular, as well as most likely to be first betrothed, if we are utterly unenlightened as to who is in town?"

Colin opened his mouth to reply, but his attention was abruptly borne away by the sight of a young maiden's face as it appeared at the door of the carriage. She was breathtaking, her heart-shaped face possessed of a pair of large, impossibly green eyes set off by arched brows, black as the hair that curled along her temples.

"If you have had your fill," Sir Anthony drawled, "you had best look away. You are utterly defenseless in the face of such beauty."

As much as the accusation stung, Colin knew it to be just. Quickly, he averted his eyes; there was no point in avoiding the Marriage Mart with all of its balls and soirees if he were to fall head over heels in love with the first new young lady to town since he broke off his engagement with one Miss Cecily Ponsonby.

"I had thought you as eager to stave off parson's mousetrap as I, Tony," Colin accused, unable to resist the return of tit for tat. "Yet you smile at her as if she were the only girl in England." He spoke in tones low enough to prevent his words from coming to the ears of the black-haired beauty as she descended from the carriage and rushed past them with a curious look from her vivid green eyes.

"I am merely considering my bets," Sir Anthony murmured, as a second young lady, this one possessed of a head of thick, blonde curls very reminiscent of his erstwhile bride-to-be, descended from the carriage to enter the shop. "Besides, I have had years to recover from my heartless wench whilst you have had less than a fortnight."

"Perhaps we ought to forswear betting on the outcome of this season as well as the enjoyment of its convivialities, Tony," Colin suggested as they headed down the street in pursuit of a round of boxing at Gentleman Jackson's establishment. "We should hardly be expected to get it right whilst avoiding the subject, altogether."

Sir Anthony looked his horror. "No balls, no routs, no parties or soirees; what else is there to do, Jonesy, if we cannot, at the very least, bet?"

Colin brushed aside the tug he felt at his back, the one that insisted he turn about and enter the shop containing the green-eyed beauty under the pretense of purchasing a pair of gloves for his sister. "Why, there is riding, hunting, shooting, gambling, and boxing, naturally," Colin replied with a gesture that indicated they had arrived at their destination. "However, am I right in thinking you are hesitant to enter?"

Sir Anthony failed to reply though his glance down the street in the direction of the waiting carriage confirmed Colin's suspicions. "You only admire her because she puts you in mind of Rebecca," Colin admonished. "However, I am persuaded she is a finer young lady than Rebecca ever was."

"Everyone is a finer young lady than Rebecca ever was," Sir Anthony replied, "except perhaps your Cecily."

"There, now, you needn't twist the knife in my back," Colin retorted. "She is *not* my Cecily. If that scallywag Rogers-Reimann is to be believed, she is presently Trevelin's difficulty."

Sir Anthony raised his looking glass to his eye through which he observed his friend. "Do I detect a reluctance to fully trust the word of said scallywag?"

"He is hardly the epitome of virtue, I confess," Colin replied grudgingly. "Still, it is not worth the risk. Her reputation is in tatters, either way, and so would mine be if we were to don leg-shackles. My father, when he heard of it, refused to hear another word. In short, the subject of our marriage was closed. When he informed my stepmother of what had transpired, she locked herself in her room for the better part of a week. As to my sister . . " Colin added, pausing to consider his words. He was inordinately fond of his sister and did not wish to overstate the case. "My sister has her come-out this year and her marriage prospects would have been sadly reduced should I, in spite of everything, have wed Cecily."

"And what of yourself, Jonesy?" Sir Anthony quizzed. "Do you not think it best to have learned the truth before it was too late?"

"Yes, to be sure! But you know as well as any that to find you are not the one to which your betrothed has given herself is a painful prospect, whether the giving occurred before or after the betrothal was announced in the papers."

"You discredit yourself, Jonesy; I was given to understand that the, er, *giving*, occurred a number of years ago." Sir Anthony sighed and patted his friend on the back. "Either way, it is a painful prospect, indeed. Is Trevelin to do the right thing by the girl, then?"

"I should say not," Colin rasped with a jab of his cane into the air. "Worse yet, it is said that her father has disowned her and that she is living on her own with no visible means of support. I hope to God it isn't true," he added under his breath.

"Either way, the fault is to be laid in Trevelin's dish, not yours. What's more, the chit passed herself off as unsullied. For all you know, five months after the wedding, you should have been presented with an 'heir'. Then where should you be?"

Colin rubbed a hand over his face. "You are right, Tony, no doubting. I only wish her character had been otherwise; either that, or my circumstances. If only I had never fancied myself in love with her," he ground out.

"Now, you mustn't go down that road," Sir Anthony implored as he took his friend by the shoulders and steered him into

Jackson's. "A few punches in the phiz will clear your head and pain you considerably less."

Colin allowed himself to be pressed into a bout though he remained unconvinced it would be in the least beneficial. As such, he was amazed by how much the pain in his face assuaged his aching heart. His mood was most improved, however, by the fist he landed on his friend's perfect nose. In spite of Sir Anthony's incipient rage, they quit Jackson's in perfect amity.

"Same time tomorrow, then, Tony?" Colin asked.

"Perhaps we had best make it day after next," Sir Anthony suggested as he took his nose gingerly between his fingers. "Once this proboscis swells as it is meant to, it will make far too ready a target."

"'Tis swollen already, Tony, just like your head," Colin quipped as he tipped his hat to his friend and walked briskly down the street. It wasn't until he reached the milliner's establishment into which the raven-haired beauty had earlier disappeared that he realized he had forgotten her entirely. Quick as a flash he calculated the likelihood that she would be first betrothed during the course of the Season but owned that he could not give her odds a full one hundred percent without first knowing the depth of her dowry or the ascendency of her ancestors.

He finally settled on ninety-nine percent, a number that was owed almost entirely to her beauty, in the case she was an orphan of indeterminate parentage. However, he resolved to discover the facts before placing his bet in the book at White's.

As he stepped down the street in the direction of home, he suddenly recalled home was now in the other direction as he had, upon his betrothal, quit his father's establishment in favor of a lease on a townhouse. Miss Cecily Ponsonby had been by his side when the neighborhood was chosen, as well as the house itself, and lastly the furnishings and the decorations. His heart squeezed painfully as he realized she had willingly fitted his house, knowing all the while she was not fit to be his bride.

Though he would have much preferred to go home and take solace in the company of his sister, he spun on his heel and strode to the new house. Having watched for his master's approach through the bow front window, the butler swung wide the door for Colin's entrance. He felt he ought to have been gratified by the obsequious actions of this new and scarcely tried servant, but there was room for no other feeling in Colin's soul but regret.

He whipped off his hat and gloves, dropped them into the butler's hands, and moved swiftly into the ground floor library to throw himself into his seat by the fire. The wing backed chair was one of a pair in a floral pattern chosen by Cecily, and he was filled with remorse that he had allowed a woman to choose the decor for a room as sacred as his private sanctum. He entirely regretted the chairs, the too-fussy drapes at the bank of windows, and the carved carpet adorned with birds bearing fanciful, impossibly long tails. Most of all he regretted that he had fallen in love with Cecily; that he had ever laid eyes on her; that he yet lived.

A quarter of an hour passed in a state of deep despondency until, finally, he decided he was too young for such bitterness and too ravenous to die. He rang the bell for the butler whom he instructed to serve supper on a tray brought to the library as he was in no mood to take his meal in the dining room. It was currently adorned with lavender wallpaper hung all around with landscapes of flower gardens and it never failed to make him bilious. The very thought led him to assign the making of plans to redecorate the entire house his first order of business on the morrow.

He hadn't long to further reflect on his woes before the door was opened by the butler, the promised dinner tray conspicuously absent.

"If you presume you might cajole me into repairing to the dining room, you are quite mistaken," Colin began, but was robbed of further speech when the butler stepped aside to reveal the very young lady with the jet black hair and emerald green eyes he had first seen on Bond Street not two hours since. He stared at her in some astonishment and fancied that her answering surprise was as artful as was the way she twisted her hands about in her muff.

"Sir, you must beg my pardon for I knew not what else to do. My mother would have had me march down Bond Street to seek help and it already well into the afternoon. I fear I should have been assumed a woman of questionable morals were I seen on the street at such a time." With a sweep of long, black lashes, she trained her gaze at the floor. "I must ask pardon for my mother. She has been in India for so long, she has forgotten the ways of London."

As the girl's voice trailed into silence Colin had but one thought: no woman could be as fair of face and form as she and be possessed of such upright sensibilities. He knew it was the pain of Cecily's betrayal that hardened his heart but he felt powerless to allow his opinion to soften towards the young lady at his door.

"And you have remembered what your mother has not?" he queried as he rose warily to his feet.

"I have been in England more recently," she replied, looking up to squarely meet his gaze. "I enjoyed my come-out in London four years ago under the auspices of my aunt."

"Ah." He picked up a branch of candles and held them up so as to better inspect his visitor. Surely, if this girl had had a London season, she should have been quickly snaffled. Yet he detected no telling lump under her glove to signify a wedding band and there was a decided lack of lace cap under the smart bonnet she wore. "What help, then, do you seek Miss . . ?"

"Miss Armistead." She regarded him steadily from her inconceivably green eyes. "My father is John Armistead of the East India Company."

Colin caught his breath before it hissed out between his teeth. "Daughter of a nabob are you?" he suggested, though he hardly dared think it to be true. Beautiful, good *and* rich? Such a possibility required too much of his trust.

"Perhaps I might explain," the butler intoned. "One of their team has thrown a shoe in the road just in front of the house."

This time Colin felt his astonishment in full. Did she think him fool enough to believe that a second encounter in as many hours was naught but coincidence? That she and her mother had followed him home after spying on him through the window of the milliner's was blatant. What they wanted of him, he had no idea, but he had been used by a woman once too often, already. "Could not the groom have walked the horse to a stables?" he asked, far too tersely to be deemed polite.

The girl's face crumpled a bit, but she quickly regained command of herself. "He was most willing to do so but Mama refused to allow him to desert her. When I parted from Miss Hale—my friend who has come to London with us from Bengal—she was suffering from a fit of the vapors and Mama, who feels London to be a very wicked place indeed, was not far from it."

Colin made no reply. Instead, he held the candles even higher to peer into her eyes as if in search of a truth she refused to utter.

"Sir!" the girl insisted. "There are two women suffering palpitations in the road before your very door and you trouble me with questions. Is it not enough to know that three females are in need of your protection?"

"Yes, of course," Colin acknowledged, his feelings a distressing muddle of doubt and shame. "Evans, have the boot boy take the horse in hand and invite Mrs. Armistead and . . Miss Hale, is it?" he asked with a questioning look for Miss Armistead who stood with such an admirable lack of temerity in his library. She nodded and he continued. "Ah! Invite them to come and join us here by the fire until the horse is properly shod." He waved a hand at one of the wing chairs to indicate that she should be seated.

"Thank you," she said as she moved to the chair with a grace that was not in the least diminished by her haste. He felt, once again, shamed as he realized how he had forced her to stand in the chill draft of the doorway far too long.

"Pray tell, by whose fire do I warm myself?" she inquired.

"I do beg your pardon, Miss Armistead," he replied, feeling thoroughly humbled for the third time in far too short a space of time. "I am Mr. Colin Lloyd-Jones, not to be confused with Mr. Lloyd-Jones, my father." He knew he ought to say more, but he hadn't the least idea what that should be. His thoughts were divided upon the subjects of her admirable poise and how the flames reflected in her glossy black curls, all the while wholly aware that these were topics of conversation to be avoided at all costs.

"I pray I do not in any way inconvenience Mrs. Lloyd-Jones," Miss Armistead ventured as she peeled off her gloves and raised her hands to the fire. When he did not immediately answer, she turned to bestow on him a smile, one which ignited her entire countenance with an even greater beauty.

As he replaced the candelabra and took up a seat across from her, he wondered yet again how such a diamond of the first water had not been spoken for during her London season or how he had failed to notice her at the time. Worse, he couldn't begin to fathom what fearful occurrence prevented her from making a sparkling match long since. Her desperation was clearly evident in the way she had pounded on his door in the dusk of evening in an overt attempt to scheme her way into marriage with him. Now she was asking, oh so delicately, if there were a Mrs. Lloyd-Jones. The whole of it was utterly mystifying.

"Sir, I beg your pardon," she murmured, her eyes wide with what looked to be apprehension. "I am persuaded I have misspoken. Pray, forgive my impudence."

The truth came to Colin's tongue before he had time to consider. "No, not at all impudent," he assured her, even as he wondered at her capacity to transform his doubt into full commiseration.

He, however, failed to reveal his marital status, an omission that prompted her to turn her bewitching gaze upon him in a manner so divested of guile he knew not where to look. Mercifully, the discomfiture of the moment was put at an end by a knock on the door and the entrance of Mrs. Armistead, her eyes owl-like behind her spectacles. She was followed by whom he presumed to be Miss Hale, whose tear-streaked face and disordered locks denoted such genuine distress, he was instantly contrite.

"Please be seated, Mrs. Armistead," he insisted as he leapt to his feet and indicated that she should take up his own chair. Miss Armistead also rose in favor of her friend, but he persuaded her to stay put, collected another chair from the corner and placed it in front of the fire with the others.

"Thank you," Miss Hale said in a girlish voice that belied her full-blown looks. "I had thought we must surely freeze to death before help came!"

Miss Armistead's gaze flew up in dismay and Colin wondered if her agitation at Miss Hale's bald admission was further evidence of Miss Armistead's impeccable manners or merely the mark of her determination to gain his favor.

"We are recently arrived from India and are not accustomed to the cold," her mother hastened to remark.

"Your rescue might have come sooner if you had sent the groom for help," he observed shortly, "rather than send a young maiden out into the night." He could not like Mrs. Armistead but feared that his manner bordered on an insolence that betrayed his refusal to be, once again, in the wrong. However, it was his instinctive desire to protect and defend Miss Armistead that troubled him most.

"I must confess it is my abject fear of the city that is to blame. You see," Mrs. Armistead continued with an unctuous smile, "I so feared being alone without male protection. I am ever so fortunate to have such an intrepid daughter as I do in Elizabeth. I knew she could not fail us."

Colin imagined a flash of understanding passed between the mother and her daughter, one which denoted their triumph at having landed themselves in such favorable circumstances, and he quickly turned to gage Miss Armistead's expression. He was not fast enough, it seemed, for he found her looking demurely into her lap, her lips devoid of the air of victory he was persuaded would adorn them.

"But, surely, Mrs. Armistead, you are aware that the streets of London are not where a well-favored young lady should be found so late in the day unless appropriately accompanied." He neglected to add that Bond Street was meant to be the sole province of males once the shadows began to lengthen, a fact of which she should certainly have been in possession, India or no.

"Oh, dear! Is that so?" she replied with a flutter of her hands. "I hadn't the slightest idea. Dearest Elizabeth did mention something along those lines, but Miss Hale was weeping so volubly that I was unable to make out what Elizabeth was saying. Dearest," she said, turning to Miss Armistead. "I had not wished to subject you to such peril. How fortunate we are that this fine gentleman was by."

"Yes, Mama," Miss Armistead replied as she reached out to pat her mother on the hand, "we are. However, it would be rude beyond bearing if we were to trouble Mr. Lloyd-Jones for a bit longer than need be. I am persuaded he was just about to sit down to his dinner when I arrived and for that I am most contrite."

"Mr. Lloyd-Jones?" her mother asked with a nervous twitter. "Don't say you are one of the Shropshire Lloyd-Joneses!" she exclaimed. "But, of course you are! How could I not have seen it immediately? Why, I grew up in the parsonage at Kempton and have many a pleasant memory of your father and uncles riding out on their lovely horses."

Colin subdued a groan. Here it was, the vexatious groveling over his family and their fulsome funds followed by the gushing recital of connections and common relations, most of which were invented out of whole cloth. Worse was his realization that the

Armistead's knew to lie in wait for him. Mrs. Armistead must have noted the family resemblance the moment she clapped eyes on him; gray eyes, dark, curly locks and a dusky complexion were the Welsh inheritance of each and every Lloyd-Jones of his acquaintance.

Drawing deeply upon the well of generations of training, he allowed the expected smile to curve his lips. "Yes, indeed" he replied as he sketched the matron a brief bow. "I believe your people are no longer living at the parsonage," he added with a sidelong look at Miss Armistead in order to know her reaction. He was puzzled by the color that suffused her face and more so by how she continued to gaze steadily into her lap. The thought had more than once crossed his mind that she must be an excellent actress, but he was forced to own that it was impossible to feign a sincere blush.

Mrs. Armistead must have taken in her daughter's discomposure, as well. "Oh, my, have I misspoken?" Mrs. Armistead asked.

"No, Mama, it's only that I am persuaded we have troubled Mr. Lloyd-Jones long enough. Perhaps he ought to be relieved of his duties as host. We shall do quite well on our own, shall we not?"

"Dinner has been pushed back, already," Colin said with a wave of his hand at the butler who had toed open the door and was listening for his prompt to enter the library. "It would not be equitable to require Cook to bring it on again so soon." With his words, the butler's highly polished shoe disappeared from behind the door that shut so quietly even Colin did not hear it. To his chagrin, he was now fully committed to the entertainment of the ladies until they might be once again on their way.

There followed a thorny silence before Mrs. Armistead made what promised to be another unfortunate attempt at small talk. "There is to be a ball at the Carruth's in two days time. As a Lloyd-Jones, I warrant you must have been written in at the top of the guest list. Have you plans to attend?"

"You honor me, ma'am, but I don't believe I have been invited to that particular ball." Colin restrained himself from looking to the mantle where lay the invitation designed to proffer him entrance to the very ball of which she spoke.

"Oh, dear! Well, then, what about the Green's do Tuesday next?"

"No, I am afraid I have not received that invitation, either," Colin replied in mild tones at odds with the pounding in his head. He hadn't an aptitude for deceit and he feared the insightful Miss Armistead saw through his denials.

"What of the Russell's; have you not received their invitation?" Colin merely gave her a terse smile, unwilling to say anything that would further expose his perfidy, but she would not be silent. "It is certain you have received word of the Ames' ball. And the Roberts'? Or perhaps the Scott-Montgomery's?"

Colin silently shook his head with each name and prayed she would run out of friends and acquaintances before he, in a too conspicuous move, jumped to his feet and consigned the stack of invitations on his mantle to the flames below it.

"Mr. Lloyd-Jones, you grace the portals of Almack's on occasion, do you not?" Miss Armistead asked in reasonable tones. They unaccountably served to soothe his frayed nerves in spite of his suspicions that she was aiding her mother in a quest to ascertain his schedule.

"Not often. In point of fact, I have sworn to a friend of mine that we should avoid all such entertainments this season." Rather than be dismayed at his revelation of such a personal nature, he was relieved to give the ladies the truth, one which had no reflection on them at all whatsoever. In spite of that, a shadow passed over Miss Armistead's face as if he had indeed dissembled at their expense.

"What a pity," Miss Hales remarked. "I am persuaded I should have very much enjoyed dancing with you."

Miss Armistead leaned forward and intently regarded her friend. However, Miss Hale seemed impervious to the silent admonition.

"You can't be anything but an exquisite dancer, what with those longs legs of yours," Miss Hale continued shamelessly.

"Miss Hale," Miss Armistead cut in. "You forget yourself. It is one thing to talk so amongst the officers back home, but you will find that few in London society shall look on you with favor if you do not mind your tongue."

"I only wished to dance with him, Elizabeth, not wed him," Miss Hale said with a pert air.

This admission seemed only to deepen Miss Armistead's vexation and she rose quickly to her feet. "Mr. Lloyd-Jones, we thank you for your congenial hospitality but perhaps it would be best if we waited elsewhere."

As it seemed unlikely that they should ever again lay eyes on one another, Colin was loathe to be so rude as to send them away. "I won't hear of it. As a bachelor who lives alone, I am most often deprived of such genteel company." As he listened to the words he spoke, he was surprised to know that they were indeed, true. Convinced that he would never again allow himself to be caught in the talons of a Cecily Ponsonby, he felt unaccountably safe admiring the disingenuous Miss Armistead from the distance his wounded heart afforded. Certainly, the heat from the fire had never turned Cecily's cheeks such a delicious shade of pink nor had her pale blue eyes sparkled as, even now, Miss Armistead's green ones did, for any reason at all whatsoever. So lost was he in his thoughts that he, at first, failed to notice that Miss Armistead still stood as if about to depart.

"Miss Armistead," he admonished as he rose to his feet, "do take your seat." When she did not immediately comply, he dared to take her by the elbow so as to guide her descent into the wing backed chair. He was unprepared for the flash of resistance she demonstrated and was utterly confounded by how the rigidity of her arm dissolved into compliance once she had raised her magnificent eyes to look into his.

She was far too beautiful to fail to recognize his admiration of her; as such, he had expected her to be immune to the veneration she had surely recognized in his expression. Instead, her face betrayed an emotion to which he could assign no name save that of wonderment and, in spite of his hand at her elbow, she descended as did a hot knife through butter, staring into his eyes all the while.

"Caught another one in your net, have you, Elizabeth?" Miss Hale twittered. "Still, it shall be of no account now that you are betrothed to your Duncan."

Colin felt as if the ground had shifted under his feet. "Betrothed?" he asked of no one in particular, unwilling to believe that he could have been so wrong about these three women. Certainly, he could not be, not so close on the heels of his having been so very wrong about Miss Cecily Ponsonby.

"Well, yes, Mr. Lloyd-Jones," Mrs. Armistead said faintly. "We have come for the procurement of bride clothes for Elizabeth, you see. We intend to vastly enjoy society whilst we wait for her intended to join her in a month or so. Once they are married, Miss Hale and I shall return to India."

Colin could feel the frown that furrowed his brow as he fell back a step and regarded the women with fresh eyes. The scheming mother now looked to be the frightened traveler she was and Miss Hale less the innocent ingénue, while the beautiful coquette was nothing but a misunderstood maiden. The shock of these revelations was nothing compared to the taste of ashes in his mouth when he realized that the gorgeous Miss Armistead was not in the least obtainable, his patent admiration of her not in the least proper, and that he had made a fool of himself over a woman for the second time in as many weeks.

With a swift intake of breath that, even in his own ears, sounded suspiciously like a gasp, he turned away from the trio of women he had so willingly assumed to be imbued with every possible unsavory intention and sunk his face into his hand. Not for the first time that night, he was grateful for the pact that he and Tony had made; he needs must never be in the company of any of these women again. The very moment a silent prayer for speedy deliverance was sent aloft, the butler rapped at the door and entered with news that the team and carriage were ready and waiting to convey the ladies to their lodgings.

Colin pulled the ravaged edges of his pride about himself in order to bid a proper farewell to Mrs. Armistead, her daughter and her friend and heaved a huge sigh of relief when the library door had shut behind them. As he stared into the fire, he recalled that Tony had warned him about gazing overlong on the face of one as beautiful as Miss Armistead and knew that his friend had the right of it. He had never felt quite so pulled in before, and never on so short of an acquaintance. His eyes went again to the invitations on the mantle and with a flick of his wrist he dispatched them to the flames. There was nothing, now, that could dissuade him from keeping his distance from Miss Armistead and all of her ilk for the remainder of the season.

Chapter Two

M iss Elizabeth Armistead did not wish to be observed. As
such, she stood behind a potted palm in a dark corner of
the Carruth's ballroom, a circumstance that had little to do with
the repeated requests by her aunt to partner a spotty-faced boy.
She was persuaded his governess should certainly arrive to carry
him home to bed any moment, never mind that he was over six
foot tall and, of all things, an earl. No, indeed, her hiding place
afforded her the opportunity to glean much from the breathless
conversations that sailed past her unawares.

From these, she discerned that a recent *contretemps* on the
dance floor had been occasioned by one Miss Ginerva Delacourt
who was rumored to have said something unforgivably shocking.
However, no one agreed on the words she spoke. Some said she
had called her dancing partner, Lord Eggleston, a simpleton while
others insisted that her words, in reference to his lordship's mother,
were "weighs a ton".

Under the circumstances, Elizabeth felt it was likely she had
merely uttered "Mother Eggleston" and was being unduly cen-
sured for what must surely be the fault of his lordship's feeble
hearing. From what Elizabeth could determine Lord Eggleston
was on the windy side of forty and had no business inducing a
young woman such as Miss Delacourt to dance in the first place.
The fact that Lady Eggleston was, indeed, doomed never again

to sit on a daintily constructed chair merely added fuel to the fire.

Elizabeth, who watched the proceedings unfold, found Lord Eggleston's behavior in the wake of his outrage far inferior to Miss Delacourt's as he had stalked off to leave her quite alone on the dance floor. This had caused such confusion amongst the other dancers in the set that they were soon seen to mill about in so disordered a fashion that those watching from the perimeters of the room began to point whilst chortling into their respective handkerchiefs. It was with a great deal of composure, chin held high, that Miss Delacourt had walked away in the opposite direction of her feckless dancing partner.

She had been met by a tiny woman with red hair upon which perched a turban whose arrangement was endangered by her ferociously raised eyebrows. It was only then that Miss Delacourt had bowed her head. Elizabeth doubted any but herself, who was free to gape to her heart's content, had seen how the young lady dashed away her tears, so deftly was it done.

Elizabeth's own eyes filled as she reflected on what she had witnessed. Not for the first time that night, she thanked her lucky stars that she was safely betrothed to Duncan Cruikshank, a man who cared for her as much as she cared for him. She need never again be concerned for her future as was Miss Delacourt and, perhaps more so, the red-haired woman at her side.

Elizabeth continued to observe as the woman marched out of the room into the colonnaded gallery alongside it, Miss Delacourt following behind, her head once again held high. With a sigh, Elizabeth began to emerge from her hiding place until she noticed that Miss Delacourt and her red-haired doyenne were headed in her direction. It would be some time before they reached the end of the gallery and returned to the dance floor to obtain the exit from the room, but Elizabeth knew that if she stirred an inch, she should be caught out. How much more appealing it seemed to regard the two women from her current position in hopes of overhearing as much of their conversation as possible.

She had not long to wait.

"What you could have been thinking, I cannot imagine!" the tiny woman demanded.

"It hardly matters now what I was thinking," Miss Delacourt observed. "I am to be vilified regardless of the truth."

"It would not be so," the older woman said as she stopped to catch her breath just the other side of Elizabeth's palm, "if you hadn't the distinction of being known to say exactly what you please. I can see that it has put you quite beyond the pale."

"Grandaunt Regina, you cannot believe that the purely innocent, though, admittedly unfortunate, remarks I made at Lady Jersey's rout are still being bandied about. That was three weeks ago."

"They are and they will until you make a respectable marriage or quit London society altogether, one or the other. For now, I think that is precisely the solution."

"Which is the solution?" Miss Delacourt asked with an arch look. "Or is it both? Though I fail to see how it matters as I have no say, one way or the other."

"That is quite enough," the woman huffed as she turned to resume her journey to the exit. Miss Delacourt once again bowed her head but not before Elizabeth heard the young lady mutter something nonsensical having to do with the superior company of roses over the *ton*.

Once they had marched out of earshot, Elizabeth drew a deep breath and emerged from behind the palm tree. The dancing had re-commenced and the high society lords and ladies chatted amongst themselves as if nothing had occurred. She was relieved to see that the brouhaha had blown over and, as a final boon the ladder-tall, young earl was occupied on the dance floor. Quickly she located her mother and aunt and made her way to their sides.

"Why, Elizabeth," her mother said sharply, "I had believed you to be doing the jig."

"No, Mama, I was merely amusing myself on my own. I suppose I wandered off a bit."

"Well, see that you don't," Elizabeth's Aunt Augusta insisted. "It is not seemly for a young lady to wander off, as you so summarily phrased it."

"Elizabeth wouldn't dream of provoking gossip, would you Elizabeth?" Mrs. Armistead urged as she turned to her daughter, her eyebrows raised high above her spectacles.

"Of course not," Elizabeth replied in mild tones she did not feel. She couldn't say why, exactly, it vexed her so much that her mother was in agreement with her sister-in-law unless it was that it happened so very rarely. "However, it is rather distressing to be chastised for my intrepid nature when it was praised only a few days since. I suppose it was due to the company we were keeping while at the home of Mr. Lloyd-Jones; doubtless you wished to present me in the best light."

"But of course I did. You are so much more than your beauty, my dear, and I wish all to perceive it," her mother soothed.

Elizabeth felt her mother's attempts to be of no consequence; Mr. Lloyd-Jones was as incapable of seeing past her outward appearance as every other man she had met, save her father and, of course, her betrothed. At first she had believed Mr. Lloyd-Jones to be different, but then he had looked at her with such naked admiration in his eyes and she knew that he was as caught up in her outward appearance as any other. She felt astonished by the keen sense of disappointment she felt upon the realization of the truth.

"Elizabeth, see here, the music has stopped and Lord Northrup approaches to ask you to dance after all!" Aunt Augusta enthused. "I cannot imagine why he hasn't worked up the courage to do so until now. If only you had allowed me to introduce you to him, you might have been dancing all the evening."

"Aunt Augusta, I am in your debt, but I do believe you have forgotten that I have come to London to make preparations for a wedding, not to find a husband."

"Oh, pshaw!" her aunt insisted with a deft unfurling of her fan.

Lord Northrup was now upon them and, to Elizabeth's dismay there was no escaping the following introductions. She assigned herself high marks for her forbearance, as well as a perfectly executed bow, but from the moment he took her in his arms and whirled her away to the strains of a waltz she made no attempt to charm him. She had been admired by more men than she could count, all of whom bore the same stunned expression on his face as the young earl. It was an expression she loathed, just as she loathed the hypocrisy of those who professed to love her, but only wished to possess her beauty.

In spite of the heat of India, she longed to go home, longed for the safety of a society that considered her no longer on the Marriage Mart. She had been born and raised in Bengal, yet she found her nature was far more inclined towards the atmospheric conditions of England. She had vastly enjoyed spending time in London during the course of her season four years prior and often wondered if her attraction to her betrothed was as much due to his very Englishness as it was his other qualities. The fact that his home was in Scotland and they would repair to Edinburgh directly after the wedding was an eventuality to which she looked forward with great anticipation. And yet, she longed for what she had left behind.

Lord Northrup cleared his throat. "What a brown study, Miss Armistead! Of what are you thinking, might I ask?"

"But, of course you might ask, my lord. However, I fear the answer isn't terribly diverting."

"No doubt one as enchanting as yourself is possessed of nothing but thoughts equally so."

"Very well, if you insist; I was thinking on my *modiste* appointment on the morrow." She inclined her head. "Pray tell, does that enchant as expected?"

"Yes, indeed!" he replied with relish, the spots on his cheeks turning white against his reddening skin. "Though I can't envisage how a new gown might possibly improve your appearance one whit."

"If you say so, but I am persuaded the opinion of my betrothed will differ when I don my new gown for our wedding."

His face turned red to the roots of his hair, most likely due to the fact that he had taken a deep breath which he held between his enlarged cheeks.

"Lord Northrup, you mustn't take on, so. Your petulance very well may be observed by any number of young ladies, all of them currently most eager to be courted by you," she said with a kind smile.

"Not one of them can hope to outshine you," he blurted out on a gust of air. "You are the most beautiful girl in the room!"

"If you say so," she replied tonelessly. "However, let us speak of you. I imagine that your mother, on any number of occasions, has led you to believe you deserve the very best of everything. And who is to say she is wrong? Certainly not I. However, I am persuaded you ought to pursue a younger lady if it is marriage you are considering." Elizabeth peered about the room, her gaze coming to rest on a very sweet-looking debutante with masses of dark hair, and a pair of fine gray eyes. "Why, I believe she will do very nicely. You must ask her to dance the next set," Elizabeth insisted as she inclined her head in the direction of the dark-haired ingénue.

Lord Northrup turned his head in the direction Elizabeth indicated and grimaced. "By that you would mean Miss Analisa Lloyd-Jones. She is fair enough, I suppose."

"Miss Lloyd-Jones; but of course!" Elizabeth wished to pose a dozen impolite questions of Lord Northrup, every one of them concerning Mr. Lloyd-Jones, but she managed to tamp down her desire. "She seems utterly charming."

"Perhaps, but she is just out of the schoolroom. I don't trail after children, I would have you know," he insisted with a fractious air.

"And you left . . ?"

"Eton," he supplied readily enough.

"How long ago?"

Lord Northrup had the presence of mind to hang his head. "I have only just taken my final exams. M' father promises he shall send me to the Continent for my grand tour when the season is up and says that I shall come home a man," he added, his former bravado returned in full.

"Miss Lloyd-Jones isn't likely to wait on you," Elizabeth noted as she watched the two gentlemen who even now fluttered about the girl like a pair of butterflies.

Lord Northrup followed her gaze and uttered a grunt. "He would never allow such if he were here to see."

"He?" she asked, tantalized.

"Her brother, of course. I have never laid eyes on her except when he was hovering around her like a suit of armor."

"In that case, it is passing strange that he is not in attendance," Elizabeth mused.

"I can't think why he should miss one of his sister's very first balls but, as you can see, he is not present."

It was then that Elizabeth remembered Mr. Lloyd-Jones' claim to have given up the entertainments of the season. She had thought it a polite fiction but perhaps she was mistaken. Whether it was the truth or he stayed away to reinforce the lie, she found it intriguing. Once a man had looked at her the way Mr. Lloyd-Jones had, there was no being shed of him. And yet, he was not present, in spite of his sister's circumstances. She found the idea vastly pleasant and a vision of his exceptionally light gray eyes, heavily fringed with dusky lashes, *would* rise, unbidden, into her mind.

"Am I wrong to presume his absence to be singular?"

"Yes, it is. It was just a fortnight ago that he was seen out and about with his intended, Miss Cecily Ponsonby."

"How very intriguing." Elizabeth was grateful to be finally provided with Mr. Lloyd-Jones' marital status. However, she declined to share her thoughts on his character, a silent narrative that was less than kind. A man who squired his betrothed about in public only to so openly admire another lady in private was nothing but a cad.

"It is not nearly as interesting as what happened the next morning," Lord Northrup said in conspiratorial tones.

"Do refrain from sharing the details, Lord Northrup. I am persuaded they can't be meant for a lady's ears," Elizabeth chided gently.

"How did you know?" he breathed.

"Whatever can you mean, my lord?"

"Don't play coy with me," he said, straightening to his full height. "Of course you have already heard it elsewhere. What does a woman have to do all day but pay calls and blether on about who has done what?"

"Why, you . . !" Elizabeth began, then thought better of it. She had no wish to suffer the same public and humiliating fate as Miss Delacourt. Taking a deep breath, she changed tack. "Lord Northrup, as I have already stated, I have no desire to hear your piece of news. Now, might we go on to discuss something more suitable?"

Lord Northrup accommodated her wish by remaining utterly silent for the remainder of the set. Elizabeth had danced with many young men, some more junior than her current partner, but could not recall when she had been treated with such childishness. It was with a mutual sense of deliverance that they parted ways and she found herself once again under the auspices of her aunt.

"Now, there, Elizabeth, that was not too painful, was it?" Aunt Augusta twitted her.

"I may truthfully say, Aunt, that despite his extreme youth and inexperience, he did not tread on my toes even the once," Elizabeth demurred.

"Well," her aunt purred in approval, "he is young, barely out of his books. The waltz has only been fashionable for a season. He must have had lessons. You doubtless gave him some much needed confidence, as well as something to boast about to his little friends."

"Little, indeed," Elizabeth murmured before turning to her mother and asking after Miss Hale.

"Why, Miss Hale has proven extremely popular. She has danced every set and more than once with at least two young men," Mrs. Armistead reported, her face beaming.

"Mama, you can't be serious. That will never do," Elizabeth chided.

"I did so try to warn her," her aunt said airily before turning her nose into the air.

"Why, Elizabeth, what is there in that to trouble us? It isn't as if she is going to form an attachment to either of them; we are off to India again in a month's time. Any unsavory reputation she might gain in London isn't likely to follow her there."

"I suppose you are correct, as long as she isn't seen as too fast. Those are the sort of girls who find themselves in difficult circumstances. She will be hard-pressed to find a husband, then, officer or no," Elizabeth pointed out.

"That does remind me! Your Aunt Augusta has, just moments ago, shared with me a delectable tidbit about our Mr. Lloyd-Jones!"

"If you are referring to his betrothal to Miss Ponsonby, whoever she might be, I have heard tell of it."

"No! That isn't it. That is to say, it does have something to say to it, however, the interesting portion has to do with his crying off."

"Hortense," Aunt Augusta chimed in, "I relayed that news in the strictest of confidences!"

"Yes, I know, dearest Augusta, but I hadn't thought you meant I shouldn't share it with my own daughter. With whom shall Elizabeth discuss it, pray tell?"

Aunt Augusta merely snorted and turned away, waving her fan as if ridding herself of a foul odor.

"At any rate, Elizabeth, is it not the most outrageous thing? Whoever heard of a man crying off from a betrothal? She mustn't have been as good as she should have been or he would not have dared."

Elizabeth thought of the man she had met and owned that it was likely he had a very good reason to break off his engagement to Miss Ponsonby. He seemed far too full of rectitude to take any action that would needlessly harm the young lady, therefore, it must have been he who was wronged. It was clear that he was the talk of the *ton*, and Elizabeth felt it a small wonder that he was unwilling to appear in company.

"Well, Elizabeth, what have you to say to that?" her mother demanded.

"That he is perhaps not the cad I first thought him," she replied.

"Cad? Of course not! Augusta has just been informing me of how he is the most eligible bachelor on the town! That is to say, he along with his bosom beau, Sir Anthony Crenshaw. I am persuaded that was he with Mr. Lloyd-Jones when we were nearly run over as we entered the milliner's the other day."

"Yes, Mama, I remember." Sir Anthony, if it were he, was indeed a handsome man, but he appeared to be a bit of a peacock. Elizabeth found Mr. Lloyd-Jones' quieter dress and manner far more appealing. He was older than her betrothed and seemed to exude a purity of manliness and sophistication that could not fail to attract.

"But of course you remember! How could one forget two such fine gentlemen?" her mother exclaimed. "And the other night, Mr. Lloyd-Jones was the perfect host and his home so inviting!"

"You have been inside Mr. Lloyd-Jones' home?" Aunt Augusta demanded.

"Yes, we have done, and he was all that is lovely," Elizabeth's mother continued. "One of our team threw a shoe in the street directly in front of his house and he was so good as to allow us to warm our hands at his fire whilst a new shoe could be produced."

"Directly in front of his house," Aunt Augusta echoed, her face turning pale.

"It truly was pure happenstance," Elizabeth hastened to assure her aunt. "We were none of us attempting to scrape up an acquaintance, I do assure you."

"It hardly matters what I think," Aunt Augusta insisted. "It is what he believes to be true that could very well turn the tide of opinion against you. Well," she said as she fanned the heat of shame from her face, "there is naught to be done about it, now. It is well, indeed, that you are not on the hunt for a husband, Elizabeth, as none shall give you a second glance once word of this gets out."

"It's been days, already, Augusta," Mrs. Armistead replied, "and though Elizabeth has not danced overmuch, Miss Hale has proven to be quite popular. If word were to get out, it should have been out already. I am persuaded such a gentleman as Mr. Lloyd-Jones shall continue to refrain from repeating the details of our visit to anyone whose opinion matters in the least."

"Let us hope you are correct," her sister-in-law said with a huff. "I am not accustomed to championing gels who make cakes of themselves."

"Aunt Augusta, once again, though I am grateful for your sponsorship, I haven't the need of it. I am only here tonight at Mama's behest. I could spend our entire holiday in London without another waltz and should happily forfeit any number of parties for the chance to walk through the park in the cool of an evening."

"That is all very well and fine, young lady, but you might, even now, be long married if you hadn't hampered the success of your own come-out when you were last in London," Elizabeth's aunt carped.

"What is this about?" Elizabeth's mother asked, her eyes round with curiosity.

"It is nothing, Mama, only that I did not put myself out to seduce a man I did not love into offering for me."

"Men, Elizabeth. Not man; men," Aunt Augusta pressed. "You could have had any one of them if only you hadn't chosen bonnets of a hue that made you look dyspeptic and gowns that hid your figure rather than flatter it, not to mention that hideous coiffure that all but obscured your face."

"If my actions indicated a degree of ingratitude, it is a sensibility I did not feel, Aunt, and I must beg your pardon for it. I was young and desired nothing more than to be admired for anything other than my beauty. Of what use is beauty when it has flown? What is there to attach a husband if he is so satisfied with my outward appearance that he has never looked beyond it?"

"Well, that is neither here nor there, but might you make a reasonable attempt to put your best foot forward this time, if only to be a credit to your aunt?" Aunt Augusta queried.

Elizabeth suppressed a sigh. "I vow to do my best not to disgrace you."

"There, then, that will do very nicely. I expect this means you shall attend the Green's do two evenings hence?"

"Augusta, you very well know we intend to attend the Green's do, as we do all the others," Mrs. Armistead averred.

"I presume this means Elizabeth shall begin to make her good intentions known immediately," Aunt Augusta said. "She may start by refraining from insulting her dancing partners. And before you refute it, Elizabeth, I am persuaded Lord Northrup's excellent impression of a blowfish was due, *entirely*, to something you said in his hearing."

Elizabeth wished to show her resentment but dared not. "You are quite correct, Aunt, but his indignation was due, *entirely*," she said, hoping this slight dig would sail past her mother's comprehension, "to his learning that I am already betrothed."

Aunt Augusta had the grace to look a bit discomfited, but this fit of compunction quickly passed. "Perhaps it would be wise to keep that piece of news to yourself. I should dearly love for you to make a sensation in society, the one you have long been due," she added as her severe frown softened into a tiny smile.

There was little Elizabeth wished for less than to make a sensation in society, but she owned that she owed much to her aunt for her sponsorship during Elizabeth's come-out four years prior. How to avoid one and fulfill the other was a puzzle she determined to chew on at length when she had some time to herself. If only she might talk it over with Duncan; he would know how to proceed. Either that or he would merely laugh and wave it all away, causing Elizabeth's fears to melt into nothingness. Only one more month and he would arrive and they could be married. Naught else mattered.

Chapter Three

Colin squinted at the missive in his hand and read it over a second time. He believed it to say that Tony was to fob off their planned boxing match in favor of tooling his curricle into the country with a young lady as companion. Surely, that could not be right. It wasn't like Tony to break a solemn vow, at least not so soon after its initiation.

Colin turned the letter over in his hands and read it yet again. Tony's explanation that the journey was to be undertaken at the behest of his grandmama did little to assuage Colin's ire. He had had the dubious pleasure of meeting Tony's grandmother, the Dowager Duchess of Marcross, on more than one occasion. There was nothing dubious as to his feelings on each and every occasion thereafter. At worst, she treated her grandson as she might a servant, at best, a sycophant who had nothing better with which to fill his time than to carry out her every whim.

Colin quelled his disappointment and noted that Tony was expected to return in a matter of days. The passage of time in between could be spent in the continued redecoration of the townhouse. The library had been Colin's priority and a visit to an antiques dealer had quickly resolved the matter of furniture. Even now he enjoyed the deep satisfaction one experienced when sunk into the butter-soft leather of a well loved chair.

Meanwhile, provisions had been made to redeem the floor through the purchase of an ancient, but well cared for, Aubusson rug and new window hangings had been requisitioned. As for the rest of the house, all that remained was for him to persuade his father that an increase in Colin's allowance was in order in spite of his lack of a wife. The original fitting of the house had made prodigious inroads into his accounts and once he was through with what was needed for the library, there would be little left for the other rooms, of which there were many.

With a sigh, he rose from his chair with the intention of repairing to his father's London abode in search of financial relief. He hadn't stirred far from the fire, however, when there came a knock at the door and Evans entered bearing a single card on a tray.

"Sir, there is a young woman in the vestibule. After the mishap of earlier this week, I hesitated to allow her entrance without first making her identity made known to you."

"Very good of you." Colin took the card and was surprised, as well as pleased, to see that it bore the name of his sister. "Ah, well, in future, Evans, you may admit my sister any time she is good enough to call."

"Very good, sir. I will show her through."

Colin had but a moment to wonder whether or not the room was now too masculine to afford comfort to a female before his sister was in his arms.

"Oh, Colin, how I have yearned for you!"

He gave her a squeeze and held her at arm's length. "And I you. But you look fine as a newly shined penny, do you not? Your new status in the world becomes you."

She blushed and favored him with a smile he suspected would hammer the heart of many a man in the weeks and months to come.

"Thank you, Colin. I must admit to an inordinate amount of enjoyment as of late," she said with a twirl of her skirts. "However, I am here to discover the reason for your absence. You have left me to my own devices far too long and I can hardly credit it! I would have thought you delirious with fever if Papa hadn't assured me that you were well enough. I haven't done anything to give you a disgust of me, have I?"

Colin laughed. "The very idea is absurd."

"Then why have you not been by my side? I must say, I have been positively bereft! I thought surely you would attend the Carruth's ball last night, but you were nowhere to be found. You can't still be troubled over that to-do with Cecily, can you?" she asked smartly though the expression in her eyes betrayed a much softer sentiment.

Finding her sympathy insupportable, he turned away to stoke up the fire. "Of course, what else? You do not expect me to recover from true love quite so abruptly, do you?"

"It wasn't true love, you know very well it was not. Is there even such a thing?"

Caught off guard, Colin swung round to read her expression. "What is this? Does the perennial romantic turn pragmatic?"

Tears sprang to her eyes at his words and she collapsed onto the newly delivered Louis the XIII sofa. Appalled, he rushed to her side and took her hand in his. "What is it, Ana? Mrs. Lloyd-Jones hasn't been badgering you over your sweet-eating tendency again, has she?"

"No, it's nothing like that. And if she were your mother as well as mine, you wouldn't be so inclined to fly to false conclusions. As if our father isn't trouble enough for one poor debutante."

"Dearest, whatever can you mean? You are the apple of his eye. What can he have done to vex you so?"

Analisa rolled her eyes. "Don't feign ignorance, Colin. You have seen for yourself how positively callous he can be. However, if you must know, he has verbally beaten all of the romance out of me. Where is the romance in being made to marry someone you have but met the once and who is so dreadfully tiresome?"

"Betrothed? Already?" Colin asked anxiously with a mind for the betting books at White's. "To whom?"

"Someone entirely unsuitable. He's about as dreadful as one could hope. Why Papa wished this deplorable state of affairs on me, I cannot imagine."

"You can't mean that he has promised you to Lord Eggleston?" Colin demanded. "He is more than twice your age and almost entirely deaf in one ear."

"No. Worse. Lord Northrup," she replied and promptly burst into tears.

"But, Ana, surely you are mistaken," he soothed. "Lord Northrup is practically a child."

"Yes . . I am quite aware!" she cried.

"I am beyond astonished that you have accepted this without presenting an argument or two. You must have told Father that Lord Northrup just won't do!"

Analisa swallowed her sobs and heaved a shuddering sigh. "How could I not?"

"And what was his response?"

"He said that I haven't the years or maturity to know what is best for me, that is what."

"One needn't be older than you to know that Lord Northrup is the worst choice of husband!"

"That is precisely the argument I posited," she said with a sniff. "And that is when he told me that I had best mind my words or my reputation shall be torn to shreds, just as has Ginny Delacourt's."

"Who is Ginny Delacourt?"

"Some nobody vicar's daughter presented last month along with myself. She has caused some undue amount of scandal over her unwillingness to hold her tongue," Analisa replied, tears welling again in her eyes.

Colin put his arm around his sister's shoulder. "There, there, now, he'll come about." In truth, Colin was rather alarmed and wondered at his father's judgment. The young Lord Northrup was not an answer to Analisa's spirited ways. An older man was called for, to be sure, though not one as far gone as Lord Eggleston. He considered soothing her by pointing out that the infamous Lord Trevelin might have been the man to whom she found herself promised, but decided it was a jest in poor taste. "In the meantime, I was just about to go in search of dear Papa over a personal matter. Should you like me to speak to him as to your betrothal?"

"Yes," she cried, seizing his hand. "Oh yes, Colin! Would you?"

"I would be delighted. However, you must be prepared to be patient. I am persuaded he shall change his mind, but it might take some time. Do you know if the matter is settled? Is an announcement to be placed in the papers so soon?"

She shook her head. "He was kind enough to suggest I become accustomed to the notion before it is made public."

"Well, then, matters are not as far progressed as I had feared. Did you take a hackney cab or were you allowed use of your mother's carriage?"

"Neither. I walked." She looked up at him, her eyes sparkling with tears. "I required time to gain command of myself."

"In that case, I shall be most pleased to convey you home." He rang for the butler and gave the order that the horses should be put to his curricle and brought round. "I expect I shall be asked to dine en famille, Evans, so let Cook know that I will not be in need of the usual tray."

He kept Analisa occupied with benign chatter until it was time to depart and welcomed her head on his shoulder when she nodded off during the journey home. That she was, perhaps, attending too many parties and not getting enough sleep was a matter of concern. He determined to speak to his father on that score, as well.

Upon their arrival at Lloyd-Jones House, they were met nearly as might have been long-lost prodigals. It seemed that Analisa had informed none of her departure and the household had been in an uproar since she was discovered to be missing. Colin's step-mother was particularly distressed and his father had just rung for the butler to request the physician to call when Colin and his sister descended upon them in the first floor salon.

"Oh, my dearest child!" Mrs. Lloyd-Jones cried from her place sprawled across the divan. Her struggles to rise were ham-pered by the disagreeable pair of small dogs that could always be found somewhere about her person. For the first time in Colin's presence, she ignored their vociferous barking and turned them from her lap in favor of clasping her daughter in her arms. "I have been positively wild with worry! What can have been so imperative that you must needs sail out of the house without so much as a by your leave?" she sobbed into Analisa's shoulder. "And, as if that were not bad enough, you left the house without a bonnet!"

"Mama, I never did!" Analisa gently extricated herself from her mother's grasp. "I fell asleep on our way home and Colin removed it."

"You fell asleep? How might one sleep in the face of such an ordeal? Where did your brother find you? At Gunter's sneaking an ice again?" her mother accused. "Or were you at the theater? Do tell me you hadn't ventured there. Theaters have such a distressing habit of burning to the ground."

"No, Mama, I have done nothing amiss other than to quit the house without leaving word."

"She came to see me, Ma'am," Colin supplied. "It seems she has mourned my absence as much as I have hers," he added with a fond smile. "However, methinks she is in need of a night or two of rustication," he said with a brow raised in his father's direction.

"Doubtless you are correct," Mr. Lloyd-Jones said in a manner so hearty as to betray his anxiety. "All is now well and supper may be served. Colin, you will join us, won't you."

"I should be delighted. And afterwards, Father, it would please me if we discussed a few matters."

"I should very much like to be present for this disputation," Analisa announced.

"Disputation? Who suggested anything so dire?" Colin directed a sly wink at his sister in hopes of warning her away from her present course of conversation.

"You will speak to Papa about my circumstances just as you promised, won't you?"

"Yes," Colin said briskly. "Certainly someone ought to address the subject of your propensity to run about town on your own, not to mention your utter lack of delicacy in falling asleep in the face of your mother's anguish."

"Oh! You are but mocking me, now," Analisa said and she turned and quit the room.

"Whatever it is, Colin, that you have to say, we shall address in private," his father said.

"Of course. I hadn't considered otherwise as I have matters of a personal nature to discuss. I do, as I've said, have concerns that pertain to Ana, as well, and I hope that you shall be willing to listen with an open ear."

"When have I done otherwise?" Mr. Lloyd-Jones demanded.

Colin felt it best to allow that question to hang on the air and turned to follow his sister out to the dining room. As he made his way, he examined his feelings and was surprised to find how frustrated he felt. He couldn't like the way his father was playing fast and loose with Analisa's future and hadn't the slightest idea how he was to convince his father to do differently.

The meal they took together was a chaotic one; most of the kitchen staff had been pressed into service to hunt for the young miss and several of the dishes were hastily replaced or served cold or not at all. This put Colin's father in somewhat of a bitter mood as there was nothing he prized more highly, save his children, than an irreproachable service and the ensuing pleasure derived from the consumption of the best meal his vast fortune could provide. Therefore, when the women left the dining room, it was with some trepidation that Colin broached the subject of his sister's marriage; the matter of enlarging his allowance could wait for another day.

"Father, Analisa has spoken to me of her betrothal. I must say, I am more than a little surprised. Lord Northrup can't have been through with his schooling more than a year ago."

"Less. However, he has plans for a Grand Tour of a year or more. The marriage won't take place until his return."

Colin heaved a sigh of relief and leaned back in his chair. "Then there is hope."

"Hope? Of what?"

"That she shall catch the eye of someone more suitable in the meantime and cry off."

"Why should she?" his father demanded. "Northrup is an excellent match. He is rich, educated, titled and far from being an old man. For what more should a young girl wish?"

Colin winnowed his words with great care. "Of course, you are quite correct on all counts. Only .. there is something a bit unsavory about him. It's not anything I might put my finger on exactly, but Analisa is of the same opinion. I am persuaded it would be best for her to wed where there is, at the very least, a meeting of the minds."

"Love; that is what you mean to say," Mr. Lloyd-Jones said, frowning. "What has love to say to the matter? It cannot feed you when you are hungry, house you when you are cold, put clothes on your back .. "

"Yes, Father, yes, I realize that these things are all frightfully important, particularly when they pertain to your only daughter. However, Analisa hasn't the practical nature that might best appreciate these circumstances to the fullest. I do believe she deserves the opportunity to fall in love with the man she intends to wed."

"I suppose you fancied yourself in love with Miss Ponsonby. Where has that landed you, dare I ask?"

Colin ignored the stab of discomfort that followed his father's words and pressed on. "What has my failure to do with Ana? She is nothing like Miss Ponsonby."

"No, she is not," his father said as he leaned across the table to pin his son in a penetrating gaze. "She is precisely like her brother, a hopeless romantic, one who perpetually views life through a romantic lens and is invariably downcast when life doesn't compare to her delusions. How is she to fare when the scales fall from her eyes and she learns her perfect husband is anything but? She needs to enter the marital state with no illusions if she is to survive it."

The truth of his father's words wounded Colin to the core. "I was wrong, then, about hope."

"For happiness? But of course! She shall be the mistress of her own home, bear children, have her own funds with which to buy whatever she wishes; all are the same circumstances which made your own mother quite content, I do assure you."

"So, there is nothing to be done but have the banns read and the announcement placed in the papers. Yet, you hesitate. Why is that?"

"As I have said, he is to be abroad for some months once the season has ended. She is only seventeen and this is her first season. Much can happen, with a man's fortune or his character, in a year's time. To be truthful, I suppose I *am* holding out for someone better, someone who might think it early days yet to broach the subject."

"Someone such as Sir Anthony Crenshaw?" Colin asked.

"Certainly he should make a very fine catch for Analisa. And yet . . even Lord Northrup is but an earl. I had thought to look a bit higher for her."

"Than an earl? Father, you can't be serious," Colin began when a new realization dawned. "Not Lord Eggleston," he heard himself say for the second time that day. "Yes, he is a duke but he is far too old for Analisa!"

"I suppose you think you could do better?" Mr. Lloyd-Jones challenged with a pound of his fist to the tabletop.

"I don't rightly know," Colin replied, nonplussed. "I hadn't given the matter a moment's thought until today. However, I do know that Analisa should be made miserable as wife to either Eggleston or Northrup. As for Tony, he is determined to stay a bachelor into perpetuity."

"Then you had best find someone else for your sister. In exchange, perhaps there is something I might do for you."

Colin leaned forward in his chair and ran his fingers along his chin. "There is one small matter with which you might be able to assist," he said slowly. "I find myself financially short. It's not serious," he hastened to reassure his father. "It's only that I have a project in mind that would suit me but that is currently beyond my means."

"Very well, then, I shall finance this project and you shall find your sister a more suitable husband. Am I correct in that appraisal?"

"Yes sir," Colin said as he stood and held out his hand. "You are most correct."

The two men shook hands and though the promise of money caused Colin to feel as if he had made a deal with the devil, his heart felt lighter than it had since Miss Cecily Ponsonby had agreed to be his wife. With a smile so broad he could feel it stretch his face he went in search of his sister.

He found her in the salon, her embroidery in her hand and a faraway expression in her eyes. "I had not expected to find you on your own," he observed, removing a cushion so as to sit at her side.

"Mama thought your suggestion brilliant and has ordered me to bed before she departs for the card party to which we had *both* been invited," she said with an arch look for her brother.

"Am I to be derided, then? I, your brother who has all but rescued your pretty neck from the noose?"

"I find I cannot like your choice of words," she said in bantering tones. "Have you rescued me or have you not?"

"I have convinced our papa that I could do better, and so I shall."

"You, do better? Am I to wed my brother, then?" she quipped.

"Ana, if you should but be serious, you should find that I am far more deserving of your praise than your reproaches."

"What is this?" she breathed as she thrust her embroidery into her lap. "You haven't convinced Papa of his folly, have you?"

"Nothing doubting!"

"Oh, Colin, you absolute dear! I can hardly credit it!" She took his hand and held it tight between her own. "For Papa to reverse his decision and in so short a space of time .. However did you manage it?"

"Well, naturally, he had requirements. In this case, they are well within my means."

She frowned. "I don't see that any amount of money should tempt Papa in this matter," she said slowly.

"Not money, you goose; I am merely to impart my services in the selection of a better aspirant to your hand."

"You!" she cried. "Never say so!"

"What is this?" he demanded. "I am the consummate individual to employ in such a case as this. For one, I love you too much to steer you astray."

"Yes, that you love me well is very true, and I do believe it has quite spoilt me. However, you daren't claim to be a wonderful judge of character!"

Colin opened his mouth to repudiate her accusation but recalled his lack in rightly judging Cecily in time to prevent his making a fool of himself. Taking a deep breath, he changed tack. "You are correct. I had thought I should merely make a list of suitable prospects and send you off to smile at them until they are well and surely smitten."

This remark brought the very smile to her face, as well as a fetching dimple to one side of her mouth. "I suppose you shall have to accompany me everywhere I go so as best to ascertain what's what. I can't say that I shall mind that one bit, Colin. I should like to see you more often."

"That, my pet," he said as he reached out a finger to flick the tip of her nose, "is quite impossible. Tony and I have made a pact; no balls or routs, card parties, soirees or even one Venetian breakfast all season long."

"Colin, whatever can you be thinking? I have never heard anything so foolish in all my life. If this has anything to do with what happened on account of that Cecily Ponsonby, I swear, I shall scream."

"It hasn't any more to do with Cecily than it has to do with Tony's long gone Rebecca, which brings to mind, what of Tony?" Colin twitted. "Shouldn't he make you a fine husband?"

A vague smile spread over Analisa's face as she sank back into the sofa pillows. "Sir Anthony is certainly one of the finest gentlemen of my acquaintance. He is sufficiently intelligent, endlessly handsome, witty as one could wish, and has an undeniable appeal that prompts all the ladies to sigh over him. However, I might say precisely the same with regard to you."

"I see, though one could do worse than marry a man you love as a brother."

"Worse, yes, and his name is Lord Northrup," she riposted, her eyes wide. "However, I am persuaded there is a man somewhere with whom I did not grow up and who is at least half as wonderful as the two of you put together. It means that you shall have to break your pact with Tony, but there is no doing otherwise. If not, I shall never be satisfied that you have my best interests at heart."

Colin looked into his sister's eyes and knew that she was entirely correct. He could not divide himself from the events of the season whilst entertaining any hope at all whatsoever that he could contract a suitable marriage for his sister. With a sigh, he stood and held out his hand to pull her into his arms for a farewell embrace. "Do not fear, little Ana. I shall dedicate myself entirely to your welfare until the matter is resolved. I believe there is a rout at the Green's tomorrow night. I shall present myself at your door at the appointed time and our pursuit shall begin in earnest."

"Oh, Colin!" she cried. "You are the best of brothers! But what am I to do in the meantime?"

"You are to repair to your boudoir and sleep every minute between now and then. You shall need it," he said with a last wink over his shoulder as he shut the door behind him.

Chapter Four

"$\mathcal{I}$ must say, I have never before attended a rout so thoroughly devoid of society," Mrs. Armistead whispered in her daughter's ear. "One would have believed the Green's possessed of a great many more friends!"

"I think it fair to say that we are, perhaps, a good deal too early," Elizabeth observed.

"Early? Never say so! The invitation was very clear. We have arrived at the stroke of nine of the clock, just as expected."

Elizabeth hoped the hot blush that invaded her cheeks went unnoticed by the few guests who had erred just as they had. "Yes, Mama, but I do believe we were meant to be late. It is generally understood by all but those currently present. Aunt Augusta warned us, you might recall."

Her mother raised her utterly superfluous lorgnette over her spectacles and studied the men and women in attendance, upon which she grunted in concession of Elizabeth's words.

"Perhaps we had best retire to the cloakroom for the best part of an hour," Elizabeth suggested "and reappear as if we had only just arrived."

"Yes, my dear, I do believe you have the right of it." Mrs. Armistead took her daughter firmly by the arm but, just as they gained the door leading to the stairs and the hoped for hiding place, their progress was impeded by the entrance of an elegant, dark-haired couple.

"Why Mr. Lloyd-Jones! We had not expected to find you here!" Elizabeth's mother exclaimed. "And who is this entrancing lady on your arm?"

Elizabeth debated as to whether or not she preferred to sink through the floor or allow Mr. Lloyd-Jones, who looked as if he wished for the same, the privilege. Of all the gentlemen they might have run into whilst in the act of retreating from a party to which they had arrived too early, it was he she least wished to meet. In light of her impending marriage and subsequent removal to Edinburgh, her sensibilities had been all that were hardy during the course of this particular visit to London, however, Mr. Lloyd-Jones was proving to be the chink in her armor. Worse yet, she could not account for it. Why should she care a farthing what he, or any man save Duncan, thought of her or her mother?

"Mrs. Armistead, Miss Armistead," he said with a slight bow in their direction, "I should like to introduce you to my sister, Miss Analisa Lloyd-Jones."

Elizabeth felt it a graceful speech in spite of the expression of alarm stamped on his features. "But, of course," she remarked with what she hoped to be equal aplomb and a far more opaque expression. "I recall you having been pointed out to me, Miss Lloyd-Jones, at the Carruth's ball. I might have recognized you on my own, you are so like your brother, but it was Lord Northrup who gave me your name." She could not fathom what it was about her comment that had caused two such equivalent expressions of apprehension on their faces, so she forged on with the pleasantries. "I do assure you that it was with the kindest of words he made you known to me. I am most happy to have been properly introduced and see that all he said, in perfect felicity, is true."

"Why, Elizabeth, is this the very young lady whose hand in marriage you suggested Lord Northrup should pursue?" her mother queried.

Elizabeth opened her mouth to respond but hadn't the slightest idea what she might say that should absolve her.

"How very unusual for one so recently arrived in London to play at matchmaking," Mr. Lloyd-Jones observed, coolly. "I cannot imagine why Lord Northrup did not cross my mind as a candidate for my sister's hand prior to his offering for her. Perhaps it has something to do with his extreme youth," he said smoothly as he leveled a look of mild censure in Elizabeth's direction.

"Why, Mr. Lloyd-Jones, I merely observed that your sister, a young lady so well-mannered and beautiful, was a far more suitable woman to look to for a wife than I. Oh dear! That is not what I had meant to say."

"And what was it you were meant to say, Miss Armistead?" he asked, regarding her with a jaundiced eye.

Elizabeth willed her ears not to burn hot with shame but knew it to be a losing battle. "Lord Northrup expressed a desire to marry in spite of his tender age and my reply had to do with the subject of his selecting his bride from amongst the young ladies whose number of years did not exceed his own. Your sister was to hand at the moment, that is all, though I maintain my assertion that she should make any man a lovely bride."

Miss Lloyd-Jones, who had previously looked a trifle vexed, was now wreathed in smiles. "Colin," she said as she rapped his arm with her fan, "one mustn't object to such pretty words. And, as I am *not* to wed Lord Northrup, Miss Armistead, I greatly fear he shall double his pretensions to your hand, a course of action I am persuaded, should they bear fruit, should make him most content."

As his sister spoke, Mr. Lloyd-Jones' grim expression relaxed into a natural smile and Elizabeth felt a surge of gratitude for Miss Lloyd-Jones' sweetness of nature.

"Truly, I meant no harm, but you are most correct, Mr. Lloyd-Jones, in that I should have taken better care to keep my opinions to myself."

"I find I quite like Miss Armistead, Colin. Why have you never spoken of her to me?" Miss Lloyd-Jones scolded.

Elizabeth saved him the trouble of answering what she assumed to be a provoking question and took Miss Lloyd-Jones by the arm to lead her into the ballroom, leaving her brother to escort Mrs. Armistead. "Company is so thin," Elizabeth mused. "I had feared we were terribly gauche to arrive so early but your attendance puts my mind at ease."

"Oh," Miss Lloyd-Jones cried, "we shall be gauche together, then. I am forever telling Colin that his aptitude for promptness does him a disservice in these circumstances, but he will insist!"

"In that case, I am persuaded your presence shall lend us countenance and we need not fear being snubbed by all and sundry," Elizabeth asserted. She paused for a moment to listen in on the murmur of conversation between Mr. Lloyd-Jones and her mother and, determining that all was well, carried on. "I hope it is not too coarse of me to inform you of my betrothal to Mr. Cruikshank. He has lately been in the military and stationed near my home in Bengal. He is even now on his way to join me in London. I shouldn't wish you to waste a moment matchmaking on my behalf."

"Never say so, for I am convinced you should be perfect for Colin," Miss Lloyd-Jones said lightly as if her words were not of the significance they implied. Leaning in to make her next words for Elizabeth alone, Miss Lloyd-Jones pressed her cause. "He has lately had a disappointment but she, aside from her alarming character of which we nearly learned too late, did not suit him in the least. You are far more to his taste and I am persuaded I should love you as a sister."

Elizabeth chose to treat her companion's words as being of no more import than her own wildly beating heart. Mr. Lloyd-Jones' previously open admiration of her coupled with his clear displeasure at her behavior and her unaccountable desire to be seen as all that is good in his eyes had her positively flustered. She dared not yield to the diversion she felt at such singular circumstances.

"Miss Lloyd-Jones, I am greatly flattered, but my betrothed and I shall be wed once he has taken up residence in London and the banns can be fully read. It is a circumstance to which I look forward with great contentment."

A tiny frown appeared between Miss Lloyd-Jones' pretty eyes. "I believe, absolutely, that these are your true intentions, Miss Armistead, and yet, I cannot help but feel there is something amiss." She searched Elizabeth's eyes a moment and heaved a sigh. "I have refused to settle for anything less than true love, and I urge you to follow the same course."

Elizabeth began to protest, but Miss Lloyd-Jones stepped away and took her brother's arm. "Colin, I should like you to host an evening of entertainment. In fact, I quite insist upon it. It needn't be elaborate, an evening of cards or, perhaps, dancing and a light supper. Does that not sound enchanting, Miss Armistead?"

"I don't know that my opinion has anything to say to the matter," Elizabeth said firmly in spite of her apprehension in the face of Mr. Lloyd-Jones' renewed alarm.

Miss Lloyd-Jones took in her brother's expression and emitted a trill of laughter. "You mustn't mind Colin, Miss Armistead, it is his dining room that he dislikes so excessively, not the notion of guests to dinner. And, of course, you must promise to attend, or I shall be very much put out."

Elizabeth looked to her mother, whose frozen features yielded no assistance in the least. "I suppose we might very well be free, depending on the evening in question," Elizabeth stammered as she allowed her gaze to flutter up to observe Mr. Lloyd-Jones' face in order to ascertain his reaction. Unlike her mother, his countenance was alive with myriad emotions, all of which appeared to be in utter conflict with one another.

"By all means, we must have the ladies from India to dine," he said easily. "Of course the invitation extends to your Miss Hale, as well," he added with a warning look for his sister who lifted her brows in surprise.

"Yet another young miss newly come to town with whom you somehow become acquainted without my knowledge!" Miss Lloyd-Jones chirped.

"She is but I do not see her here tonight," Mr. Lloyd-Jones remarked.

"She is under the weather," Elizabeth's mother explained. "This English climate is to blame! However, I am persuaded she shall be soon recovered."

"Well, then," Miss Lloyd-Jones said, "it is settled. Needless to say, we must petition a few gentlemen to join us. It would not do to have an uneven party. What say you to Sir Anthony, Colin?" she suggested, her face alight with mirth.

"Ana!" Mr. Lloyd-Jones snapped, his face turning a bit red. "Excuse me ladies, but I require a word in private with my sister." Before she had the opportunity to object, he placed an arm around her shoulders and led her off.

"Well! I never!" Mrs. Armistead berated. "I have a good mind to rake him over the coals!"

"Mama, please!" Elizabeth hissed. "I beg you, do not cause a scene. I am persuaded Mr. Lloyd-Jones has a perfectly acceptable excuse for his behavior. In point of fact, I believe he has mended his ways already and is poised to seek us out and beg our pardon." Elizabeth knew her words bent the truth nearly to the snapping point, but he had, indeed, turned his head in their direction. That he had turned away again after treating her to what seemed to her a scathing look that raked her from head to toe was a snub that hurt far more than she was willing to admit.

Forcing away the inexplicable tears that started in her eyes, she concentrated on what it was they ought to do next. "Come, Mama, I feel we are in need of some refreshment." Together they walked in the opposite direction of their erstwhile failed decampment and went in search of cold lemonade and a plateful of bonbons. They ate, huddled together in the corner of the salon, whilst Elizabeth mentally went over the conversation with the Lloyd-Joneses in an attempt to determine of what she could have been guilty that should earn her such barefaced scorn.

It would seem that her mother's thoughts ran along the same lines. "Do you know," she murmured, "I do believe it was not well done of us to trespass on Mr. Lloyd-Jones' hospitality when first we met. I ought to have sent the coachman in pursuit of assistance just as you suggested. If so, we would not, even now, be in such bad odor with Mr. Lloyd-Jones," she added with a sniff.

"Why? What could his opinion of us possibly matter? By the end of June, you shall once again set sail to India and I will be a married woman on my way to Scotland. We shall none of us see neither hide nor hair of Mr. Lloyd-Jones for the remainder of our lives, and, I must say, we shall most likely be happy not to."

"But, Elizabeth in spite of his sometimes unpleasant manner, he is an excellent catch!"

Elizabeth was stunned. "But, Mama, how can you say so? I am to be married to Duncan in little more than a month. We are promised to one another. I consider myself married at this very moment in all but deed."

"Yes, but Elizabeth, he is so rich!"

"I have no love for money." Comfort, however, was another matter. Life on the moors of Scotland promised to be forsaken and excessively frigid.

"And so well-connected!"

"Duncan and I shall be enough for each other. And soon enough there shall be children." However, there would be no Miss Hale or any other young lady with whom to pass the time. The only woman for miles around promised to be Duncan's mother who was sickly and in need of care.

"I daresay I haven't seen so handsome a man since your father was young."

"Handsome men are thick on the ground. Do you not recall his equally handsome friend, Sir Anthony? Besides which, I prefer men who are interesting." And yet, there was something about Mr. Lloyd-Jones that attracted her as had no other man. It was really most provoking.

"Interesting! Mr. Lloyd-Jones is extremely interesting. I doubt I have met a more interesting man in all of my life. Have I told you that I lived in the neighborhood of his family in my youth? Such fine young men, all of them, and the ladies no different. I should have been proud to marry a Lloyd-Jones and that is not an exaggeration, I do assure you."

"And yet, no Lloyd-Jones offered for you. To think, you might be his aunt, even now, if one had," Elizabeth said with a wry smile. "And I, his cousin."

"That is neither here nor there," Mrs. Armistead replied with a swat of her hand. "You are well aware that I was entirely besotted with your father from the moment I laid eyes on him. Which brings to mind; Mr. Lloyd-Jones has a very fine set of eyes. I can't recall seeing another quite as fine, not even amongst his family. Should you marry him, your children should have eyes just like his."

Elizabeth sighed her frustration. "Our children will have mine or Duncan's eyes, and though they will not be gray, they shall be every bit as beautiful." One trait they would not inherit were the scars that Duncan's eyes had born since the accident, the one that left him blind and entirely incapable of loving her purely for her beauty.

"That is all very well and true, Elizabeth dear, but you know what it is I meant, about the eyes, that is to say."

"Yes, Mama, I do, and I can only wonder at you. If you objected to my marriage to Duncan, you might have aired your opinion before our first meeting with Mr. Lloyd-Jones. As it is, I can only assume you have been seduced by his comeliness, a virtue that is as inconsequential as it is ephemeral." At least, she could only assume that a man's beauty was fleeting if her father were meant to be regarded as an example of youthful winsomeness. And yet, she could not deny that Mr. Lloyd-Jones' propensity to blow hot and cold towards her was only one of his attractions. His eyes, sometimes light and piercing, at other times shadowed and striking, were such that she had woken having dreamed of them on more than once occasion. The way his dusky hair curled about his temples was also very pleasing and she owned that his lips were shaped in a manner most becoming.

"I am only pointing out that it is as easy to fall in love with a rich, handsome man as it is a blind soldier-turned-farmer."

"Mama! I must beg you to refrain from such talk! Now, I do believe more guests have arrived. I intend to return to the ball-room and pass the time with more congenial company." Elizabeth then turned on her heel and marched out of the room with as much refinement as she could manage. Her ears and cheeks felt hot and she knew that she must look a trifle fearsome, but she found that nothing would abate her anger. She passed along the edge of the dance floor where a number of couples were enjoying the music, including Mr. Lloyd-Jones and his sister, their dark heads close together and as handsome as two people could ever wish.

She quickened her pace so as to put the Lloyd-Joneses beyond her line of vision when, to her horror, they looked up and took notice of her. Quickly, her face hotter than before, she turned away and all but ran towards the exit. She had not got very far, however, when she felt a hand on her shoulder. Startled, she whirled to come face to face with the very one she hastened to avoid. He appeared to be suddenly far more amenable than she had known him to be, his expression one of openness and even suppressed mirth. She thought she had never beheld a more welcome sight in all her life and the intensity of her feelings nearly robbed her of breath.

"Mr. Lloyd-Jones," she said, panting from her exertion a bit more than comfort allowed. "I had thought you dancing with your sister." The words were out before she thought better of them and she was left to wish she had not given him the satisfaction of learning she had been mindful of him. The slow smile that started in his eyes to finally reach those full, well-shaped lips was the final blow to her self-possession.

"Miss Armistead, my sister insists that I tender my apologies. In point of fact, I hadn't the need for her to tell me so; I realize that I was insufferably rude. However, I must assure you that it had naught to do with you that prompted my actions. I hadn't thought how my concern for other matters should be perceived by you and your mother." He held out his hand and waited until she placed hers in his grasp. "I do beg your forgiveness," he said and bowed over her hand, kissing the air a hair's-breadth above her fingers.

Elizabeth had never known her heart to beat at such a rate nor her stomach to be so aflutter. She suspected that her countenance bore the self-same expression she had seen on so many faces of those young men who admired her and she loathed herself for it. Yet, there was nothing to be done; she found Mr. Lloyd-Jones to be the most attractive man of her acquaintance.

Bearing in mind the fact that outward appearances revealed the very least about any individual, she collected herself and convened her thoughts on which words should form a sensible reply. "Mr. Lloyd-Jones, you have done nothing for which to berate yourself. As for myself, I do not hold you in less esteem for any action taken here this night. On the contrary, I do not believe I have ever been the recipient of so pretty an apology, especially one over such a trifling offense."

He drew himself up to his full height as she spoke and now stood so near that he seemed to tower over her. It was a wholly pleasant sensation, as if he need only spread wide his arms and she should be entirely swallowed up in his shadow. With most men of her acquaintance, it seemed very much otherwise, including Duncan who needed her so very much.

"How very kind of you to overlook my slight, Miss Armistead. Since you are present tonight for the purpose of dancing, might I be allowed the privilege of leading you out onto the floor at the beginning of the next set?"

"Well, I . . Yes, of course. I should be delighted," Elizabeth stammered. "I have always believed dancing to be the most amiable course of exercise."

He looked as if he wished to say something but checked himself just in time, whereupon he smiled, and said, "In this particular instance, I shall be most delighted by the company."

Elizabeth had been the recipient of hundreds of pretty, even lavish, compliments, but none had pleased her as had these words of Mr. Lloyd-Jones. "I, too, look forward to it, I assure you. However, I am afraid that your sister has been left alone too long on the dance floor."

Without a word, he hastened off to rescue his sister whilst Elizabeth waited for the wobbling in her knees to pass. If this, truly, was what the young men of her acquaintance experienced when they beheld her, she once again considered herself most fortunate that Duncan was blind and immune to such a bewildering happenstance. Why Mr. Lloyd-Jones seemed immune to her, despite his acute eyesight, was a question whose answer she looked forward to discovering.

While she waited for the next set of music to commence, she went in search of her mother and disclosed to her the news that she had accepted an invitation to dance with Mr. Lloyd-Jones. "I am quite aware that you are beside yourself with delight, Mama, however, it is only a dance. Dancing is why we accepted the invitation here tonight in the first place, is it not?"

"But, of course, Elizabeth, it is only a dance, but who knows to what it might lead?"

"Mama, why must you insist on being so vexing? If you have no reverence for the promise I have made to another man, I am persuaded that Mr. Lloyd-Jones has. I cannot imagine that he has a single solitary design beyond that of dancing with a fellow guest."

"I am merely pointing out that one dance might lead to a second and so on and so forth," Mrs. Armistead said with a sniff.

"What is this 'so on and so forth'?" Elizabeth requested. "No, never mind, I have no wish to know. We have been invited to dine at his establishment, is that not enough?"

"Oh, yes, it is quite, quite wonderful. I daresay he has a beautiful home and most likely constructed quite recently, too, not one of those hovels dating practically back to Shakespeare."

Elizabeth wished nothing more than to laugh, but the music had now ceased and Mr. Lloyd-Jones and his amiable sister were even now approaching. "Mama, please do behave yourself and pray do not say anything you shall wish unsaid."

"I?" she asked, her eyes wide. "I have never regretted a single word that has escaped these lips."

"I am persuaded that is perfectly true," Elizabeth murmured to herself just as Mr. Lloyd-Jones reached her side, his hand outstretched and waiting for hers. Briefly she considered telling him that she had changed her mind for she was suddenly very afraid. What if dancing in the arms of this captivating man resulted in a lifelong discontent with the lot she had chosen for herself? However, her hand moved as if of its own accord to place itself in his and before she had a chance to demure, he had escorted her out onto the dance floor.

To her great relief, the musicians struck the chords of a contra-danse and her time in conversation, not to mention his arms, would be limited. She found, then, that she could smile and enjoy the dancing with no self-recrimination. She could not compare it to time spent similarly with Duncan as his lack of vision did not allow them the opportunity, but she found it far superior to dancing with the young officers who failed to vanquish the desire that flared in their eyes when they gazed at her.

Too soon the music came to a halt. Elizabeth expected to be immediately led back to the auspices of her mother, but it seemed that Mr. Lloyd-Jones had the opposite intention.

"Would you object to another dance with me; the next waltz, perhaps? I find it much more conducive to conversation and I find myself keen to learn from you of India. You must have had a fascinating childhood."

Elizabeth looked down at her hands. "If any of the soldiers with whom I have danced had suggested anything as beyond the pale as a second dance of an evening I would, of course, be forced to decline. However, as I am betrothed to another, I trust there will be no misapprehension between us. I find that I should like, very much, to tell you about my home, but only if you tell me about yours. I am more than a little captivated with the land of my ancestors."

He did not immediately respond as the music had once again been sent aloft and, as it was indeed a waltz, he took her hand and placed one of his at her waist. "Shall we begin?"

She rested her left arm along his shoulder and took a deep breath; the waltz had not been long performed in Bengal and she had no wish to mortify Mr. Lloyd-Jones. She had not long to contemplate her thoughts, however, for soon they were whirling about the room together and she could think of naught but keeping up with him. He was an exceedingly skilled dancer, or so she supposed though she had few but the young officers stationed in India with whom to compare.

"Well, then, Miss Armistead," Mr. Lloyd-Jones said as he looked down into her eyes, "this seems a most opportune time to divulge to me the fascinations of India."

"But where shall I begin?" she asked whilst silently observing that, in order to converse, she was forced to crane her neck at an awkward angle. However, if she did not, her forehead grazed against his chin in a too-familiar fashion she was powerless to prevent. Indeed, he swept her about the room with such authority, it seemed as if she need only submit and he would execute the dancing for the both of them.

"Perhaps you might start by telling me about your family. Your mother I have met and your friend, Miss Hale, but have you no sisters? Brothers? Have they enjoyed growing up in India as much as have you?"

"I am possessed of two younger brothers who, I am persuaded, are every bit as irascible as they should have proved to be had they grown up in England. My mother has resisted sending them to be schooled abroad, but I expect it is a disagreement my father shall presently win. Mr. Cruikshank and I shall look forward to hosting them for the course of their holidays as well as the heaving of a sigh when we see the backs of them, I suppose."

"I should have liked a brother or two," Mr. Lloyd-Jones remarked, "though I often feel as if I have enough to do in looking after my sister. She is not in the least wayward and yet she seems to find herself in more than her share of scrapes."

"Miss Lloyd-Jones? Never say so!" Elizabeth insisted as she realized that the pain in her neck was due to the fact that he held her entirely too close for proper conversation. "She seems the epitome of pleasing comportment," she added a bit faintly.

"Oh, entirely! I haven't the slightest qualms when it comes to her behavior. And still, the most appalling commotion seems to rise up round her like a sudden thundercloud burst onto the scene of a pure blue sky."

"Somehow I do not believe you. She is a lovely girl, in every way. I wish I had a sister as kind and merry as she."

Mr. Lloyd-Jones bestowed on her a beatific smile, one that denoted his great affection for his sister. "Yes, I am most blessed in her. As such, I find I am particular as to whom she should marry."

"More so than your parents?" Elizabeth asked with great interest in spite of the pain in her neck and the ensuing faintness that, moment by moment, grew more imminent.

"My mother is no longer with us," he replied as a dark cloud passed over his face, "and while Analisa's mother is all that she should be, I can hardly hope to stand against my father in this matter, let alone his wife. But that is neither here nor there. We were meant to speak of India, were we not?"

Elizabeth managed a little nod but felt that if she were not allowed to ease the pressure to the back of her neck, she should surely swoon. "Mr. Lloyd-Jones, I do not believe I have ever experienced waltzing thus. I confess to feeling as light as a feather in your arms, however, if you were to loosen your hold just a trifle, I should find conversation more comfortable."

Immediately, he loosened his grip, a circumstance she instantly regretted as she knew she was safer in the tight circle of his arms. As matters stood, she was doomed to fall to the floor. The room began to swirl about her and her vision narrowed until all was utter darkness.

Chapter Five

Colin stared at the white face that lolled against his black coat sleeve and knew he had never seen anything so beautiful in all his days. It was his last thought before the humiliation assailed his senses; the fault for her fainting could be laid entirely in his dish. Why he had gripped her so tightly in his arms was anyone's guess. It wasn't that she seemed in need of his strength; she did not seem the least bit frail—quite the opposite—and yet, in spite of her efforts to conceal it, he sensed in her an unaccountable vulnerability.

More likely his rigidity on the dance floor was due to his anxiety with regard to his deflated confidence as a result of his broken engagement. The breaking of his pact with Tony, and at such a rapid rate, did nothing to improve Colin's opinion of himself, either. It hardly mattered that he was thoroughly justified in the breaking of both promises, he still wanted nothing more than to curse, competently and at length. However, he did not; the girl in his arms was in need of a gentleman and he was the one at hand.

Quickly, he scanned the room for an unoccupied piece of furniture, preferably a sofa of some length where she could be arranged in comfort. He spotted one on the far side of the room and instantly began to bark at the circle of onlookers. "This lady has fainted; do allow me to pass!" When the crowd did not immediately part, he cradled her more tightly in his arms, her head protected along the inside curve of his shoulder while he engaged the outer to butt against those in his path.

Analisa ran to his side and he was only too grateful to order her about. "Find her mother and have her meet me at the sofa by the fireplace. No, wait!" Concerned that it would be too warm and stuffy by the fireplace, he changed direction and headed to a different sofa, this one beneath a window. "Here, Analisa, she shall be here," he called in what amounted nearly to panic. Appalled at his heart-pounding apprehension, he forced himself to slow down and succeeded in placing his burden on the sofa without further mishap.

The moment she was no longer in his arms, she began to stir. "Where am I?" she asked as her head swayed to and fro.

He fell to his knees at her side and took her hand. "All is well," he said, vastly relieved that his words were indeed true. "You shall be right as a trivet in a moment."

At his words, her head turned in his direction and she opened her eyes. For a moment, she seemed sadly bewildered but then her gaze fastened onto his face and she smiled at him with such sweetness that his heart seized up in a most peculiar fashion.

Suddenly, she frowned and uttered an "oh" of alarm as her hand slid from his grasp. Pushing herself upright, she looked about. "I fear I have created a scene. Is my mother nearby?"

Colin turned to look about the room and spotted the approach of Mrs. Armistead. "She is nearly upon us." He rose to stand and stepped away to allow Miss Armistead's mother to tend to her daughter. It occurred to him, then, that he was no longer strictly required, yet he had no wish to depart before she had entirely recovered. "Do you wish to go home? Shall I have your carriage brought round?" he asked for lack of any better reason to remain at Miss Armistead's side.

"Oh, please do," Mrs. Armistead replied as she chafed her daughter's hands and pinched her cheeks. "I shall take you straight home to Aunt Augusta's and tuck you into bed, my sweet," she cooed.

Reluctantly, Colin turned away and went in search of a footman. After some thought, he realized that should he order his carriage be brought round with the Armistead's, he could insist on his willingness to escort the ladies home in his own conveyance. Miss Armistead would be afforded the company of Analisa while those who saw them leave together would refrain from speaking ill of the girl who had the great fortune to be escorted from the party in the company of the Lloyd-Joneses.

Satisfied with this arrangement, he found himself suddenly eager to host the ladies at a dinner in his home as Analisa had suggested. It would give him the opportunity to make amends to Miss Armistead and perhaps she should regale them all with the promised tales of India. He returned to the Armistead's and informed them that once they had proffered their *adieus* and retrieved their wraps, his carriage would be at their disposal.

"Oh, but we have our own carriage, Mr. Lloyd-Jones," Mrs. Armistead blustered. "It is not as if we arrived in anything as pedestrian as a hackney cab. Elizabeth's Aunt Augusta is very good ton, I shall have you know!"

"Yes, of course she is, Mrs. Armistead," he assured her, though he hadn't the slightest idea who Aunt Augusta might be. "I hadn't meant to imply anything untoward; I only thought to escort you home in my carriage. It would be a boon to me, as I am more than a little alarmed and shall feel better when she is safely home. My sister shall come along, as well, to lend us countenance, and your carriage may follow along behind. Does that suit you?" he asked with a little bow.

"Oh, yes, indeed it does," she cried as her spectacles slipped to the end of her nose. Hastily, she adjusted them, her hands, one full of a pointless lorgnette, shaking. "I do assure you that Elizabeth has not fabricated her condition so as to prevail upon you in any way. How I should scold her if she had!"

Colin observed how Miss Armistead turned at her mother's words so as to hide her blushes, but she was not quick enough to keep them from his observation. "The thought hadn't occurred to me," he hastened to assure them. "As proof of my good will I wish to renew my sister's invitation to dine at my house; shall we say Thursday next? I intend on serving a great many delicacies for your enjoyment, ones that cannot be had in India." He hadn't any earthly idea what those foodstuffs might be, but he was determined to find them out. He also decided that alterations to the dining room would commence the moment he had breakfasted in the morning.

"How very lovely, Mr. Lloyd-Jones! Elizabeth and I shall very much look forward to it, won't we my dear?" Mrs. Armistead crooned. "And now it is time that you got to your feet."

Colin wasted no time in assisting Miss Armistead to a standing position and refused to let go her hand until she had proven she was no longer in the least faint.

"Thank you, Mr. Lloyd-Jones," she said quietly. "I am persuaded I don't know what could have happened. One should think my sea legs would have been of more benefit to me in this instance, should they not?" she asked, smiling up at him.

It was with some difficulty that Colin resisted the impulse to fall headlong into the depths of her emerald eyes. "I must take the full blame for your mishap, Miss Armistead, sea legs or no. Now, do feel free to lean against me as we depart," he instructed as he took her arm. "We shall force ourselves to go slowly, shan't we? Doubtless both carriages will have arrived out front once we gain the steps down to the street."

She followed his directions without comment and, though she leaned on him very little, she felt scandalously near. He thought how completely different was his life but a fortnight ago when he knew he should die of grief over his broken betrothal. It seemed but a blink of an eye ago and yet, here he was, very much alive and enjoying every moment.

Their journey through the now voluminous crowds of the ballroom and down the stairs staggering with the weight of party-goers on their way up was not in the least conducive to conversation. The silence between them continued, however, as they waited in the chill night air for the carriages, which did not arrive as quickly as promised, to heave into view. However, once they had seated themselves in his comfortable coach lined with ruched gray satin, the squabs covered in petal soft velvet, and the door had shut behind them, Analisa ensured that it would be a most memorable ride.

"So! I do believe I heard Colin give a date for his dinner party. Please say that it is an evening you are free, Miss Elizabeth," Analisa urged.

"I really couldn't say for certain. Mama, do you agree that we ought to check with Aunt Augusta before we accept any invitations? She might have accepted one on our behalf for the same date and has not of yet divulged the matter to us."

"Very true." Mrs. Armistead wagged her head sagely. "Lady Augusta would take it amiss if we were to accept an invitation without her approval. Not that she would disapprove of our dining at Lloyd-Jones House, to be sure," she added nervously. "It is only a matter of being made sure she has not already accepted an invitation on our behalf for the self-same night, don't you see?"

"Yes, of course," Colin assured them but he could not help but feel their protestations were on account of something else. He thought perhaps Miss Armistead would venture a more illuminating comment if there were a silence to fill. As such, when Analisa took a breath to speak, he squeezed her hand in his own as warning.

The brief silence stretched on into an awkward breach and Colin wondered if perhaps he had got Miss Armistead all wrong.

Finally, she drew a deep breath and spoke. "You have both been so very kind and attentive. I am persuaded Aunt Augusta shall understand should it be required to break an engagement for the sake of your party. I imagine her possible ire might be greatly reduced should she receive an invitation, as well. I am aware that having yet another lady to the party might lead to difficulties and yet I am persuaded you shall have no trouble finding enough gentlemen to balance the table should Miss Analisa be in attendance."

"An excellent notion, Miss Armistead," Colin replied, "and expressed so prettily! I should be honored to add your aunt to the guest list. I have a few ideas of my own as to which gentlemen to invite, but I wonder if there are any you would most especially wish to attend?"

Miss Armistead's expression was difficult to read in the darkened carriage, but he could well enough detect the note of censure in her voice. "Certainly Miss Analisa's assessment on the matter should be of far more use than mine. After yourself, I can have no reason to wish any other gentleman in attendance save my betrothed, who will not as of yet have arrived from India."

Colin admired Miss Armistead's address. He admired, also, her appearance but owned that her admonishment stung. "Analisa, as you can see, I have been appropriately upbraided. I daresay I shall regret the question based on your response the last time I posed it, but, pray tell, whom should it please you to invite to balance out the ladies?"

"I shan't mock you again on account of Sir Anthony, have no fears on that score," Analisa chirped. "Meanwhile, I do believe it far easier to call to mind the names of those I shan't wish invited. Let's see, I suppose we must ask four gentlemen to make the party even. We can't ask Papa, as Mama will come along and then we shall be right back where we started."

"Shall I invite Lord Northrup just to tease you?"

"Colin, no! If not for my comfort but for Miss Elizabeth's. You mustn't forget that now that I made it clear I shan't have him, he shall be demanding her hand instead. I am persuaded she should find it not in the least pleasant or she would not have fobbed him off on me in the first place, is that not so Miss Armistead?"

"Indeed, it is so," she said, laughing, "but, pray, do not exclude him on my account."

"I believe Osterley and Plimpton should make excellent conversationalists," Colin suggested. I plan to insist that the ladies from India share with us the stories of their adventures there, and the two gentlemen named should prove worthy foils in that endeavor."

In spite of the darkness, Colin knew Analisa wrinkled her nose in disdain. "Oh, pray, not those two! They battle between them as to who is to be allowed to speak most already as it is. Should you have hopes to allow anyone else the slightest moment to converse, they are quite, quite doomed. No, I believe you should ask Mountbank, Mr. Laraby and Billingham. I shall leave the fourth to you as long as it is not one of those two gossips."

Colin silently congratulated himself on his skill in bringing Analisa round to exactly the point he wished her to be. "Thank you, dearest. Now I know precisely whom I shall begin to consider as potential grooms for you."

"Oh, Colin, don't be absurd! You know Mr. Laraby has been betrothed this age and Billingham is poised to offer for that Runyon girl."

"You are quite correct, Analisa, however, in spite of my respect for the vows of matrimony, a mere betrothal is no impediment should you desire to have him."

The silence that followed his remark was so thick he felt as if he might merely reach out and fill his hand with it. "I must beg your pardon, Miss Armistead, for such a clumsy remark. In light of my recent broken betrothal, of which I doubt not you have heard tell, and the honor in which you hold your current betrothal, I cannot have failed to offend. Please do me the kindness of viewing it in the light it was offered; as adulation for my sister of whom I think most highly, love more dearly, and for whom I wish the best of all things."

"I find I cannot doubt your love for your sister, sir; she is all things admirable as well as amiable."

"As are you, my dear Miss Armistead," Analisa was quick to proffer.

However grateful Colin felt for Miss Armistead's words, he could not help but note how they failed to absolve him. "Perhaps it is arrogant to suppose my motives for refusing to honor the promise I had made to Miss Ponsonby should be of the least interest to any of you. However, I find I wish to speak of it, with your permission."

"By all means, sir," Mrs. Armistead cried, "you have my leave to speak."

Though he would have preferred to know her daughter's opinion on the matter, he pressed on. "Thank you. In truth, I should never have cried off on my account alone in spite of my having every reason to do so. If Analisa had been safely married prior to now, I still might have married Miss Ponsonby. As matters stood, I was not at liberty to make such a choice this season of all seasons. I wish Analisa to make the best match possible for her happiness and having Miss Ponsonby for a sister should have reduced her opportunities to literal ashes."

"But of course, you did just as you ought," Mrs. Armistead declared. "It is my fervent opinion that you have acted with honor, sir!"

"Such is the world, Ma'am, that I could not treat both young ladies with honor despite my wish to do so."

"I hesitate to speak to the subject, Mr. Lloyd-Jones," Miss Armistead said, "on the chance you are still in love with Miss Ponsonby, but I can only assume your own honor should prevent you from crying off if she, indeed, had been worthy of you."

Colin felt his heart fill again with gratitude at the generosity of Miss Armistead's words. "You are correct in that she misled me, took advantage of me, and passed herself off as someone she is not. However, I did not wish to see her so publicly disgraced. I did believe myself to be in love with her, I must confess, but the depth of her betrayal put an end to such finer feelings. I hope that I might have found a way to overlook her offense if she had but confessed the truth to me at the outset of our association. The fact that she did not was that which I found so intolerable. Sadly, due to the manner in which her circumstances were made known, I had no hope of keeping it a private matter between the two of us. In the end I did the only thing possible, no matter the personal cost."

"Truly, Colin," Analisa said, "I do believe you are well rid of her, the airing of her dirty linen, regardless. I am persuaded you only believed yourself to be in love while it is certain she did not love you nearly as well as you deserved."

"But, surely, there is more to marriage than romantic love," Miss Armistead interjected. "What of regard, admiration, compatibility, friendship and objectives in common?"

"I have been all of my life a single man, Miss Armistead, but I have observed many marriages. What you say is true, yet, you have left off one of the most important aspects, one that serves as the foundation for any successful relationship; that of trust. Without trust, there can be no faith in future happiness."

"I should happily applaud you, Colin," Analisa said a bit smugly, "if you hadn't allowed your disappointment in one woman to destroy your trust in all of her kind."

"Whatever can you mean? Do I not trust you?" In spite of his protestations, Colin knew his sister had a valid point. Had he not instantly mistrusted the motives of Miss Armistead and her mother from the moment they had met?

"I am not at all the same thing and you know it. This silly pact you have with Sir Anthony to avoid all entertainments this season in order to keep your heart fortified against further injury is that to which I refer."

"We only hope to support one another in our mutual heartbreak," Colin said as he put his arm around his sister and squeezed her shoulder as warning to mind her words.

"Heartbreak! Heartbreak? Rebecca broke Sir Anthony's heart. . what? Two seasons ago? It should have mended long since. Pray tell, you shan't be so willing to eschew the company of women as long as he and over a woman who has proven to be even less deserving of your love than Rebecca was of his?"

"I do not believe our cases to be in the least similar," he replied with yet another warning squeeze for Analisa. "Sir Anthony's proposal of marriage was rejected at the outset whilst Cecily and I spent months planning our lives together. If I were to mourn over the loss for twice as long as he has mourned Rebecca, it should not be in the least indecorous." However, he was astonished to note that he no longer felt the least grief over Cecily or her betrayal. Indeed, to his further astonishment, at the moment the only burden his heart bore was the possibility of risking the loss of Miss Armistead's good opinion.

"Well, Miss Armistead, what have you to say to that?" Analisa queried exactly as if Miss Armistead's assessment was of as much consequence to Analisa as it was to Colin.

"Once again, my sentiments do not come into the matter," Miss Armistead insisted. "Though, I confess to feeling sorry for you, Mr. Lloyd-Jones, that you have been forced to endure such a drastic state of affairs. A broken heart is one thing, but to be faced with such a decision, one that affected everyone you hold most dear and promised to be the cause of such scandal, should have been more than I could have borne."

Her speech was followed by another silence, this one more companionable and far less unendurable. Colin felt his heart yet again swell with gratitude at Miss Armistead's generosity and was content to merely say nothing as he absorbed the balm to his wounds. However, it would seem that Analisa was of a different opinion.

"I find I do not believe you, Miss Armistead, not in the least."

"I fear I did not hear you aright," Miss Armistead said faintly.

"But of course you did, my dear. I do not believe you to lie, only to be mistaken. I am persuaded you might bear a burden as great, if not greater, than has Colin. There is something about you that I can name naught but noble. Your manners are impeccable, you are unfailingly kind and your integrity is without end. You are made of sterner stuff than Colin, and that is the truth."

Miss Armistead laughed with delight, a sound belied by her words. "You should not say so if you knew me well, Miss Analisa, but I thank you for your kind opinion."

"It is not mere kindness," Mrs. Armistead hastened to add. "It is true, my Elizabeth possesses all of those virtues and more. I have been quite, quite proud of her, I must say."

"I thank you, as well, Mama, but you should know better even than they. I blush to think of the moments when I have disappointed you and Papa."

"Moments are what they were, my girl, mere moments. I shall stand by my words, my dear. Mr. Cruikshank has no idea what a bargain he made when he won your heart."

Colin saw, through the shadows of the carriage, how Miss Armistead bent her head and suspected she would say no more on the subject.

"Well, it would seem we are all pattern cards of erect behavior, are we not?" he bantered. "I shall expect nothing less at my dinner party Thursday next. Specifically, in spite of the fact that you are a woman whose heart and hand are fully engaged, Miss Armistead, I trust you shall still regale us all with tales of growing up in India, shall you not?"

"But, of course, I should enjoy it vastly," she replied.

"You must be certain to ask her how she met her intended, Mr. Cruikshank," Mrs. Armistead proclaimed. "It is a story worth hearing, I do assure you."

"I would not miss it for the world." Indeed, Colin was willing to hear any amount of stories about Mr. Cruikshank in hopes that they revealed what sort of man could command the heart of a girl such as Miss Elizabeth Armistead.

"My mother makes it sound far more exciting than it was. I have told her she ought to consider becoming a novelist along the lines of Mrs. Radcliffe but she insists such an undertaking is beneath her dignity."

"Dearest, you know what they say about ladies who read lurid novels," her mother replied. "What they must say about those who write them, I shudder to think. Besides, I am persuaded Mrs. Radcliff is, in truth, a man."

"Oh! What a rapturous idea!" Analisa said as she threw her hands into the air. "I should be quite jolly should that prove to be the case."

"Analisa!" Colin rebuked. "I hadn't known you read Mrs. Radcliffe!"

"But, why ever should I not, dearest? Her books are most entertaining, are they not, Miss Armistead?"

"I haven't had the pleasure," she replied without the slightest hint of censure in her voice. Her reticence made it difficult for Colin to determine whether or not she was a reader of novels at all whatsoever, a fact about her which he suddenly yearned to know.

"We must rectify that as soon as possible!" Analisa exclaimed. "I can't be positive, but I should be willing to bet money that Colin has at least one of her novels in his collection."

Unsure as to what should afford him the least credit in Miss Armistead's eyes, to have read Mrs. Radcliffe or not to have read her, he remained silent.

"Oh, come, Colin! Don't say you cannot recall as I do our conversations on the subject of *The Romance of the Forest*. You said how queer it was that the author chose to call one character Peter and another Pierre as they are essentially the same name. You claimed to have read it through to the end in hopes that the reason for this choice would be made obvious, but it never was. I must admit to having been so vexed by it that it quite ruined the story for me. Yet, if Colin had never mentioned it, I should not have noticed it at all."

"Then I suppose it would be safe to say that I read *The Romance of the Forest* through to the end at the very least," Colin grudgingly admitted. "If you, Miss Armistead, find that the hours weigh heavy on you as you wait for your Mr. Cruikshank, I shall be most happy to conduct a search for it if you should wish to borrow it."

"I thank you most sincerely. I should be delighted to pay a visit to your library. English books are few and far between in India and once I marry and have made my home on the family farm, I daresay there shall be a sad lack of printed material there, as well."

"I am persuaded it shan't be that primitive," Colin suggested. "Where is this farm?"

"It's in Sutherland, very close by a breathtaking beach, or so I am told."

Her reply caused Colin to wish he had not made so bold a statement as Sutherland was nearly as primitive as one could wish. His fervent desire that such a fate not befall the glowingly alive Miss Armistead struck him with such force, he nearly gasped aloud. "There is naught to farm there but seafood. Unless, perhaps, they raise cattle?"

"I . . I don't know. I feel of a certainty that he referred to it as a farm. It hardly matters, though, as long as we are together. I am looking forward to escaping the relentless heat of India. I have so enjoyed the bracing weather during the course of my visits to London."

"The highlands of Scotland," Analisa ventured, "are hardly the same thing. I'm afraid you shall find that the winters are quite brutal and the summers hardly better."

"Well," Miss Armistead replied a bit shortly, "as I have said, I am anticipating the change with much enthusiasm."

There was another silence, this one of the uncomfortable sort that stretched out until the carriage came to a halt.

"It would seem we have arrived at the home of Lady Augusta," Colin pointed out. "Do extend to her my invitation to dine. I shall be sending one through the post within the next few days, as well."

"Yes, of course we shall share the happy news with Augusta immediately we lay eyes on her," Mrs. Armistead assured him. "Good night."

"Good night," Miss Armistead said in her turn. "And thank you. We do so much look forward to dining at Lloyd-Jones House."

Colin watched her follow her mother out of the carriage and up the steps to Lady Augusta's Georgian townhouse so like his own and hundreds of others in the city. Yet, the girl who walked so regally through the front door was unlike any he had ever known. He knew his time was limited, but he determined to get the measure of Miss Armistead before it ran out.

Chapter Six

Elizabeth had been most surprised to see Mr. Lloyd-Jones at the Green's soiree in light of his insistence that he had not been invited to that particular do. It would seem that he did not generally run in the same circles as Aunt Augusta as he had denied having been invited to all of the parties to which the ladies from India had planned to attend. And then there was the curious pact he had made with his friend, Sir Anthony, one which made Mr. Lloyd-Jones' presence out and about in society highly unlikely. Therefore, it was with more than a little astonishment that she saw him the very morning after their last meeting when out with her mother, Miss Hale and Aunt Augusta on a shopping expedition.

As they had passed Hatchard's, Elizabeth felt a sudden craving for an enthralling English novel of the variety so difficult to procure in India. Nothing would do but for her to be let down at the book shop with arrangements to meet the other ladies at a later time and it was with a song in her heart that she had entered and made her way straight through to the back of the establishment. As she had rounded the end of the last bookstall, she had been immediately favored with the profile of Mr. Lloyd-Jones as he examined a painting hung on the wall.

Quickly, she stepped back around the stall where she hoped her examination of him would appear less unmistakable. He looked particularly well in his dark blue, double-breasted frock coat and buff pantaloons, his dark curls spilling over the snowy folds of his intricately tied cravat. Idly, she noted that she had never before seen a man with such a long fringe of black eyelashes or eyes such a light shade of gray. Never before having found herself in just these particular circumstances, she wondered if it were polite to speak to him or if it would be best to look away and pretend as if she hadn't taken notice of him. The decision was withdrawn from her, however, when he turned to see her watching him and stared back at her with a piercing look from his penetrating eyes that made her as weak in the knees as melted wax.

"Why, Miss Armistead," he greeted her as he swept his hat from his head. "What a pleasant surprise." Somehow she had already forgotten that voice, one rich as cream and so low it sent her stomach to fluttering in a manner most distressing.

"We were out," she stammered, "and when we passed by, I found I must stop. Our discussion of Mrs. Radcliffe's novels reminded me of how I do so love to read. My mother and the others will be back to collect me presently," she added, turning towards the door as if she expected to see them enter at any moment. It was the most inane string of sentences she had uttered in her entire life and the pursuant humiliation froze her lungs. The rational portion of her brain urged her to breathe even as she noted that if he continued to stare at her in such a speaking way, she should surely suffocate and cease to exist except as a lifeless bundle of India muslin at his feet.

He smiled as if her thoughts had been read aloud and treated her to a canny look from the corner of his eye. "I am delighted to know that you enjoy reading," he said as he ran a finger over the spine of a book that stood on a shelf between them. "I have found many hours of pleasure in so doing. But, see here," he said as he turned back towards the painting, "perhaps you should be kind enough to tell me what you think of this."

Free from his gaze, her lungs began once again to take in air. With a deep breath, she moved to stand in front of the picture that had him so absorbed. Instantly, she recognized it as depicting a common scene from India, that of the gaily dressed native ladies as they moved about the stalls in the open air market, their baskets balanced on their heads and their children following along behind with fistfuls of their mothers' saris in their hands. The market stalls were aglow with colorful awnings spread below with equally colorful fruits, as cows, dogs and chickens wove in and out of the scene just as they were wont to do.

"Why, it is as if the artist plucked this from a scene of my childhood! I wonder how it came to be here. It is a scene of India, I am sure of it."

Mr. Lloyd-Jones' well shaped lips broke into a smile so breathtaking it could only have been rendered for the sole purpose of breaking her heart. "I thought it must be. It is quite beautiful."

"How very lovely!" she managed to say in unexceptionable tones in spite of the way her lungs rattled against the sudden thunderous beating of her heart. "I wonder if it is for purchase."

"With your leave, I should be happy to inquire about it."

"Oh, yes, would you? It should make a perfect memento for the farmhouse, to remind me most pleasantly of India."

Mr. Lloyd-Jones nodded and sketched a brief bow, whereupon he strode to the clerk who handled purchases. With their heads so close together, Elizabeth could hear nothing of what was said, but momentarily Mr. Lloyd-Jones returned to her side and divulged a sum of money that, though well within her means, was more than she wished to pay for something so self-indulgent.

"You are so very kind to have inquired and I thank you for having done so, however, I had not thought how presumptuous my intentions have been. How could I bring a painting so personal to my taste into what shall be the home of another? I daresay I shall not have much say in the furnishings as long as Mr. Cruikshank's mother lives."

A shadow seemed to cross the face of Mr. Lloyd-Jones and she thought perhaps he frowned a little before his lips turned, once again, into a smile. "Your mother-in-law is expected to stay on after your marriage? In what sort of dwelling? Something a bit bigger than a crofter's hut, I should hope."

Elizabeth worried that he might be exactly correct, but she would not allow him to think so ill of Duncan. "Certainly something larger, of course! Though, I hope not too grand as I shall be helping to care for Mrs. Cruikshank. She is ailing, and I have no wish to be tramping up and down stairs all the day long."

"I pray that I do not overstep my bounds, Miss Armistead," he replied, his smile looking more and more fixed with every passing moment, "but I must say that it seems an arduous life. Your Mr. Cruikshank must be all things wonderful for you to be willing to sacrifice so much for him."

"It is not so much," she said with a shrug, though she knew her words to be a lie. There would be Duncan to care for, as well as his mother, and the farm, whatever that entailed, exactly, and the running of the house on top of that. "There are servants, to be sure, and local fishermen who come in and help when there is the need."

"Indeed."

Why that one word should convey such a wealth of meaning, Elizabeth did not perceive, nor did she have any desire to puzzle out his intent. This, however, made it impossible to formulate a sensible reply. She turned again to the painting and made as if she examined it for the artist's name, one that turned out to be an illegible scribble and worthless as the topic of a new line of conversation.

They stood together in silence and gazed fixedly at the painting. Elizabeth felt that his thoughts were most likely more plentiful than his words, if the manner in which he turned his hat round and round in his hands was any indication. Finally, he seemed to come to a decision, placed his hat on his head, sketched a bow in her general direction, and strode away.

As Elizabeth watched him go, she felt her heart plummet into her stomach. She had said or done something that had disappointed him, but she could not begin to fathom what it might be. She was unable to collect her wits enough to select a book and when Katherine, Miss Hale, found her some minutes later, she was more than ready to join the other ladies in their shopping.

"Come, Elizabeth, we go next to the dressmaker's," Katherine insisted as she took her friend's arm and led her from the shop, "for I am persuaded I never had more reason to have a new gown made up than I have at this very moment."

"Why, has something particularly fortuitous happened whilst we were apart?" Elizabeth asked though she was only half interested in the reply.

"But of course! We encountered Mr. Lloyd-Jones in this very street not five minutes since. He was very attentive to me and asked after me most particularly. He wished to know if I planned to attend the dinner party you spoke of only this morning. To think, I have come all of this way to witness your wedding and might very soon be a married lady, myself!"

Elizabeth felt a surge of some unnamed emotion fill her breast. "Whatever can you mean by that, Katherine? Surely, you have no aspirations in that quarter!"

"If by 'that quarter' you mean Mr. Lloyd-Jones, why ever not?" Katherine asked with an arch air. "He might be a mere quarter to you but in my eyes, he is possessed of all the four quarters that make up the perfect man."

Elizabeth laughed in spite of herself. "And what are those, silly goose?"

"He is handsome, rich, well-spoken," Katherine said, ticking off fingers, "and thoroughly unattached."

"Yes, all you say is true, except for the last." Irked, Elizabeth forced herself to look down the street in anticipation of the shop where they were to meet the older ladies. "I am persuaded he is still in love with the young lady to whom he was most recently betrothed." Once the words were out, Elizabeth knew them to be untrue but she could not account for why she had said them.

"What has that to say to anything?" Katherine asked with a shrug. "He shall not marry her, of that I am certain. Even if he were to change his mind, it is too late. Her name is sunk below reproach and, if you are to be believed, he loves his sister too well to look back, now."

"My opinion does not greatly differ from yours on such matters. However, I should not wish to wed a man who loved another, no matter the circumstances. I should wish better for you, as well."

"You needn't worry about me on that, score, Elizabeth. I do not ask for love. Also, I am weary of soldiers! I wish to marry a man, not a boy, one who has property and privilege. I want to be someone, perhaps even a lady or a countess. Is that too much to ask?"

"It would depend, I suppose on the man. Mr. Lloyd-Jones certainly could not give you a title, and yet, unlike yourself, he comes from a landed family, one whose parents should not wish him to marry the daughter of an upstart mushroom such as your papa."

"And yours is not?" Katherine cried.

"I never said he wasn't. I am not the one under discussion, Kate."

"Yes, but you could be. I see the way he looks at you. You need only snap your fingers and he is yours."

Elizabeth laughed though she was far from amused. "And yet, he has done nothing, said nothing, to make me believe he prefers me to anyone else. There have been no notes or flowers, no lovelorn poetry, no lingering below my bedchamber window, nothing!"

"Elizabeth, I am surprised at you! Those are the actions of the young boys that pine after you at home. A man such as Mr. Lloyd-Jones doesn't stoop to such drivel."

"Oh?" Elizabeth remarked with some uncertainty. "In what manner does the admiration of such a man differ?"

"Well, he most surely would invite her to go out with him, perhaps for a walk, or a ride, or even offer to accompany her to the sweets shop."

"Is that all?" Elizabeth asked, unimpressed.

"No. He would pay calls on her, invite her to dance more than once of an evening, invite her and her family to dinner," Katherine said with growing enthusiasm.

"Aside from the dinner party to which we are both invited," Elizabeth pointed out, "Mr. Lloyd-Jones has taken none of these actions." She failed to mention the two dances they had had the night prior, but she was persuaded that it was of no consequence. "As you shall recall my saying, dinner was originally his sister's notion."

"We shall see," Katherine quipped. "Though, I daresay it hardly matters. You would never leave Duncan. It would break his heart."

"And even more so, mine!" Elizabeth insisted as she pushed open the door to the dressmaker's upon which they had just descended.

They walked into the shop and all disagreeable feelings fell away as they gazed on an impossible number of bolts of gorgeous cloth. The muslin was beneath their notice as it was plentiful in India. However, the velvets and wools were of such quantity and depth of color that Elizabeth thought she might weep. There were also rows of other fabrics too heavy for use in Bengal, all most suitable for walking dresses and riding habits as well as a veritable treasure trove of ribbons and fripperies to trim bonnets and hats. Long elbow-length kid gloves, another article of clothing not much used at home, claimed Elizabeth's fascinated attention.

"Look here at the shawls!" Katherine breathed. "To think that one should need a shawl of such length and thickness! Though I suppose London winters are quite cold."

Elizabeth sighed her approval. She loved a ball gown as much as any other young lady, but she felt a particular yearning for cold weather clothing as they had rarely been of the least use to her. To own a velvet pelisse, a red wool cape, sturdy jean boots and gloves that felt like butter from the tips of the fingers to the hem of one's tiny, puffed sleeves seemed the pinnacle of her fashionable desires.

"Oh, there you are, my darlings," Elizabeth's mother called. "Lady Augusta and I have been discussing styles with the dressmaker. I am determined that you should each have a new gown for the dinner at Lloyd-Jones House."

Elizabeth felt a blush rise in her cheeks at her mother's shameless gloating. At the same time, Elizabeth owned that it was very pleasant to contemplate the construction of a new gown, English made, and up to the very minute in London fashion.

"I have decided," Katherine announced, "that none other will do but this emerald green silk."

"But your eyes are blue," Lady Augusta announced. "I am persuaded you shall look a veritable seraph in the blue satin."

"No. I thank you, Lady Augusta, but my mind is set on the green."

Elizabeth felt her heart sink as she could hardly choose green now. It was her best color and one she wore as often as possible. She owned an emerald green sari that she donned for masquerade balls and very formal Indian occasions, however, it was broken up with bands of other colors. In India, such a length of uninterrupted green was only available in ribbons and as tiny sprigs on the muslins she wore all year round.

"Then, Elizabeth, you shall have the blue, won't you?" her mother suggested. It is such a lovely color and I am persuaded it shall make *such* a gown!"

Elizabeth was about to concede when her eye was caught by a red silk that seemed to glow with an ambient light of its own. "What about this one?" She crossed the room to pull a length of the red silk from the bolt and held it up to the light from the window. "It is so lovely and deep."

Lady Augusta, who looked a bit discomfited, turned a baleful eye on her sister-in-law who, in turn, looked her disapproval. "I don't know . . It's a bit daring, don't you think?"

"How can you say so, Mama? I am a nearly married lady, not a debutante. I am persuaded this shall be just the thing for formal dinners in Scotland and red is the primary color in Duncan's family tartan. If I were to wear a gown in this red with a tartan scarf, it ought to be all that is proper."

"I do agree," Lady Augusta conceded. "Though, we shall have to look elsewhere for the tartan. Prinny brought it into fashion in eighty-nine, but that was long ago when your mother and I were young brides."

"I shouldn't wish to be a burden," Elizabeth began, reluctantly.

"It is no trouble, we shall have to be clever, that is all! Now that you have made an account of it, I am persuaded it shall be all that is proper and will look excessively well on you, my dear," her aunt continued.

Elizabeth admitted to feeling very well pleased. The tartan in question bore bands of green, as well as blue, and it would be not at all amiss to complement the gown with the parure of emeralds given her by her father as a wedding present. "Then it is settled. All that is left is to consider the style of gown. What shall you have, Katherine?"

But Katherine seemed sulky and out of sorts and did not answer.

"That is all right, Elizabeth, we shall leave your mother to assist Katherine with her gown. I am persuaded she will be absolutely lovely in whatever she chooses. Why don't you come with me and we will speak with the dressmaker as to the sort of gown you wish."

"Of course, Aunt," Elizabeth replied dutifully even as she fretted over Katherine's demeanor. It almost seemed as if she was envious, but Elizabeth felt they had been the best of friends far too long for such unpleasantness. She made a mental note to have a good, long cose with her bosom friend the moment they had some time to themselves.

"Now, Elizabeth," Aunt Augusta said as she put her arm around her niece and drew her towards the back of the shop. "Bear in mind that I had not the pleasure of watching you grow up, however, I must say, you have made excellent strides since you were in London last. I am most pleased with your deportment, manners and willingness to let your natural beauty shine. I propose that we make this new gown as fetching as may be and that we order up a few other pieces, as well. I understand that gauzy muslins that leave little to the imagination are *di rigueur* but they won't be best appreciated in the wilds of Scotland. You must have sturdy morning gowns, stout walking gowns and shoes and riding habits. You will find that you cannot have enough wraps of every kind; shawls, capes, cloaks, mantles, and of course, at least one spencer, pelisse and redingote each."

"Goodness, Aunt, you make my head spin! Shall it truly be as cold as all that in Scotland?"

"Oh, no my dear, colder! My list is what one would need to survive the English countryside of a winter."

"Then, I suppose we had best get started. I should not like to shiver my way through winter."

"Exactly. And since this is not the same establishment at which we have ordered up your wedding gown, the seamstress shall require you to be properly measured out. When she is done with your measurements, I shall expect you to have considered and we will make a list of all that you will need, not just to survive the winter, but as a young bride. You will need warm underclothes, as well," Aunt Augusta said with a sad little shake of the head.

"I . . I suppose I had not considered the need for so many new clothes. It is fortunate that Papa was very open-handed with funds and I shall be able to bear the expense."

"Precisely, so you must not stint on a single thing. Remember, you must have gloves for every occasion and bonnets, too," Aunt Augusta pointed out as she disappeared from the little room they had entered so as to leave Elizabeth alone with the seamstress.

Elizabeth gave the seamstress only enough of her attention to do as she was bid. She turned the rest of her mind over to the tallying up of a new wardrobe and concluded that the purchase of several new trunks would be required to cart her clothing out to Scotland. She supposed ball gowns would be of little use in Sutherland, but she intended to have a new one made up as well; it would be well worn by the time she quit London.

After what seemed like hours, an order for a grand, new, wardrobe for Elizabeth and several new gowns for Katherine had been successfully concluded, leaving the ladies free to dwell on the state of their stomachs.

"I believe I have never been more famished," Elizabeth's Mama declared with an enormous sigh. "And, to think, I had little more to do than sit in a chair and admire everything upon which my eyes fell!"

Secretly, Elizabeth thought that her Mama's task of contenting Katherine in her present mood whilst placating the shop girl, whose patience had worn thinner than muslin in more than one instance, took the prize for most arduous of the day. "Well, then, Mama, you shall choose where we should go to take refreshment."

"Gunter's! I should love it above all things! I have patronized his shop, of course, but it was so long ago. Elizabeth, do you know, they offer ices in the most exotic flavors; burnt filbert, bergamot, and parmesan of all things!"

"Yes, Mama, I too, have been to Gunter's once or twice with Aunt Augusta when I was last in London. I think it sounds a splendid idea. What say you, Katherine?"

"Whatever you say should suffice for us all, I daresay," Katherine replied with a saucy air. "However, if I had just now ordered up such a quantity of gowns, I should take care not to add to my figure or you shall not be able to get into them once they arrive."

Elizabeth subdued a gasp of dismay. "I am persuaded you are too kind, Katherine," she said meekly. "I am not entirely certain what I have done to deserve such a good friend as you have been to me for so long and daresay you are perfectly correct. I shall only have a taste of Mama's ice, depending on whether or not she chooses to eschew the parmesan."

Katherine's only response was to take Mrs. Armistead by the arm and walk forward so briskly that Elizabeth and Aunt Augusta were quite left behind.

"I should mind that girl if I were you," she advised. "It is clear that she does not have your best interests at heart."

"I should be surprised if that were true, Aunt. She is not herself today for some reason. I expect I shall have it out of her when next we speak."

"Mark my words, Elizabeth, that girl is inclined to stir the pot."

Elizabeth knew not what to say that would not put her aunt in the wrong. As such, she found it best to remain silent for the remainder of their journey to Gunter's. Once they had arrived, however, Elizabeth did her utmost to include Katherine in every remark.

"I am so well looking forward to our dinner with the Lloyd-Joneses, are you not, Katherine?"

"But of course," she said, lifting her spoon in so pretentious a fashion that Elizabeth knew not where to look. She had never known her friend to put on airs and could not fathom why she should now so do.

"And you, Aunt? Do you not anticipate that Katherine shall experience an evening of surpassing divertissement?" Elizabeth knew she overstated the case, but she was bent on teasing a more congenial mood from Katherine.

"I am of the mind that we shall all enjoy ourselves immensely," Aunt Augusta replied. "Mr. Lloyd-Jones was good enough to send his man to inquire of me what his menu for the evening should entail, based on the delicacies that are not easily obtained so far across the sea. I am persuaded you all, Katherine included, shall be delighted with the treats he has in store for you."

"Oh," Elizabeth's mama declared, "I can hardly stand the wait! I have so longed for a taste of good English cooking."

"You have experienced the best of English cooking whilst staying in my home this past se'nnight." Augusta turned her nose up in the air.

"Yes, of course. I hadn't thought . ." Mrs. Armistead said into her plate.

"What Mama means to say, Aunt, is that she looks forward to an entire evening dedicated to the sort of food we don't often eat or simply cannot find in India. Do you not think that is just what she meant, Katherine?"

Katherine favored Elizabeth with a mulish look and said nothing.

"Very well, then, Katherine, if the very idea of dinner with the Lloyd-Joneses is to cause you such misery, I very much look forward to it having been eaten and done with."

All the ladies ignored this piece of impertinence and it was Elizabeth who was miserable as she watched her companions eat their delicious ices. Indeed, she felt so out of sorts that she thought perhaps she was sickening with something. By the time tea had been taken and the journey home commenced, she was persuaded that she was entirely unwell. It was with a great deal of relief that she took to her bed where she stayed for the remainder of the days left until dinner at Lloyd-Jones House.

Chapter Seven

*B*y the morning of the dinner party, Colin felt that he must escape the house or run mad. Carpenters, plasterers, painters and seamstresses scurried hither and yon as they rushed to do the master's bidding in time for the much anticipated dinner. In all the chaos, he had all but forgotten his promise to escort Analisa to her round of soirees and balls. He presumed that she was still inclined to speak to him when she arrived for the dinner she had so insisted upon, the dawning of which marked four days since he had last seen a living soul, save those in his employ. He hoped he still recalled how to make polite conversation for his guests, though he knew he had weightier concerns with which to flay himself.

The newly decorated dining room was one such concern; green and blue draperies against walls papered in gold and mustard was a hazardous combination, but one he felt he must risk in light of the new painting. His purchase of it was the only choice of which he was absolutely certain and he had enjoyed repeating the blues, greens and reds, as well as the yellows and gold from the picture in the fresh decor of the room where it hung. Though Miss Armistead had admired it every bit as much as he, he felt no qualms in purchasing it; she had been given the opportunity.

He thought it looked very well between the pair of long, paned windows that looked out onto green grass and blue skies that mirrored those on the canvas while the mahogany wainscoting complemented the skin tones of the natives pictured. The rest of the decor would have to take care of itself for he found he minded very little if it were far from perfect; it was now the room he loved best.

"Beggin' your pardon, sir, but I must get by."

Colin turned to find a worker as he strong-armed a floor candelabrum through the doorway and quickly stepped out of the way. As the man placed the enormous piece, one of a pair of Nubian slaves holding aloft a brace of candles, on its feet, Colin admired the rich Venetian paint colors that adorned the wood and gesso piece. He found that he greatly anticipated the moment when its twin was in place and the candles lit so as to fully illuminate the painting he had grown to love so much already.

When all was in readiness, the candles were lit, as well as the fire in the grate. Colin drew back the draperies to allow in as much sunlight as possible, looked round the room and was greatly pleased. For the remainder of the day, he shadowed his cook to ensure she followed his instructions to the letter, hounded the butler as to the seating arrangements and forced himself to refrain from haunting the dining room. When evening finally arrived, he lingered over his toilette and, for the first time in recent memory, discarded one imperfectly tied neck cloth after another.

By the time he was ensconced in the salon adjacent to the dining room to await his guests, he felt his nerves were standing on end. However, once he caught sight of green silk skirts emerging through the doorway, he sensed that all was right with the world. Those skirts were the precise shade as the upholstery on his new dining room chairs, the very same color of Miss Armistead's eyes, and he knew, deep in his bones, it was the hue she would wear to his dinner party. When he looked up to behold the somewhat wan face of the girl in the green gown, he knew a bit of a jolt. It wasn't only that the face belonged to Miss Hale; it was clear to see that green was not her color. It seemed almost as if the gown were wearing her rather than the other way around.

And then Miss Armistead came through the doorway, utterly resplendent in her deep, red round gown, her eyes like pools of emerald fire, her black hair done up in dozens of glossy ringlets that framed her creamy face, and his world was turned entirely upside down. He knew in that moment that he was doomed to pine after another man's wife for the remainder of his life. "I . . Miss Armistead, you look enchanting!" he exclaimed as if she were the sole occupant of the room besides himself. He remembered himself quickly, however. "As do you Miss Hale, Lady Augusta, Mrs. Armistead. We are to abide here for a time before dinner is served, but I own that I am most eager to proceed to the dining room."

"I have heard tell," Lady Augusta replied, "that you have been at great pains to redecorate your dining room to your own tastes. I must say, we are all most eager to view it, however, wouldn't it be best if we were to wait for your other guests?"

For a moment, Colin thought she was jesting with him, and then he recalled that Analisa had not yet arrived. "Yes, of course, my sister; I daresay she shall arrive at any moment."

"And what of the other gentlemen invited?" Miss Armistead asked. "Hadn't we best tarry here for them, as well?"

Thunderstruck, Colin prayed the alarm he felt did not show on his face. "Oh, yes . . the other gentlemen. I don't believe I have received acceptances from any of them. Perhaps Analisa has done."

"What is it I am to have done?" Analisa asked as she entered the room.

Colin went swiftly to her side, drew her back into the hall, and firmly shut the door behind them as he dismissed the footman who lingered nearby; his attention seemed too sharp for comfort. "You shall be appalled when I tell you, but I failed to issue invitations to any save those already arrived. I don't suppose you thought to speak to any of the gentlemen we considered, have you?"

"But of course not!" Analisa protested. "I had thought you had that well in hand. I can see that you are helpless without a woman to serve as your hostess."

"I had thought you to be my hostess, Analisa. Was that not understood?"

"No, it was not. Need I remind you that I am just out of the school room and as such am unsuitable for such a role?" she asked, a bit cross. "Well! We shall simply have to make do but it shall seem very odd, there is no doubt of that. I pray that we might count on Lady Augusta to refrain from speaking of this to her friends. As for the others, they will all be gone from London by the end of the season and we may breathe far easier then."

"Yes, but how might I excuse myself for such a lapse? There was so much conversation on the topic of having an even number of ladies and gentlemen, how do I explain?" Oh, no!" he cried as the whole truth dawned on him. "I told Cook that dinner would be for ten. I was very particular that she should have enough food for five hungry gentlemen. She will have my head on a platter, I have no doubt! And Evans! I insisted that he go out at the last minute and acquire more port as I was without any doubt that more was needed."

Analisa favored him with a most grave expression, whereupon her eyes began to twinkle and she dissolved into laughter. "Oh, Colin, it is above all things rich! I am persuaded we shall have a marvelous time, just the six of us, and no one shall be the wiser. But, yes, we must arrive at an explanation that bears scrutiny, to be sure!"

"I am most relieved that you have arrived at the same conclusion as have I," Colin said a bit disdainfully.

"Yes, well," she replied, quelling her laughter, "I believe we might do well enough if we simply tell them the truth."

Colin silently considered this proposal but found he must reject it. He could hardly claim that his mind was so taken up with what should be Miss Armistead's wondrous reaction to his having built a room around a painting she admired that he simply forgot to invite the gentlemen. No, that would never do. "I suppose I might say that I had some rather onerous business matters that claimed my attention."

"Oh, Colin, you mustn't! They know you have arranged to redecorate an entire room to be ready for this evening, and you have managed to do so in an exceedingly short period of time in spite of business matters, am I not correct?"

"Yes, I have, but just," he said wryly. "I could claim that, in my eagerness to have everything perfect for tonight, the inviting of the others slipped my mind." It was close enough to the truth to slip as easily from his tongue as the issuing of invitations had his memory.

"I suppose that will have to do. Now," she urged as she adjusted his neck cloth and brushed a speck of dust from his coat sleeve, "you must simply loosen up. They will assume you are dissembling if you walk in there with your shoulders up around your ears."

Colin took a deep breath and allowed his shoulders to drop. "Shall I pass muster, then?"

"Yes," his sister said as she gave him a twinkling look. "I have always maintained that you are the handsomest of my brothers."

"I am your only brother, you dullard," he taunted as he pulled her hand through to rest on his arm.

"Yes, but if I were to say what I am truly thinking, you should become unbearably puffed up."

"Since I do not know what it is you are thinking, I am unable to comment as to your accuracy. However, I suspect I might say the same of you," he said with a doting smile. "And now we shall sally forth and take our lumps, shall we not?"

Together they pushed open the door and walked into the salon.

"They are returned," Lady Augusta announced as if the others in the room were quite blind. "Is there anything about which we should be aware?"

MISS ARMISTEAD MAKES HER CHOICE

"Nothing untoward, Lady Augusta," Colin answered. "Only, it seems that we might go into dinner immediately if it is quite ready. I must apologize for our uneven numbers. I was so eager to arrange matters in the dining room that I neglected to issue invitations to any besides those already present. It is unfortunate but there is nothing to be done about it but eat twice as much as intended. I pray Cook shall not take me to task for working her harder than was needful."

"Then it shall just be us," Miss Armistead replied. "I own, it is a pleasant notion and I find I am most anxious to take in the beauty of your newly decorated dining room."

Colin was so well-pleased that he wondered how he could bear the thought of Miss Armistead going off to Scotland for any reason at all whatsoever. "Then there is nothing for it but to proceed."

"Colin, I shall just pull the bell and remain here to let them know below stairs that we shall be waiting in the dining room," Analisa said.

"Thank you," Colin said with a wink for her eyes only. He hoped she knew how much he owed her and decided he must go out first thing on the morrow to arrange for flowers or chocolates or perhaps a jeweled pendant to be delivered to her without delay. "As it is a most casual affair, there is no need to proceed in any order," he said in hopes that Miss Armistead would push her way past her elders to be led into dinner on his arm. As she did not, he was left with nothing to do but throw open the connecting doors from the salon to the dining room. Lady Augusta stepped forward in what he supposed to be expectations that she should have his arm, but he held his ground and indicated that they should pass into the room ahead of him.

Last of his guests to enter was Miss Armistead, who uttered a gratifying gasp of delight as she turned about to take in all its charms. As her red gown swept the antique crimson and cobalt Persian carpet beneath her feet, he could not help but think how her ensemble might have been custom made for just such a

room. Aside from the virtues of her gown, the blues and greens
threaded through her long, red scarf were a perfect match for
those of the draperies and the green of her eyes, as well as the
emeralds about her creamy neck, all of which were of a hue with
the velvet cushions of the chairs that encircled the table.

He knew the very moment that she realized the single painting
in the room was the same they had first seen together at the book
shop. She did not immediately say anything but moved to stand by
it when she thought the other ladies, who were wandering about
the room in abject admiration, would take no notice of her. She
glanced over to where he stood, perhaps to ascertain whether or not
he watched, and when she saw that he did, she appeared to pause
to consider. The allure of the painting seemed, however, to be more
than she could withstand and it was not long before she turned to
regard it openly.

He found he could withstand it no less and found himself suddenly next to her, drinking in the vibrant scene. "Pray, do tell me if
I have done wrong. I was persuaded you did not wish to own it."

"Oh, but I did want it, quite desperately," she replied, her gaze
never leaving the canvas. "I merely felt it unwise to purchase it. You,
however, have done no wrong in my mind; quite the contrary. I am
gratified to know that it is here and so happily admired. You have
masterfully arranged the entire room in celebration of it."

"I am delighted that you noticed. It is a beautiful painting and
I'm afraid I have a decided weakness for all things beautiful. I hope
it is not too bold of me to say that it brings me pleasure for reasons
other than its beauty, as it never fails to bring you to mind each
time I cast my eyes upon it."

She remained silent for so long, he feared that he had, indeed,
been too bold, and was relieved, when she spoke, to find that he
had not.

"It pleases me to think that you shall remember me and that,
when I think of this painting, as I shall every day of my life, I shall

picture it here, in this room, its owner admiring it every bit as much as have I."

A suitable reply was beyond Colin's powers at the moment; so moved was he by her words that he was made to relive again the emotions he experienced when she first walked through the door that evening. He knew himself to be the least knowledgeable person when it came to determining what it felt like to be in love, but he could say, in no uncertain terms, that what he felt for Miss Armistead was unlike any sensibility he had ever known. It was certainly one far deeper than what he had felt for Cecily Ponsonby.

"Now it is I who fears she has done wrong," Miss Armistead said quietly. When he did not immediately reply, she turned to gaze at him and he was astonished to see the same glow of admiration in her eyes for him as she demonstrated for the painting. They stood staring at one another so long that he forgot entirely every reason why he should not act on an overwhelming desire to put his lips to hers. Recalling their circumstances just in time, he noted that her cheeks turned bright red as she turned hastily away and he knew that she had somehow ascertained his longing.

"Sir, I see that you have pressed a pair of Nubian slaves into service so as to illuminate your painting," she said over-brightly.

"I found I could not resist them. The blue of their jackets so exactly matches that of sky in the picture."

"Or, one could say, the same as the color of my eyes," Miss Hale remarked from where she stood behind them.

Colin hadn't heard her approach and could not say how long she had stood there. It was a most discommodious sensation. "Yes, indeed, Miss Hale," he said far more politely than he wished. "I am not the least loathe to admit that your eyes are of a deep hue not often found anywhere but in paintings."

She smiled her pleasure at his compliment but made no further remark.

"I own myself surprised," Miss Armistead said, perhaps in an attempt to steer the conversation in a different direction, "that a fashionable man such as you have no little, black boy to ride on the back of your carriage whilst you tool about London."

"Me? What should I do with such a fellow? Besides which, it should be an expensive prospect. I'm told children that age eat their heads off."

"Does this signify that you are in no hurry to fill your nursery?" Mrs. Armistead asked from across the room.

He was more than a little dismayed that his private conversation with Miss Armistead had become a battle royal, but he hid his ire well. "No, not at all. I am more than happy to feed my own children any amount of food, especially if it should make their mother happy." He said this with a smile that he just managed to refrain from bestowing on Miss Armistead. "However, a servant is something else entirely. It's a matter of economics. I find that little, old ladies with no teeth eat the least."

"Well, this little old lady," Lady Augusta chimed in, "has all of her teeth and she means to make the most of them."

"Dear Aunt, you make yourself sound an ancient and we all know that is not the case in the least," Miss Armistead insisted.

"Truer words were never spoken, Miss Armistead," Colin readily agreed. "The four of you make an enchanting quartet, all of whom I hope to please with my plans for the evening."

"I shall be most amused to see how you carry out the dancing portion of the entertainments," Analisa remarked. "I do not intend to sit idly by whilst you dance with each of us in turn."

"Ah, Analisa, I see that you have joined us. So, what is it you suggest, then? That the ladies should dance with one other?"

"Why ever not?" Analisa asked with that twinkle in her eye that spelled her enjoyment of his predicament. "It shall doubtless prove *tres amusant*. This is why we are here *ensemble*, is it not?

I should particularly enjoy getting to know Miss Elizabeth, as I should be most pleased to call her, a good deal better before she takes herself off to Scotland."

"In that case, you shall have first place on my dance card," Miss Armistead replied with an answering twinkle.

As Colin had immediately wished for that particular place, he found it difficult to share their amusement. "I have no wish to dampen your zeal, but the menu for dinner is such that you are all likely to be too full to take a step. That is, if you wish to spare me trouble with my cook. She is excellent when it comes to food, however, her temper leaves much to be desired."

With those words, the butler entered the room. "Sir, if it suits you, dinner is now served."

"Thank you, Evans, it suits me admirably." Colin turned to take in his guests. "Shall we all be seated? Do feel free to ignore the place cards as at least four of them allotted are decidedly *de trop.*"

A chorus of laughter rose up at his words and there was a general hubbub as the ladies took their seats. Colin was surprised and a little injured when Miss Armistead eagerly took her place at the center of the table rather than at one of the two nearest his own position at the head. As a result, his dinner partners were Miss Hale and Lady Augusta, the two ladies he felt the least desire with which to converse. Mrs. Armistead took up the place across from her daughter and Analisa was farthest away, a circumstance that prompted a feeling of having been abandoned. However, he was confident that once the food began to arrive that there would be much to discuss.

With the help of Lady Augusta, he had chosen the menu with great pride and was very much looking forward to the reactions of the ladies from India. Though generally a dish reserved for breakfast, he greatly anticipated their reaction to a British staple, bubble and squeak, along with gooseberry on mashed turnips and Naples biscuits. Also to come were

Welsh rarebit on toast, Salmagundi, white soup, jugged hare and meat pasties. Desert would consist of molded ices, flavored and shaped as various fruits, made from Gunter's own receipt. Colin was delighted when he learned Cook was capable of creating her own ices and decided he should do himself a sad disservice were he to cause her to tender her resignation on that count alone.

As the meal progressed, the blissful reaction of the ladies was all that he could have wished. The items that could not be had in India or required a British cook of some expertise to replicate with any success were all happily hailed and discussed at great length, and the ices were an absolute triumph. However, the delight of the ladies did not please him to the extent he had anticipated; certainly it was nothing compared to the pleasure he felt at the words with which Miss Armistead demonstrated her approval of the painting and it's well thought out setting.

He felt Analisa's eyes upon him from her seat down table and saw that she had guessed his thoughts.

"Ladies," Analisa said brightly, "I believe we must do our best to work off our dinners. I, for one, wish to dance, do you not?" she asked with a look for Miss Armistead.

"But, of course. You shan't wiggle out of your promise as easily as that," she replied.

"Then, let us leave Colin to his own devices for a bit whilst we all retire to a room where we can freshen up. Colin, you have a room set aside for the use of the ladies, do you not?"

Colin did not. Or, at least, if he was possessed of a chamber prepared for such activities, he was unaware of it. In hopes that his former betrothed had thought of providing whatever was needful for afternoon callers, he rose and pulled the bell. "Evans shall escort you thither. Pray tell if there is anything else you need."

"I believe our lack of male guests requires that a footman or two be sent up to assist in moving the sofa and rolling back the carpet in the salon so we might commence dancing the moment we are returned."

"To be sure," he replied with deep gratitude for his sister's prudence.

Evans entered and the requests were made, whereupon he led the ladies from the room with absolutely no sign that there was no portion of the house given over for the use of females and their needs. Once the door had shut behind the last of them, Colin collapsed into his chair, grateful for small miracles.

By the time the ladies returned, the footman had prepared the room and Colin had recovered enough to spend a moment going through the music at the pianoforte. "I had hopes that you should be willing to play for us, Analisa." The fact that he had forgotten to engage musicians was all of a piece and he loathed to admit it in the presence of Miss Armistead.

"Of course I shall play, Colin, but surely there is another young lady present who possesses such skills. We shall take turns," she said with a glance at the faces of the other ladies.

"I play," Miss Armistead readily admitted, much to Colin's chagrin. He had hoped that she lacked the skill, making her available to dance all the evening.

"Very good!" Analisa cried. "Come and turn the pages for me, Miss Elizabeth. We shall observe the others and speak snidely of them beneath our breaths," she added with a smile that utterly belied her offensive words.

"I am persuaded you shall have nothing but praise for myself and Mr. Lloyd-Jones as we waltz," Miss Hale replied loftily.

To his surprise, Miss Armistead and Analisa turned upon one another the self-same smile, one that indicated a wealth of meaning, all of which was a mystery to him. It cut him to the core that neither seemed the least interested in dancing with him. He envisaged an evening of longing to hold Miss Armistead in his arms whilst he danced with most everyone else.

"Well then, Miss Hale," he said duteously, "I shall be honored to partner you in a waltz if we are able to persuade Analisa to play one for us. However, as the innocent young maiden she is, she might not wish to participate in anything so scandalous," he mocked with a sidelong look for his sister.

"Yes, of course I shall!" Analisa replied. "Fortunately, my brother is an accomplished musician and keeps abreast of all the latest pieces. Ah! Here is just the one."

"Is that the very truth? Do you play, indeed?" Miss Armistead quizzed.

"Not as well as my sister, but I do enjoy it."

"He plays far better than I, do be assured of that! I shall have him play something for us later this evening," Analisa insisted.

"I should be happy to do so but, as you can see, my work has been cut out for me," he said with a smile that took in every lady in the room.

Miss Hale stepped forward and placed her hand in his. "Dancing is not work, sir, but pure poetry. Do begin, Miss Lloyd-Jones, or we shall waste the evening in idle chit-chat."

None seemed capable of disobeying such a command and Colin and Miss Hale were in motion with no further delay. As conversation was entirely possible in such a setting, he felt he was expected to speak. However, whatever was said between them should be heard, at the very least, by the two older ladies who sat on the far side of the room from the pianoforte and who took no pains to hide the fact that they were actively eavesdropping. With a last covert glance at Miss Armistead, he cleared his throat and attempted to land on a suitable topic of conversation.

"I had momentarily forgotten, Miss Hale, that you spent your childhood in India, just as has Miss Armistead. Perhaps you might regale me with tales of Bengal. I find that my interest in the subject grows with our every meeting." Colin meant his comment to encompass all the ladies from India, but it was clear Miss Hale thought otherwise.

"If I had known you were so interested in my childhood, I most certainly should have filled your ears, for it is all most exciting. Not for me, of course," she was quick to add. "I am, in fact, quite accustomed to lions and elephants, you understand, though, I must confess, I never tire of spotting a leopard as they are rarely seen during the day."

"I am vastly relieved to know that, Miss Hale, as I am persuaded that the young ladies of Bengal are not allowed to wander about at night. Now I need not be apprehensive as to whether or not you shall become dinner to a leopard."

He could not say why he looked to Miss Armistead as he spoke, and though she did not turn to find his eyes on her, he was gratified to see that she smiled in reaction to his remark.

"I have an elder brother, just as your sister does, but I am persuaded you are far more kind to her than Harold shall ever be to me," Miss Hale said in tragic tones.

"In that case, Miss Hale, I am in hopes that he is not often at home. What does he do?"

"He makes money, stacks and stacks of it, just as Papa does. I have never bothered to learn precisely how they get their hands on it. I have been told that the mind of a woman is too genteel for such things."

Colin felt unable to serve her remark with an appropriate reply, especially in light of how Lady Augusta rolled her eyes in disgust at Miss Hale's déclassé words. "Do you have sisters?" he asked in hopes of changing the subject.

"Yes, indeed, all of them still in short skirts and excessively tiresome," she said with a jaded air. "I should hardly say so, but I do not look forward to going home. I should much rather stay in England," she added with a moue that he was persuaded was meant for him in spite of the way in which she turned her blue eyes to the wall.

He stole another glance at Miss Armistead and saw that, this time, she did not smile. In point of fact, she looked more than a little low and he wondered what could account for it.

"Has your father sent you here to find a husband, then? I should have thought there were more than enough British officers in Bengal from which to choose now that Miss Armistead has made her choice." The words were out before he ascertained the unpleasant light in which they put Miss Hale. Now that they were said, however, he could not think how to unsay them. His gaze flew once again to Miss Armistead at the pianoforte in hopes that she might discover the means to rescue him.

"I do believe that what Mr. Lloyd-Jones meant to say," Miss Armistead began slowly, "is that one hardly need send one's daughter to England to secure a husband, is that not so, Mr. Lloyd-Jones? After all, it is common knowledge that I failed to receive a single offer the year I enjoyed my London season. Love and happiness were waiting for me back in India all along."

Though Colin could not like all that Miss Armistead said, he could not help but compare her to his sister with most favorable results. Both seemed to say the right thing, always, in spite of the lively sense of humor they seemed to share. In contrast, Miss Hale, whose vivid blue eyes were even now filling with tears, had proven to be more than a little indiscreet.

"My dear Miss Hale, I am persuaded there are dozens of young soldiers back at home who are pining away for you. Marriage to any one of them should return you to the British Isles post haste."

To his extreme discomfiture, rather than Miss Hale's mood being bolstered by his words, she burst into a proper bout of tears, whereupon Miss Armistead abandoned her post at the pianoforte, took Miss Hale in her arms and drew her a few paces away while Mrs. Armistead and Lady Augusta looked on in horror. "Mr. Lloyd-Jones, I should be most grateful if you and your sister played something lively, as a duet. Wouldn't that be diverting, Katherine?" she asked of her friend.

Miss Hale, who had already begun to rally, nodded her head and sniffed.

Colin immediately moved to the pianoforte and quickly located just the right piece of music, a Mozart variation that required four hands. He was delighted to play it with his sister as he had longed to do since he had purchased the music. However, the notion of having Miss Armistead at his side as they played was one he could not readily dismiss.

An image of her seated in the shadows of a dark and cold hovel in the wilds of Scotland, one entirely devoid of a pianoforte, a proper library or even a book, rose unbidden in his mind. He shivered and Analisa turned a wide-eyed look on him that indicated she had felt the tremor that passed through him. He feigned not to notice and diverted his attention to the hoped-for recovery of Miss Hale. He saw that Miss Armistead had a masterful command of the situation but hoped he might take an action that would somehow make amends. "Miss Hale, I daresay you play. Are you familiar with this piece? I am persuaded Analisa should yield her place in your favor."

Smiles wreathed every face at his suggestion and Miss Hale eagerly took Analisa's place at the pianoforte.

Chapter Eight

"The time has arrived for you to partner me, Miss Elizabeth," Miss Lloyd-Jones urged. As the two of them clasped hands, Elizabeth was only too happy to finally have the opportunity to dance. To her satisfaction, the older ladies seemed to be enjoying themselves as they clapped their hands and stamped their feet in time to the music. All in all, it was vastly diverting and it served to distract Katherine from her wounded feelings.

However, the new arrangement put Mr. Lloyd-Jones in proximity to Katherine's clumsy attempts to attach him. Why Elizabeth should be in the least put out by the thought of Mr. Lloyd-Jones and Katherine together, she could not say. And yet, she was vastly relieved when, the moment the piece was finished, Mr. Lloyd-Jones rose from the bench and favored Katherine with a bow. "I feel privileged to have played with such a fine musician, Miss Hale, but I find I must return to my role as the only suitable partner available to a room full of ladies, all of whom have clearly demonstrated their love of dance."

"Never say so, Colin! I feel supremely suitable, indeed," Miss Lloyd-Jones claimed, her face alight with laughter.

"Very well, then, I shall seek my quarry elsewhere," he chided.

"Ho! Not I, you rogue!" Lady Augusta said when his eye fell upon her.

"Mrs. Armistead then?"

Elizabeth thought for a moment that her mother would accept if only Miss Lloyd-Jones had not quite literally pushed Elizabeth directly into Mr. Lloyd-Jones' path.

"Miss Elizabeth has not yet had her turn to dance with you, Colin," Analisa pointed out.

Once again Elizabeth stood so close to Mr. Lloyd-Jones that she was forced to experience discomfort in order to look up at him. To her relief, he took a step back but her consternation was doubled when he took her in his arms in preparation for a waltz. Katherine, however, immediately began to play a polonaise, a circumstance that greatly appealed to Elizabeth who lost no time in urging her mother and Miss Lloyd-Jones to join them.

"We can hardly give a satisfactory appearance of marching if there is not at least one other couple, is that not so?" Elizabeth queried.

"But of course," Miss Lloyd-Jones replied, whereupon, she navigated herself so briskly to Mrs. Armistead's side that Elizabeth had no choice but to take Mr. Lloyd-Jones' arm or risk seeming uncivil.

"How very pleasant," Elizabeth remarked as they began to march, "as this is a dance much given to conversation, whilst being utterly devoid of the danger of fainting."

Mr. Lloyd-Jones laughed and Elizabeth noted that he appeared to be at ease for the first time that evening.

"Well, Miss Elizabeth, if I may call you thus, has the moment arrived when you might tell me of your version of a childhood spent in India?"

This obvious reference to their conversation at the book store brought a smile to her lips. She looked up to read his expression but hadn't the opportunity to speak before her mother interpolated her opinion on the subject.

"I do believe she should inform you, first, as to how she met her betrothed. It is a story quite dramatic, I do assure you."

"Mama," Elizabeth said as she turned to bend a look of warning on her mother. "I met him at a dance along with many other soldiers that night, as I recall."

"Your birthday fete could hardly be deemed an ordinary event! I was at great pains to take care that it was exceptional," her mother said with a sniff. "Still, I do not refer to that particular meeting. There is no doubt that he admired you most excessively from that night on, but I speak of the occasion when you began to admire him in return."

"Somehow I think there are few who should be entertained by such a story," Elizabeth said in a low voice.

"You needn't relate it if you do not wish to," Miss Lloyd-Jones suggested warmly, followed by what Elizabeth thought to be a look of consternation cast upon Mr. Llyond-Jones.

"Truly, Elizabeth was a great heroine. I am vastly pleased at her courage and strength," her mother insisted. "If she does not relate the story, then I shall."

"Very well, then," Elizabeth agreed. "I shall tell you the circumstances to which my mother alludes as she is sure to embroider it past all recognition." She looked to Mr. Lloyd-Jones to ascertain his feelings on the subject but he wore a slight smile that said nothing of his thoughts. "India is truly a far different country than is England, but those of us who hail from Britain pass the time much as you do. Though it rarely is truly cold in Bengal we do have a rainy season of some duration. In point of fact, it rains so heavily during the same months you enjoy summer that one must grasp upon any opportunity to spend time out of doors. I love to ride and on this particular morning, I had taken advantage of a clear sky in order to acquire exercise."

"Are you a horsewoman, then, Miss Elizabeth?" Mr. Lloyd-Jones queried.

"Yes, a tolerable one. However, my enjoyment of it is doubtless far greater than my abilities. On this particular morning, I was a few miles from home when it began to pour. I was just about to turn back when I heard a cry. I was riding alongside the river and could see where a horse had struggled and slipped in the mud of the verge between the road and the bridge."

"This is the part that is so very astonishing," her mama interrupted.

"I dismounted as I did not wish to suffer the same fate of who ever might be found and very carefully made my way onto the bridge so as to look down below without fear of being washed into the river. It was all very muddy, but I could see the red of his coat .. and there was red for other reasons, as well," she added in a small voice that she feared revealed too much of her horror.

"It is difficult for Elizabeth to speak of this, but he was injured and bleeding quite severely," her mother revealed.

"And this was Mr. Cruikshank?" Mr. Lloyd-Jones queried.

"Yes, it was," Elizabeth replied. "It was required that the horse be shot, of course, but that was not the most distressing part. Mr. Cruikshank had been struck in the face by the hoofs of the horse. I'm afraid I wasn't terribly useful except that I rode for help which, thankfully, was found not too far off."

"It was a service of inestimable worth, of course, as it saved his life," her mother added. "However, it was the weeks she spent by his side at hospital that buoyed his spirits and prevented him from succumbing to his injuries."

"There was a good deal of infection," Elizabeth explained, "and there were surgeries, as well. I am aware that there is no common sense about it, but I felt somehow responsible, having been the one who discovered him. I found I was unhappy and fretful if I were not by his side and, as Mama has said, I spent a good deal of time at his bedside, reading and talking. It resulted in our becoming acquainted with one another."

In spite of Katherine's spirited playing, the atmosphere of the room became a bit somber and Mr. Lloyd-Jones in particular appeared to have been greatly stirred by her story.

"Mama, you should not have so insisted on my relating such an affecting tale," Elizabeth scolded lightly.

"Pray, do not regret your words, Miss Elizabeth," Miss Lloyd-Jones cried, "as I do not. It has shown me a deeper view of your character. Indeed, I must say that it is little wonder that I love you so."

As if these words of affection were not enough, Elizabeth was astonished to feel Mr. Lloyd-Jones' hand upon her own where it lay against his arm. It occurred to her, not for the first time, that the Lloyd-Joneses were creatures of such friendship and goodwill that she would sadly miss them when she married and repaired to Scotland.

"I must add my words of admiration to my sister's," Mr. Lloyd-Jones said quietly, as if for Elizabeth's ears alone. "It is clear that you are possessed of more than your share of virtues of every kind."

Elizabeth looked up to deliver a heartfelt denial of his words but when she looked into his eyes she encountered an expression so extraordinary that she failed to remember what it was she had wished to say.

"I pray that Mr. Cruikshank appreciates the treasure he has in you, Miss Elizabeth," Mr. Lloyd-Jones said as he curled his fingers over hers against his arm. "I am persuaded that I should never doubt such love."

The steps of the dance separated them for a moment but when they again came together she said in a low voice: "That you should acknowledge the sincerity of my feelings for him means more to me than I can adequately express. It has constituted in me a willing trust that you are, indeed, my friend." This capitulation from admirer to friend created a sensation in her with which she was most unfamiliar. Once a man had been caught in her net, as her friend had so put it, Elizabeth had never known a man to concede so quickly. It troubled her even as she found that she greatly appreciated his honoring her feelings. "And I, Mr. Lloyd-Jones," she continued, "do greatly admire your regret in being forced to end your betrothal, as needful as it is said to have been."

"I thank you for your kindness and hope that we are, in truth, friends, Miss Elizabeth." He followed his words with that smile of his that broke her heart, if only because she might never again bask in its glow. "I pray that it shall ever be so."

"Do you know," she began a bit hesitantly, "I believe, you are the only male outside of my family for whom I have felt such a kinship. It is as if I might say anything to you without fear that you should take my confidence as a sign of anything more than friendship."

His laugh was rueful, but his words were all she could have wished. "You needn't me to tell you that your beauty is such that it must routinely put a period to even the notion of mere friendship in the mind of any man possessed of a pair of eyes. Surely, you must have enjoyed male friends when you were too young to think of marriage."

"No, never. By the time I was even the least interested in anything but dolls, I bore the appearance of a woman grown." She thought her reply sensible enough in spite of her distraction at his remark. "I wonder, Mr. Lloyd-Jones, as to your choice of words. I don't believe I have heard anyone phrase it quite as have you."

"What words would those be, Miss Elizabeth?" She was grateful that he leaned his head close to hers so as to catch her reply as she dared not speak any louder.

"Those having to do with 'any man possessed of a pair of eyes'."

This time his laughter was free of strain. "That is quite simple; he would have to be blind not to be swayed by your beauty, that is all."

"Yes," she said firmly, "I have had that thought and, at risk of sounding haughty, I do believe it to be truth. It has long been my burden and my curse. That you see it all so clearly is a blessing I had not looked for."

"Miss Elizabeth, I can't speak to anything akin to a burden or a curse, indeed, I can hardly credit such a notion. Nevertheless, I do comprehend how difficult it must be for anyone, man or woman, to see past your appearance. I am obliged to your mother for insisting upon the story you related to us of your betrothed; it has demonstrated to me that you have an inner beauty that eclipses that of your so exquisite face."

The balm his words afforded her soul was spoilt by a sudden doubt; there had been too much talk of blindness for her to feel easy. "Have you been speaking with my mother, sir?"

"If by that do you ask if I have exchanged words with her when you were not present? No, I have not. When should I have had the opportunity? And of what should we have spoken?"

"Pray, do not be wounded, sir. It is my mother whom I accuse of having sought you out, but I believe that I was wrong to suspect her."

He looked down at her from the corner of an eye that gleamed with mirth. "Ah, I see. I suppose it would be fruitless to ask what intelligence you fear she might have divulged."

"Yes, you do comprehend, most fully, Mr. Lloyd-Jones, and for that I am most grateful."

There followed a prolonged period during which the four of them marched in companionable silence. Miss Lloyd-Jones was the first to brook it.

"Miss Elizabeth, when I entered the dining room this evening, I could not help but notice your interest in the painting my brother has selected to replace the quite tiresome one that had formerly hung in that selfsame spot. My eyes were drawn to it quite frequently during dinner and I must admire your taste in art. Colin has promised to take me to view the treasures at the British Museum day after next and I am persuaded you should enjoy it every bit as much as we. Do you find that you are free to accompany us? Of course, my invitation is meant to include you, Miss Hale."

Katherine's skill at the pianoforte required too much concentration for her to speak, but her smile proved that she willingly fell in with the plan.

"I can't think why we all shouldn't be quite free," Elizabeth's mother remarked. "Augusta, are we engaged day after next? We have all been invited to the British Museum with the Lloyd-Joneses."

"If we are already engaged, we shall simply make our excuses," Aunt Augusta declared.

"Oh, I am mortified," Elizabeth whispered to her dancing partner. "I would find an outing to the museum delightful but I simply cannot exclusive of Mama and the others. She and Miss Hale are determined to spend as much time with me as possible as we soon shall part. I pray their presence tomorrow shall not inconvenience you in any way."

"Not at all. It shall be my pleasure to escort five lovely ladies to the museum. Indeed, I cannot think of a more pleasant way to spend an afternoon."

"I know that they shall both be very grateful." That Katherine would be extremely vexed if she were to be left out of the excursion was a fact Elizabeth refrained from revealing. If there were to be a romance between her friend and Mr. Lloyd-Jones, it would be without her assistance.

"There is no need. I, that is to say, Analisa and I shall be grateful for the company. Is Miss Hale a lover of art as well as yourself?"

"I cannot say that it would be accurate to label even myself an art lover," Elizabeth said with an unaccountable stab of annoyance at Mr. Lloyd-Jones' interest in Katherine. "I so admire your new painting because it depicts all that is familiar to me, so much of which I have left behind, perhaps never to see again. However, I find that I am every bit as interested in paintings of life in England, as a history lesson, I expect, more than for a love of art."

"It is true, we British have excelled at depicting history, both national and personal, with the expert strokes of a brush."

"Precisely! It is to that which I refer. I find I cannot get enough of it; not the history, nor the art, nor the books. I most recently spent four days abed with an abominable cold and passed the time most pleasantly with one book after the next."

"You were recently ill, Miss Elizabeth?" he asked with some consternation. "I pray that you do not experience a recurrence. Springtime in London can be quite chilly."

She smiled, ruefully. "I see you did not miss my presence at all of those parties we had been so adamant we would attend."

"Would you believe me if I said that I have not attended a single function since last we met? The redecorating of the dining room has taken up most of my time and energy. I half expected Analisa to give me a dressing down in front of you ladies tonight as I have not escorted her to a single ball or rout five nights running."

"She is a most loyal sister. I am persuaded I should have taken out an ad in the paper and exposed all to your perfidy." Elizabeth laughed.

"Never say so! It is most self evident that you are made of kindness. And yet, you retain such a liveliness of spirit, in spite of all you profess to have endured, that I can only wonder. Analisa has that same liveliness but has nothing of which to complain. Her parents capitulate to her every wish and I must count myself complicit in that, as well."

"Are they not your parents, too?" Elizabeth asked.

"Our father, yes, but my mother succumbed to sickness when I was very young. I do not even remember her, at least, not with any great detail."

"That is sorry news, indeed, Mr. Lloyd-Jones," she replied, remembering that he had spoken of his mother's early death when last they met. "But how remarkable that you and your sister bear such a resemblance to one another."

"You are not the first to remark on it, nor shall you be the last. Yet, it is not in the least odd amongst the Lloyd-Joneses; we are both much like my father just as he is much like his siblings and father, in turn. It is how your mother recognized me the day we first met."

"Not immediately, but yes, I believe you are correct. I recall that she commented on your likeness to the previous generation. I expect your children shall bear all the exact same characteristics even if you were to wed someone such as Miss Hale? Her coloring is quite as striking as is yours."

"I'm afraid there is only one way to know for sure, Miss Elizabeth," he replied in a tone so enigmatic she could not know if the prospect of marriage to Miss Hale were a welcome one or not.

She pushed aside the sudden dashing of her spirits and reminded herself that her present happiness in her pending nuptials should be her wish for all about whom she cared. It was then that the music came to a triumphant end and there was naught to do but remove her hand from Mr. Lloyd-Jones' arm, the same one yet covered by his warm fingers. She yearned for nothing more at that moment but that the two of them should remain exactly as they were, but she could find no means to justify it. In spite of the much coveted kid glove that adorned her hand, the cold that assailed her skin when it was free was nearly unbearable and quickly, she clasped her hands together.

"Are you chilled, Miss Elizabeth?" Mr. Lloyd-Jones asked. She wished most fervently to deny it but felt that she was likely to shiver from head to toe if she did not focus all of her energies on the prevention of it. The realization that she stared mutely at him only came when music once again flowed from the pianoforte and her attention was diverted. She saw that it was Miss Lloyd-Jones seated at the instrument, she heard that it was a waltz that she played, but none of it seemed in the least tangible until the moment Mr. Lloyd-Jones put his hand at her waist and, without a word, whirled her into the dance.

She supposed it was to avoid the debacle of their last waltz that he took such great care to hold her at arm's length. Yet, she wished he would grasp her so tightly that she could not be faulted if she were to rest her cheek against his chest, her head tucked under his chin while he spun them about the room. There was a peace she felt in his arms that was unlike any she felt, even in the embrace of her papa, in whose presence she felt like a child no matter her years. The mere existence of her intended husband served only to remind her that she must lend her strength to others whilst fearful that the strength demanded should run out before it was no longer needed. As she compared one circumstance to another, she was astonished to learn that, in the arms of Mr. Lloyd-Jones, she was exactly enough.

They spoke very little as the room turned about them. Their eyes met frequently, whereupon they smiled at one another with no constraint, almost as if they had been acquainted the whole of their lives. She was aware that there were others in the room but, presently, her mother and aunt seemed to her as inanimate as the sofa upon which they sat and Miss Lloyd-Jones became one with the pianoforte. Even Katherine, who moved about the room so that her presence always came as a bit of a surprise, soon faded into the scenery. All of it seemed perfectly natural, none of it new or in the least startling, until the music came to an end and Elizabeth found that her cheek was indeed against his chest and his chin rested on her head, their joined hands no longer stretched out but folded in and resting against his heart.

She came to herself as if from a dream and was appalled to find that, as she drew her head away, a few of her curls stuck to his chin. "Oh," she breathed, "I do believe I fell asleep," she claimed in hopes that such a minor lapse in propriety would deflect the others from the knowledge of one far greater.

"Of what did you dream?" Mr. Lloyd-Jones asked quietly, his gaze so intense she felt scorched by it.

"I can't recall," she said brightly as she turned away to rub at her cheek, the one she feared bore the imprint of the weave of his coat.

"I do believe my Elizabeth has not fully recovered from her indisposition," her mother said in a voice that quavered just a little. "Perhaps, Augusta, we should return home and put her to bed."

"Yes, I do think that would be best," she replied as she rose to her feet. "I do so dislike to cut Katherine's evening short, but you do not begrudge your friend her health, do you, Katherine," Aunt Augusta said in that tone of voice that brooked no argument.

"Why should my sensibilities be taken into account?" Katherine replied in dulcet tones. "I have grown quite accustomed to my place in the shadow of the beautiful and always sought out Miss Elizabeth Armistead. Indeed, I believe it was at *my* birthday fete that she and Mr. Cruikshank announced their betrothal," she said, her voice rising in volume until one could deem her hysterical. "Why should tonight be any different?"

"My dear Miss Katherine," Miss Lloyd-Jones cried as she rose from her seat at the pianoforte. "You mustn't discount yourself, so. I am persuaded you are sickening with something," she offered as she put a hand to Katherine's forehead. "No doubt it is with the selfsame illness from which your dearest friend has not yet fully recovered."

"Yes, Kate," Elizabeth said upon receiving a pointed look from Miss Lloyd-Jones. "I am persuaded she is absolutely correct. Do take my arm," she directed as she went to her friend's side. "Mr. Lloyd-Jones, perhaps you might have our carriage brought round?" she asked cheerfully.

He sprang to pull the bell and went to assist Katherine by taking her other arm.

"Oh, I *am* sorry the evening has ended so soon," Miss Lloyd-Jones soothed as she offered a hand to assist Elizabeth's mother to her feet. "Let us hope that both ladies are fully recovered for our visit to the museum. I find I am *so* looking forward to it. It should not be the same if we are without a single one of you."

Elizabeth turned her head to favor Miss Lloyd-Jones with a grateful smile. "You are so very kind. I am persuaded we shall all be as healthy as horses by then, shall we not, Katherine? Though, perhaps I had best stay in and rest whilst you go and enjoy yourself."

"I wouldn't hear of it, my dear Elizabeth," Kate said in surprisingly happy tones. "You have been in the better part of a week, already, while I have attended all the parties at which you were meant to appear. How odd in me to have forgotten. I should not wish you to stay in when you only have a fortnight or two before you leave us for good."

"I do believe it to be a bit more than a fortnight or two," Elizabeth said with a low laugh that belied her apprehension. "Once Duncan arrives, there are still the banns to be read and that requires another fortnight and a half."

An uneasy silence fell upon the group that was blessedly interrupted by the entrance of the butler.

"How might I be of assistance, sir?" he asked.

"Please have Lady Augusta's carriage brought round at once," his master requested. Once the door had shut behind the butler, however, the heavy silence returned.

"Perhaps we ought to make our way downstairs," Miss Lloyd-Jones suggested. "I am persuaded that, by the time we have arrived, the carriage shall be waiting. I *do* so hope you all sleep well so that we might enjoy our outing, all six of us together."

Mr. Lloyd-Jones opened the door, took Katherine by the arm, and led the way. Elizabeth took his sister's arm and squeezed it gently. "You must be such a comfort to your brother. I must take a leaf from your book and practice more kindness when dealing with my own brothers."

"Oh, well! I am persuaded elder brothers are far more tolerable than younger ones, though I should have wished to have discovered the truth of that statement from my own experience. I should so enjoyed having been possessed of a sister, as well."

"One day, when Mr. Lloyd-Jones marries, you doubtless will," Elizabeth said firmly.

"Yes, and I am ever so happy that it is not to be Cecily Ponsonby. Do you know," Miss Lloyd-Jones continued, "I daresay

I should make a lovely sister a requirement of the man I intend to marry. That shall ensure that I have one I am happy to love."

"It is said that when you marry a man, you marry his family," Elizabeth replied though she was soon to wish she hadn't. The words echoed in her mind throughout the journey home, up the stairs to her bedchamber and were still there when she prepared to lay her head upon the pillow. What sort of family would her marriage bring her? What sort of woman was the bedridden Mrs. Cruikshank? And what of his siblings who were all older and living in the city?

It was with great relief that she bid enter whomsoever it was who scratched at her door just before she blew out her bedside candle. "Oh, Mama, it is you!" Elizabeth cried upon that lady's entrance. "I am so glad!"

"Yes, dearest, I thought you might be. Hadn't we better have a bit of a cose about what has occurred? I don't know what can have possessed Katherine, but I am more than happy to assure you that you did not deserve a word of what she said."

"I must confess I hadn't any idea she felt that way. I ought to have surmised, however. I feel a most thoughtless friend."

"Well, dear, the fault for such beauty, talent and kindness cannot be laid in your dish. You were simply made that way. Oh, my!" she exclaimed, "I have never been more proud of you than I was tonight! Your ensemble might have been made for such a room and you glowed like a ruby in a jewel box, you did."

"Mama, you know that was not my intention. Of course I enjoy a lovely gown, but I chose it on account of the Cruikshank clan tartan, not to outshine Katherine."

"No, of course you did not, though I daresay any of us could be accused of outshining the poor girl. Why, with that gown the same color as the chair and the wallpaper the same shade as her hair, she all but faded into the scenery. I was put out of sorts when she so insisted on the green silk, but I do believe it all worked out in your favor."

"Favor? Pray, do not speak so, Mama! I have no need to impress anyone but Duncan," she said before she realized the utter folly of such a notion. "I consider myself the most fortunate of women," she said, lifting her chin proudly, "that I need never be concerned that I shall lose the love of my husband because I fail to make a positive impression on him. I shall grow old and gray and he shall never know of it."

"You are most correct about that, my dear. Always and forever, in his mind, you shall look precisely as you do now—as beautiful as the day you were born."

When Elizabeth finally did lay her head upon her pillow, she found that she had a new notion to trouble her; that of the perennial beauty she would always be to Duncan. She had thought that she wished to marry him because he could not love her for her beauty. However, it was true that he had seen her often enough prior to the accident. She wished so much to be loved for more than her outward appearance but perhaps her comfort rose from the fact that, in his mind's eye, she would be always as beautiful as the day they met.

It was a sobering thought and one that spoke ill of her character. If only she might feel the truth of those qualities she possessed that made her worthy of the love for which she yearned.

Chapter Nine

The morning after his party, Colin found himself by the fire in the dining room. The fact that he was possessed of a perfectly lovely breakfast room was beside the point; he now enjoyed the dining room every bit as his library, and he would breakfast where he pleased in spite of his butler's protestations. As he sorted the morning post, Colin was at first delighted, then more than a little suspicious, when his gaze settled on the crest, impressed in wax, of Sir Anthony Crenshaw. Why he was not in town to call in person, Colin could not begin to fathom. Certainly he had long ago completed the task set him by his grandmama.

Colin broke open the seal and spread wide the single sheet of vellum.

Dearest Jonesy,

I am held prisoner at the Barrington estate near Bedford. The quarantine is meant to extend through the 15th of May. I count myself fortunate that I have not yet broken out in spots (have I had the pox? I do not recall) and that I am confined in tandem with two very pretty, young ladies whose skin as of yet remain unblemished. If only Avery were not under the same roof, I should be vastly enjoying myself. If I find you are responsible for his exquisitely timed arrival, it shall be pistols at dawn.

Affectionately,

A

"What claptrap!" Colin bellowed aloud. "I have never read such a quantity of drivel in all my life!"

"Might I be of service, sir," Evans panted as he entered the room at a run.

"But, of course not! You could no more terminate a quarantine than construct a gown. And I don't know that they should allow you near the place, what with the pox run amuck. Besides which, you might end up a prisoner, as well."

"Sir?" Evans asked, his face perfectly composed except for his eyes, which were more than a little frenzied.

"It's not as if I believe a word of it," Colin continued. "This is just Tony's way of getting out of our pact."

"How, sir? I presume this Tony of whom you speak might escape his agreement only through death or illness, however, I cannot determine if it could possibly occur via the pox or imprisonment."

"Neither! Both! Don't you see? None of it is the least bit factual. He has invented the whole of it."

"In that case, sir, I am most relieved. Is there anything else?"

Colin looked at the butler and let loose the pent up air in his lungs. "No. I was merely taken by surprise. You must excuse my outburst."

"Very good, sir," the butler said as he turned to quit the room.

"Oh, and Evans, be a good man and have my breakfast brought in here from now on, will you?" Colin requested. He waited until he was alone before he jumped to his feet and began to pace the room. It wasn't that he felt the least sorry for Tony; he had brought this predicament on himself. No, it was the pair of pretty young ladies with unblemished skin who had Colin feeling a bit nonplussed.

And then it dawned on him. "*Tres bien, alors!*" he said to the painting on the wall. "If he sees himself absolved of our agreement, so shall I. I will attend every ball, rout and soiree and will do so with as much ardor as I please. But first, I am persuaded I am in need of a new waistcoat."

Breakfast was served promptly and Colin ate with good appetite to see him through a full day that included a visit to his tailor. He had promised that he would construct a waistcoat made to Colin's exact specifications and to be delivered before the day was out. The visit with the tailor was followed by a visit to his club for a meal, and then a ride through Hyde Park to survey the landscape. If Tony was allowed such proximity to two young ladies, surely Colin should be allowed, at the very least, to peruse the new crop of debutantes of the season, many of whom should be seen riding out in their carriages to take the air.

To his astonishment, he spotted his sister out for a ride in the crack-of-fashion, canary yellow curricle that belonged to the Corinthian, Sir Henry, who was seated by her side.

Colin cantered up to the vehicle and lifted his hat in greeting. "Analisa, I see that you have made a fine beginning in your hunt for a husband." He was gratified to see a wary expression enter Sir Henry's eyes. "Is he aware that you have declined one offer already?"

"I say!" Sir Henry cried. "We are only out for a ride through the park; there is no harm in that. I will have you know that we were properly introduced at the Ames' do night before last."

"One of the many you promised to escort me to," Analisa said with a bat of her lashes for her brother. "But you needn't worry, Colin. Sir Henry is perfectly safe. We should never suit."

"I am? We shan't?" Sir Henry demanded huffily. "Why ever should we not?"

"Now, don't be provoked, Sir Henry. You know as well as I that you should prefer we remain friends, isn't that so?" she said with an arch look for Colin.

"Mere friends do not live in one another's pocket, Analisa," Colin pointed out even as he wondered why she should wish to be seen in the presence of such a coxcomb.

"I shall be sure to relay your notions on the subject to your dear friend, the soon to be Mrs. Cruikshank."

"What does my friendship with Miss Armistead have to say to anything?" Colin demanded.

"Ah, then it is perfectly unexceptionable for you to live in her pocket, but I should not be seen with Sir Henry, here, even though I should never deign to marry him, not in a million years."

"Again, I say!" Sir Henry entreated.

"Analisa Lloyd-Jones," Colin warned in his most authoritative voice, "what game are you playing at? Have you forgotten that it was you who insisted I invite the ladies from India to the museum, as well as to my own home for dinner?"

"No, of course I haven't," she replied, suddenly contrite. "But, Colin, dear, you must allow me to conduct myself as I choose in these matters. Do you not trust me?"

"But of course I trust you, Ana," he claimed, reigning in his restive mount. "I simply don't like you being seen out and about with this dandy; that is all."

"I do believe I have been insulted yet again!" Sir Henry cried. "Miss Lloyd-Jones, do you wish to proceed with our drive or should you prefer to be let down in the street this instant?"

Colin was as astonished as Sir Henry when Analisa gave her suitor a glance that took him in from head to toe. "I believe my brother is correct. I am persuaded I shan't have a difficult time enlisting his aid in seeing me home," she said, whereupon she alighted from the carriage and smiled up at her brother as he dismounted.

The two of them waited until Sir Henry had tooled his eye-catching vehicle from view before bursting into laughter. "Analisa, you minx! I am persuaded he shall be soon regaling his cronies at White's with tales of your double dealing, and where shall you be then?"

"Double dealing? I shall have you know, I was perfectly amenable to riding out with Sir Henry today. It wasn't until you registered your disapproval that I thought better of it."

Colin linked her arm with his and drew his horse behind them, reins in hand. "I am delighted to learn that you have seen sense. Might I ask if you have plans with any other exquisites? They do dress like men of means but I am persuaded father prefers to wed you to a peer."

"He does, does he now? I don't know what makes him think I am worthy of such *elan*," she said with an impish smile.

"Do not disparage yourself, Ana. However, I do find you need guidance when it comes to marriage prospects. It is clear that I have been derelict in my duty. That being said, I have had a *communique* from Tony and I am now free to attend as many social events as even you should choose. To whom do you go tonight?"

"The Russell's but I hardly think you should like to go there. Cecily is their god-daughter, after all."

"Never mind that," Colin said. "They shall be as eager to forget their connection with her as am I. As for the visit to the museum tomorrow; were you genuine about how it might look should I be seen too often in the company of Miss Armistead?"

"I did not mean to imply it was only Miss Armistead about whom I am concerned. There is also Miss Hale to consider."

"True. However, should I be seen squiring Miss Hale about town, there should hardly be any stir. She is to return to India very soon and that will be the end of any tittle-tattle."

"Are you so sure she wishes to return to India, Colin? I am persuaded she would enjoy marriage to a resident and to remain here as much as Miss Armistead."

It was a surprising notion. "Do you truly believe that?"

"Why, yes I do. I would not have said it, otherwise."

"But you can't mean that the sole reason Miss Armistead intends to wed her betrothed is to live in England?"

"I do believe you to be correct; it is not the sole reason, I am most sure of it. However, I am every bit as certain that she does not love Mr. Cruikshank."

Colin felt a grin stretch across his face and he turned away from his sister to hide it from her view. "So, you feel it your duty to rescue her from a loveless marriage. Is this what lays behind your schemes?"

"Do be serious, Colin, do! And do not say that you aren't pleased; I know you are smiling, I can hear it in your voice. My motivation for throwing the two of you together is quite simple; I believe she shall make you a most excellent wife and myself an amiable sister. After months of feigning to love Miss Ponsonby and failing miserably, I find it a welcome notion, indeed."

Colin felt the smile fade. "She shan't fall in with your plans. There is no mistake about that. Whatever her reason is for having chosen Mr. Cruikshank, she is entirely attached. And there is her character to consider; she has made it perfectly clear that she won't easily forgive herself if she should fail to honor her promise to him."

"We shall see about that. Perhaps even as soon as tonight," she suggested as she tipped her shining face up to his. "And there is always tomorrow."

Colin declined to say so aloud, but he had hopes of discovering the ladies from India at the Russell's do. However, it was not to be. To make matters worse, he received so many compliments on his imperial green waistcoat that he dared not wear it again the following day. He was persuaded Miss Armistead should appear in her best color sooner rather than later, but it seemed that such a happy convergence would have to wait.

He awoke earlier than he wished after a long night at his sister's side fobbing off unwanted advances from nearly every man present. Analisa insisted that they merely wished to dance with her, but he had a darker view of the matter. Once he was awake, however, he thought of little else but Miss Elizabeth Armistead. That she had agreed to join him and his sister on their visit to the museum was splendid, indeed. That no note crying off had arrived seemed nearly miraculous, especially in light of the ladies' absence at the Russell's ball the night prior. It was early days yet, however, and he forced himself to occupy his time with something useful, with only periodic journeys to the front hall to ascertain whether or not a correspondence had arrived.

He had not forgotten that most of the house was still in need of modification and his thoughts turned continually to the garish suite of rooms that Cecily had once hoped to occupy. A bed-chamber, a sitting room and a dressing room, done up in mawkish shades of lavender, lilac and violet comprised the rooms deemed for the use of the lady of the house. However, Colin felt that any true lady of fashion should prefer something a bit more modern such as Pomona green and primrose.

It should require that the brand new carpet be taken up, replacement draperies for the bed and windows be devised and the wall-paper be stripped and rehung but he would be glad to bear the expense; he knew in his heart of hearts that he should never wish to call on his wife in a room that spoke so clearly of Cecily. Instructions to his housekeeper on how she should apprise the decorators took up the better part of his morning until at last, the hour for his departure for the British Museum had arrived.

He tooled his curricle as far as his father's establishment whom he had hopes had been enjoined by Analisa to allow them the use of the family coach as they were to be so large party. Colin, pleased to see that the coach was already in front and waiting when he arrived, had but enough time to hand off the reins of his vehicle to a groom before Analisa was seen springing down the front steps of the townhouse.

"You are looking quite the thing," Colin said as he handed his sister up into the carriage. "And yet, such a vision is not sufficient to force my eyes open after last night's festivities. If only they had not slipped into the wee hours of the morning."

She waited until he was seated across from her to reply. "Do not say that you regret having escorted me there. I am fatigued beyond bearing, but it was ever so delightful. I can't think of a time when I danced so often or for so long!"

"You have only been out for a fortnight, m'dear. There will be other balls, *many* other balls, at which you shall dance all night and find it difficult to stir from your room before two or three in the afternoon."

"How terribly exciting! Now, let us discuss Miss Armistead and how you are to win her heart."

"We shall do nothing of the sort. It is clear as crystal that she is very much looking forward to her upcoming nuptials and life on that wild, deserted stretch of Scotland," Colin insisted.

"Oh, but you don't believe that, do you? I suspect she hardly does herself. She has made a grand gesture and she requires your help in getting her out of it."

"And how should I do that?" he asked with the realization that he truly desired to learn the answer.

"I don't know, at least not yet. However, you are older and wiser than I and I am persuaded that, between the two of us, we shall think of something that answers."

"Ana, you know that she will never cry off. It is not in her to be so false. It leaves me with very little to choose from. I can hardly snuff him out," he said with a rueful laugh. "Aside from the immorality of it, what is there in such an action that should make her love me?"

"Oh, but you do not understand," Analisa insisted. "She already loves you quite desperately. The fact that she does not know it yet is a mere trifle."

Colin stared at his sister for some moments before he replied. "Have you run quite mad? For a chit of seventeen to know enough of love to recognize it in another young lady, that is one thing. However, for you to say she does not know even her own heart whilst you do is bold, indeed."

"Oh, Colin, shall you never learn?" Analisa asked as she arranged her skirts to advantage. "Women are so very perceptive about one another even while they remain without a notion as to their own state of mind."

"I see," Colin agreed in spite of his reservations. "Am I to apply that to you, as well?"

"Oh no, not I!" she said in some astonishment. "How can you ask? Have you ever known me to be in any doubt as to my own mind? The very idea!"

Colin laughed outright. "Somehow I thought you should say precisely that."

"Do be quiet, Colin, and let me think on how we might solve the problem of her current engagement."

Colin sighed. "Am I to believe that you shall have arrived at a means for me to woo Miss Armistead under Mr. Cruikshank's nose in the next moment or two?" he asked as he tugged at his gloves and adjusted his hat.

"But, what else?" Analisa asked in all sincerity.

"My dearest Ana, life does not always cooperate with our desires though there is no mystery as to why you should believe otherwise," he said with a wry smile. She was not best pleased by this revelation and the two of them kept their own council for the remainder of the journey. Colin spent most of it in hopes that the apprehension he felt did not show in his face or manner.

The coach came to a halt in front of Lady Augusta's townhouse and it seemed an inordinate length of time before anyone came to the door once the driver had alighted from the box and rapped. Just when Colin thought perhaps no one was home or they were all still abed or had, perhaps, succumbed to a sudden fatal illness, the door turned on its hinges and Miss Hale squeezed

through the doorway before the driver had a moment to divulge
his purpose.

"Oh!" Miss Hale cried through the open window of the carriage as she peered inside. "I have been so looking forward to our
little tryst!"

"Doubtless you have, as well?" Colin teased his sister, one
brow cocked in surprise. "Though, we mustn't forget the others,"
he said as he opened the door from the inside and let down the
steps. "They are coming as well, are they not?"

Miss Hale's smile fled. "Yes, of course. I am persuaded that
Mrs. Armistead should not let me attend without her chaperon-
age. Naturally, it should have been vulgar to deny Elizabeth and
Lady Augusta the chance to come along, as well."

Colin looked to Analisa and beheld the self-same expression
of consternation gazing back at him. "Miss Hale, we are delighted
that you are well and able to attend the museum with us," he said
as he reached out his hand so that she might enter. "We should
not have dreamed of excluding a single one of you," he said firmly.

Miss Hale only took his hand in reply and entered the coach,
however, she waited so long to take her seat that Colin was forced
to stand, bent over, face to face with her. "Miss Hale, please do sit,"
he asked.

"I suppose I should yield the forward facing seat to the older
ladies," she remarked as she sat on the bench opposite. Colin could
hardly be less gallant and was forced to sit next to her. When the
other ladies were handed up they availed themselves of the places
next to Analisa while Miss Hale indicated that he should slide to
the far side so that Miss Armistead was left to take up the seat two
places down from him. As such, Colin was denied anything much
more than a glimpse of her profile through the lace trimmed brim
of a fetching toque. It was old rose in color and matched a very
smart spencer, both of which served to accentuate the rose of her
cheeks.

"Good afternoon Lady Augusta, Mrs. Armistead, Miss Armistead," Colin greeted them in turn. To his dismay, Miss Armistead afforded him nothing more than a glimpse from beneath her lashes and a very low "Good day". He was tempted to wonder what he might have done to offend her but, after a thorough review of every word they had spoken two nights previous, knew there was nothing.

"Miss Elizabeth seems to be in a lusterless frame of mind, today. May I inquire as to why?" he queried.

"I can conceive of no reason, Mr. Lloyd-Jones, why you should find me in a mood other than contemplative. I am most eager to explore the treasures of the museum, as are each one of us, I do assure you."

Colin shot his sister a look to gage her reaction, but her face revealed little and she remained silent.

"I daresay you were out quite late at some ball, though not at the Russell's, is that not correct?"

"You are quite wrong, Mr. Lloyd-Jones," Lady Augusta replied. "Elizabeth's mother and I determined that it would be best if the girls stayed in so as to be assured that they were both free of illness. We did not wish them to miss their outing today."

"I am humbled by your wisdom," Colin said with an inclination of his head. "My sister and I have been anticipating our visit to the museum today, as well."

"I am persuaded that I did, at one time, visit the museum when I was quite young," Mrs. Armistead remarked. "But that was some time ago. I understand that there are many new and marvelous items to be viewed as of late."

"Yes," Colin was happy to confirm. "There is the marvelous Rosetta Stone of which I am persuaded you have heard as far away as India and the Townley sculptures which have prompted our visit here today. Sadly, the Elgin marbles have not, as of yet, been moved to the museum but it is said that they will be by this time next year."

"I do appreciate antiquity as much as the next lady, I hope," Lady Augusta replied, "though I am not anxious to view the sculptures of which you have spoken. I have heard tell of the young man, in particular, who hasn't a stitch of clothing to his back. It is not suitable for the eyes of decent women, I daresay."

Colin smiled. "As I have not seen it as of yet, I am not in a position to verify or dispute, however, I have been told that it is wondrous to behold. Surely, a piece of cold marble, no matter how it is formed, is not the same as when adorned in flesh and blood."

"Do not be in such a pother, Augusta," Mrs. Armistead suggested. "It is art and, as such, it can only be unexceptionable."

Colin could not help but wonder how Miss Armistead viewed this exchange and longed to be able to read her face. Worse were his thoughts along the lines of how he was to get ahold of her arm as they descended from the carriage with Miss Hale between them. Doubtless she had foreseen this very circumstance and had devised a plot to place herself at his side so as to be the one on his arm. If so, she must have counted herself rewarded as, once free of the carriage, there was naught for him to do but offer it to her as Miss Armistead had already moved on ahead with her mother and aunt.

"Well," Analisa murmured as she took his other arm, "we are thwarted for a time but not defeated."

Colin ignored her and concentrated on ensuring all of the ladies made it up the first flight of stairs and through the front door of the establishment. Lady Augusta in particular was already showing signs of wearing thin. Once they were safely inside, he returned his attention to Miss Hale. "I don't believe I posed you the question; are you a lover of art?"

"Oh, yes, I find it is a pleasant means to expand one's mind. I am a dab hand at watercolors, but I have longed to make an attempt at oils."

"Then I am persuaded you shall enjoy the gallery of portraits. What say you, Miss Armistead? Shall we go first to the paintings before and then the sculptures?"

She turned to look over her shoulder as she replied, but the brim of her bonnet was such that he saw very little of her expression. "I would be grateful if you put Katherine's wishes above mine. I am content to view whatever she decides."

"Well, then," Analisa whispered, "we now know which way the wind blows.

Colin refrained from turning away from Miss Hale so as to whisper in his sister's ear, but his thoughts were such that he wished to unburden his mind of them. That the women from India had determined that he should make an excellent catch for Miss Hale was more and more apparent, but he could hardly credit it. Certainly Miss Armistead had enough feelings for him as to constitute a natural desire for her friend to wed elsewhere. He hoped he did not credit himself too generously, but the fact that Miss Armistead was, at the very least, drawn to him was not in any doubt.

And then he recalled her comments as to her interest in paintings, particularly those that depicted British history, and he felt his mood rise. "Let us do as Miss Armistead suggests and grant Miss Hale her wish to see the paintings." Delighted to have discovered a way to make both of the younger ladies happy, he steered them to where entrance tickets could be purchased and bespoke six.

"Mr. Lloyd-Jones, how kind," a flustered Mrs. Armistead said. "Certainly it was our intention to pay for our own tickets!"

"It is my pleasure, Mrs. Armistead," Colin replied and turned in hopes of finding her daughter close to his side and the natural choice for his arm. She, however, was across the hall admiring the broad sweep of stairs that led to the upper gallery.

"It is impressive, is it not?" he asked of Miss Hale who seemed far more attuned to treasures closer at hand. She took his arm and led him off to view the cluster of columns that supported the ceiling to either side of the entrance to the main gallery.

"Yes, indeed, it is! It seems to be nothing but steps, steps and more steps. I do believe I shall be done in by the time we have arrived at wherever it is they have hung the paintings. It was quite farsighted of you to lend your assistance as I am persuaded I am the lady of the party least likely to manage such an ascent!"

"Not at all, Miss Hale. I cannot believe that you, as the youngest of the group, save my sister, should have any trouble at all whatsoever. I expect it should be wise of me to offer my arm to each of the other ladies, in turn."

"I suppose that is only proper," Miss Hale said slowly. "But of course, you are always all that is proper, Mr. Lloyd-Jones," she added with a simpering smile.

Colin subdued a sigh in the face of Miss Hale's glaring attempts to incite his favor and turned to his sister. "And what of you, my poppet? Does your heart quail at the sight of so many stairs?"

"Should it?" she asked, her eyes wide with suppressed levity. "Indeed, I shall prove to you my lack of need for anyone's arm, even yours," she retorted as she let go his arm and made her way up the stairs on her own.

"That leaves one arm free for one of the ladies from India," Colin invited, "both of whom must be as bitter towards the prospect of a great many steps as Miss Hale."

"Mr. Lloyd-Jones," Miss Armistead replied as she turned away from her inspection of the vaulted ceiling to join in the discussion, "I profess to be quaking in my boots."

Colin lost no time in extending his free arm to her which she gratefully took. As the three of them proceeded up the steps, he felt that the tide had turned.

Chapter Ten

Elizabeth did not know when she had enjoyed herself more. To gad about on the arm of a handsome gentleman in a public place was an unknown indulgence in Bengal. It was most stimulating, even heady, and if the day never came to an end, she would have been most pleased. This, in spite of Aunt Augusta's propensity to puff along beside them or lag behind. There was also the need to usher Elizabeth's mother away from one treasure after another as they did their utmost to turn a blind eye and a deaf ear to Katherine's hopeless attempts to attach Mr. Lloyd-Jones' interest.

Katherine displayed a lack of decorum in other ways, as well, none of which failed to vex all within her orbit. She disdained the portraits for depicting a quantity of personages most unattractive when she had hoped for landscapes; she proved that she cared nothing for books when she recommended they skirt the library section and made them each an object of fun when she viewed the Townley sculptures, most particularly "the man with the oatcake in his hand".

"It is not an oatcake, Miss Hale, but a discus," Mr. Lloyd-Jones explained. Katherine exposed her ignorance when she treated his words to laughter as she tugged on his arm to lead him away. Elizabeth, however, would have liked to linger and indulge her fascination with the ability cold marble has to take on such a likeness of life.

Mr. Lloyd-Jones turned to her, then, and, as if he did not wish to be overheard, leaned shockingly near. "I should be delighted to escort you hither on a day when Miss Hale is engaged so that we might peruse history to our heart's content."

Elizabeth had the presence of mind to nod her agreement in spite of the disorder of her emotions she experienced at his closeness. She had most usually perceived men much as she did a marble statue; untouchable and stiff. From them she always was expected to keep her distance, to not become overly familiar, to observe and admire but never to know. She had come to understand the minds of the men close to her such as her father and Duncan, and she had stood on ceremony as she had danced with any number of them. However, as she clung to Mr. Lloyd-Jones' arm, she enjoyed a lively awareness of the differences between a man carved of stone and one of living flesh.

His warm breath against her cheek, the manner in which his shoulder brushed against hers, the rippling of his muscles under her hand, the warmth of her elbow caught tight against his side, each sensation served to call forth a delicious affinity for a form she had often seen as little more than a suit of clothes with a head. Every inch of her seemed to yearn for his touch, and yet, she had never so yearned for Duncan's physical attentions. She had not even particularly enjoyed the small, dry kiss he had bestowed on her the evening prior to her departure from India. It had been the only kiss they had shared in all the weeks they had been betrothed and she had not felt the lack of it until now.

The day, however, did come to an end and Mr. Lloyd-Jones had delivered them all to Aunt Augusta's house with vows from both parties that they would see one another soon. Every fiber of Elizabeth's being had rebelled at the parting, one which promised to be of short duration. It was nothing to the peaceful emotions she had experienced when she had parted from Duncan for the long sea voyage.

Later, as she dressed for dinner, she reflected on her feelings and was persuaded the contrast was due to the fact that she planned to spend the rest of her life with him while she only had little more than a fortnight to enjoy the company of the Lloyd-Joneses before Duncan's ship arrived. Her belly clenched at the notion and she wondered why that should be so. A voice at the back of her mind whispered that perhaps she did not love Duncan and she was marrying him for all of the wrong reasons.

Angrily, she pushed the unworthy thought away and redirected her attention to the final fitting for her wedding dress she had experienced the day prior. The gown was every bit as lovely as she had hoped. The wedding was to be at St. George's at Hanover Square and the long train at the back of the otherwise fairly simple muslin gown was quite dramatic. The bodice was tucked with a trim of lace that flared to make up the quarter length sleeves and leaves and scrolls were embroidered in white down the front of the skirt and around the entire edge. It was quite simply delicious but far simpler than her father could afford. Elizabeth felt it foolish to spend a great sum of money on a dress her groom would not be able to see but owned that the train was a personal indulgence. After all, it wasn't as if every guest at the wedding would be blind.

The very thought led her to wonder if she should invite the Lloyd-Joneses to her nuptials. They had become such dear friends in such a short time and she had no doubt they would grow dearer as the weeks went by. She made a mental note to ask her mother and aunt after dinner as to what was expected and how she might go about it.

As it turned out, the evening meal was a bit tiresome in light of Katherine's smug remarks with regard to the progress she was making in her pursuit of Mr. Lloyd-Jones. However, her pretensions turned to outright anger when the butler brought to table a note from Miss Lloyd-Jones addressed to Elizabeth alone.

"What could Miss Lloyd-Jones have to say to Elizabeth that should not apply to me?" Katherine asked petulantly.

"I don't know, Kate," Elizabeth said with a great show of patience. "I shall open it and perhaps discover the answer to your question," she added as she broke the seal and unfolded the thick vellum. "Why, how lovely! They have asked that we accompany them on a picnic tomorrow, all four of us once again."

"I am most sorry, girls," Aunt Augusta said, "but these old bones are not accustomed to such a quantity of staircases in one afternoon. Doubtless I shall not be able to get out of bed tomorrow let alone dispose myself on the ground to consume grapes straight from the vine."

Elizabeth felt her heart plummet at her aunt's words. "But, Mama, you shall go, won't you? We shall miss you, Aunt, but cannot Mama serve as chaperone well enough?"

"Yes, indeed, if Hortense wishes to, I can think of no reason why you should not all go."

"I think it sounds an excellent notion," Elizabeth's mother replied. "The two of you shall look a picture with those matching sprig muslins you had made up last year."

"Yes," Katherine announced, "I find saffron to be quite complementary."

Elizabeth contemplated the muslin to which her mother referred, one worn with a straw chip bonnet tied with a wide saffron satin ribbon, and knew a curious sense of defiance. Certainly her mother knew that saffron was far from her best color. Soon Elizabeth would be married to a man who would have no care as to how she looked or what she wore. For once in her life she wished to dress to be admired, for as long as she had remaining to her as a maid.

"I do believe I left that one behind, Mama."

"You never did! Well, then, I suppose you shall have to don one of the new ones we recently had made up."

"Yes, I suppose I shall," Elizabeth said as offhandedly as she could manage under the glare of Katherine's ire.

"I am ever so glad of the smart parasol trimmed in jonquil I picked up during our last shopping expedition," Katherine interjected. "I had thought to use it first once I returned to the heat of India but I am ever so glad I bought it as it shall be the perfect thing for a picnic."

"Yes, Katherine, indeed, and I am persuaded Miss Lloyd-Jones addressed her missive to me so as to be all that is proper. If she had addressed it to you, it might have been deemed by Aunt as too forward. As I am betrothed, there is nothing untoward about it."

"Yes! You are betrothed!" Katherine cried as she jumped to her feet. "Why must you be endlessly reminding us?" With that, Katherine began to cry and rushed from the room.

Elizabeth looked to the others and saw the self-same expression of astonishment on their faces as she herself felt. "I had not known that Kate was envious of my marriage. Could it be only that she shall miss our friendship?"

"I think there is more to it than that, my dear," Aunt Augusta replied. "Was Katherine known to Mr. Cruikshank prior to your engagement?"

"Yes, indeed, but what that has to say to the matter, I couldn't say."

"Did she spend time with him, dance with him, sit in the corner with him conversing at balls prior to his accident?"

Elizabeth looked to her mother in bewilderment. "I can't say. I was not in the habit of following his movements at that time. Mama, do you remember them together at all?"

"But, of course! I must say, I had thought they were very close to an understanding at one time. His accident put an end to that, however. Her father would not agree to a marriage, even if Mr. Cruikshank had made his intentions clear."

"You don't suppose she fancied herself in love with him, do you?" Elizabeth asked faintly.

"I imagine you shall never know unless you were to ask," Aunt Augusta said with a frown.

"Oh, I had no idea!" Elizabeth insisted. "I feel dreadful. How she must have been hating me all of this time. I had not thought her capable of such forbearance. If it had been the other way around, I am persuaded I should have wished to pull her hair out."

"We don't know that her heart has been injured, my dear," Elizabeth's mother soothed. "Perhaps it is merely that you are embarking on a new and exciting adventure and she is not."

"That could very well be the root of it," Lady Augusta agreed. "Either way, the best course is to continue to treat her with tolerance, just as you have done."

"Yes, Elizabeth," her mother agreed, "I have been exceedingly proud of you. Katherine has been most tiresome of late," she added with a tsk.

"Mama, I wonder if we are, perhaps, looking at this from the wrong way around. It seems to me that her disposition has changed for the worse only since we have met the Lloyd-Joneses. Indeed, her attempts to attach his interest have been most manifest. Though, what power my betrothal has that should make her cry, I cannot say."

"Can you not? Truly?" her aunt demanded.

"No." Elizabeth looked to her mother who bit her lip and stared owlishly back at her.

"Perhaps it is because Mr. Lloyd-Jones sees only you, Elizabeth," Aunt Augusta claimed.

"Whilst Mr. Cruikshank sees nothing at all," her Mama said in a small voice.

"What?" Elizabeth asked, scarcely able to credit what she was hearing.

"Mr. Lloyd-Jones has eyes only for you," Aunt Augusta echoed.

"Whilst Mr. Cruikshank has eyes for no one," her mother muttered under her breath.

"Yes, Mama, Mr. Lloyd-Jones has beautiful eyes," Elizabeth impatiently conceded.

"Whilst Mr. Cruikshank has no eyes a' tall," her mother whispered, nervously fingering the bit of lace that edged her handkerchief.

"Mama! I shall not allow you to be so unkind with regard to the man I am to marry. Katherine's path to Mr. Lloyd-Jones is quite, quite clear," Elizabeth insisted in spite of the pain that gnawed at her belly.

"But he loves you, Elizabeth; you!" Aunt Augusta insisted. "This means Katherine shall always be a dim star in orbit around the sun. It must seem monstrously unfair to her that you should have the affections of both men with whom she has become infatuated."

"Yes," Elizabeth said sadly, "I comprehend it now. Only, I have done nothing to attach the favor of either of them. I saved Duncan's life because I happened to be the one present and I spent time with him for nearly the same reason. Miss Katherine might have spent as much time with him if she so chose; even more! And Mr. Lloyd-Jones . . If only she had been the one to step out of the carriage that night in front of his house, it might be she for whom Mr. Lloyd-Jones feels an attachment."

"You make them out to be as fickle as fish," Aunt Augusta pointed out. "They have not fallen in love with you because you were present; their love for you depends entirely on who you are."

"I . . I wish, quite desperately at times, that I could be certain of that," Elizabeth said quietly.

"My darling girl, this is not why you have agreed to be Mr. Cruikshank's wife, is it?" her mother asked. "Because his very blindness makes him the only man you can trust to love you for yourself and not for your appearance?"

Tears started in Elizabeth's eyes as a wave of despair overtook her. "I do not know, Mama. There are moments when I think perhaps that is the right of it. And yet, I am truly attached to him. I love him! I know that to be true!" she said fiercely.

"It is entirely possible to love two men at the self-same time, Elizabeth," her aunt remarked. "The pertinent question is whom you love best."

Elizabeth dried her tears with her serviette and bowed her head. "I do not know. I have only known Mr. Lloyd-Jones for such a short time, it is absurd to think I could love him even as well as Duncan."

"Yet, he makes you feel differently than does Duncan, is that not correct, my love?" her mother asked.

Elizabeth did not wish to answer the question but her head nodded without her leave. A fresh bout of tears flooded her eyes and streamed down her cheeks. "Duncan is even now on his way to these shores. How shall I tell him that I was wrong to accept his proposal? And who is to care for him? If I do not marry him, he shall be alone with his mother with no means of support."

"That is not your concern or your responsibility, my dear," her mother replied.

"I do believe she has a point, though, Hortense. It would be quite callous, indeed, if she were to cry off for the sake of a man she has known but little. Chances are she is only suffering from the doubts that assail every bride prior to her wedding. She has made a promise to this young man and he is depending on her to see it through. Besides which," she said with an offhand air, "it is not always wise to marry the man one wants the most. It leads to expectations that are so very often dashed. A well to do, handsome young man such as Mr. Lloyd-Jones might not make the most comfortable of husbands whereas I am persuaded Mr. Cruikshank shall."

"Yes," Elizabeth said, feeling stronger. "That is precisely how I feel. I am ever so comfortable in his presence. I cannot say how much that has meant to me. What I feel for Mr. Lloyd-Jones is likely mere infatuation. It will pass."

"But who can make you happy?" her mother pleaded.

"Whomever I choose, Mama, I am determined to be happy. If I were to break my promise to marry Duncan, if I were to desert him, I do not know if I could live with myself, and I am the one person I cannot escape for even a moment."

Elizabeth's Mama rose and went to put her arm about her daughter's shoulders. "I can think of no one with whom I should rather spend a lifetime. As for now, I am persuaded that you are still done in from your illness. Why don't you go to bed, now, my darling. Things will look brighter in the morning."

Elizabeth was only too happy to oblige and, after saying her goodnights, did not delay in making her way from the room. She knew that the two of them whispered to one another at her expense the moment she turned her back, but it was the remark made by her mother just as Elizabeth closed the door behind her that taunted her throughout the night: "He must wed her for her dowry, for, what shall he do without it?"

The bright morning sunshine brought with it a dull headache and a sense of foreboding. Elizabeth lay abed as she waited for the clearing of her mind that would allow her to think in a straight line. She recalled that she was in England, in her Aunt Augusta's house, and that she had been waiting for word from her betrothed that his ship had docked and he was making his way to her side. It was with a rush of pleasure that she suddenly remembered that she was to attend a picnic at the invitation of the Lloyd-Joneses and the morning was bright, indeed.

She hopped out of bed and went to her clothespress. She hadn't any better idea of what she should do than she had had the night before, but she felt that she should not burn her boats in the meantime and was determined to dress like a woman who had not given up. As it proved to be a lovely day, she would have no need of her new red wool cape but the green and gray plaid pelisse trimmed in imperial green satin should be perfect. It was worn with Pomona green jean boots and a very smart chip straw bonnet with emerald green ties. For underneath, she intended to don a simple muslin gown in green sprigs with a matching sash. All in all, it would make a fetching, entirely English ensemble that promised to be vastly becoming.

The hours leading up to the arrival of the Lloyd-Joneses seemed an eternity to wait. Elizabeth so longed to ascertain for herself if Mr. Lloyd-Jones felt anything distinctive for her than he did for Katherine and the waiting seemed very hard. The ladies waited in the first floor parlor while Elizabeth and Katherine, who was dressed in the promised saffron, took turns peering out of the window in hopes of sighting the carriage as it pulled up to the house.

"Do remain seated, girls!" Aunt Augusta cried. You are giving me the megrims. We shall be informed of their arrival tout suite, have no doubts as to that!"

Katherine let fall the lace curtain she had pulled aside from the window and took her seat while Elizabeth clutched her hands more tightly in her lap. She was persuaded Katherine looked the veriest child but had not realized how very much the same Elizabeth must have looked in her aunt's eyes. "I do hope you feel better directly," Elizabeth said. "Is there anything we can procure for you in town on our return journey?"

"No, child, I should not have left my bed this morning, that is all. I am persuaded I shall be fully recovered by the time you return. You must be certain to tell me all about it, won't you?"

"Yes, of course we shall," Elizabeth's Mama assured her with a knowing look.

Elizabeth sighed. At least her current dilemma had brought her Mama and her husband's sister together in a spirit of amity that had long been denied them.

When at long last the carriage was heard to arrive, Katherine had shot through the door and down the stairs only to reappear on Mr. Lloyd-Jones' arm, her bonnet, gloves and parasol arranged to perfection, a few minutes later.

"Ladies, my sister waits in the carriage. She and I are both delighted that you are to come with us today," he said with a bow for each. "If we hurry, we ought to be able to make it back in order to have ices at Gunter's before returning to our various abodes to dress for dinner."

"I cannot conceive of a more perfect manner in which to pass a lovely spring day," Elizabeth remarked. "I have collected my sketchbook and pencils in hopes that we shall come across a view worthy of drawing."

"You draw, Miss Elizabeth?" He looked as if he were about to drop Katherine's arm to come directly to Elizabeth's side but seemed to remember himself just in time, his face turning a bit dusky with what she could only deem chagrin.

"I do. I find it excessively relaxing."

He inclined his head and gave her a warm smile. "Then, perhaps we should be on our way. Lady Augusta, we have received your missive and are saddened that you are not to join us."

"Oh! Do go on, Mr. Lloyd-Jones. You have no need of an old woman such as myself to slow you down."

"Not at all. We have room for each of you and have packed enough food to feed an army."

"That is tempting, I must say," Aunt Augusta mused, "but I am persuaded I should take my rest today."

"Very well, but you shall be missed." Mr. Lloyd-Jones then held his free arm out to Elizabeth's mother whereupon Elizabeth greatly astonished herself with the speed that she put herself forward and took his arm out from under the nose of her Mama. Elizabeth was rewarded for her resolve with a wide smile and a sly wink from the corner of Mr. Lloyd-Jones' light gray eyes that positively undid her.

With no further ado they quit the room, made their way down the stairs and out the front door to enter the carriage. Katherine was first to be handed up followed by Mrs. Armistead. Elizabeth was next and she entered the carriage fully prepared to do battle. As such, she took up the seat next to Katherine suspecting that Mr. Lloyd-Jones would eschew the place next to her mother with the desired result: he and Elizabeth were successfully seated side by side for the duration of their journey.

She had only a moment to applaud her faultless logic before she was assailed with unfamiliar and disquieting sensations. Whether it were because her father was too strict or her opportunities too few, she had never before been seated next to a man in close quarters other than her father or uncle, husband to Aunt Augusta who still lived when Elizabeth was last in London. So, it was with both a shiver of apprehension and a frisson of delight that she acknowledged the impressions that beset her during the course of their ride.

In order to distract herself, she opened her sketchbook and proceeded to draw Mr. Lloyd-Jones' in three-quarter profile, a view that included his gray beaver hat and exceptionally tied cravat. She propped the cover of the book at such an angle that he was not allowed to see what it was she drew and was delivered from exposure by Katherine through the offices of Miss Lloyd-Jones, who kept Katherine in animated conversation throughout the journey.

She did not allow the conversation between her host and her mother to fall on deaf ears, however, and she made certain that she noted every word that passed between them.

"Mr. Lloyd-Jones, where are we to picnic today? There were many out of the way places in the Shropshire countryside where I . . that is to saw, *we*, grew up, but everything in London seems always to be teeming with humanity."

"You are most correct, Mrs. Armistead. We shall spread our cloth at Hyde Park. It is not such a crush this early in the afternoon as it shall be later on. We should be expected to wait an hour at the gate simply to gain entrance at such a time of day if you can credit it."

"Oh, my! But it was ever thus, as I recall," her mama replied.

"Yes, I suppose that is so. After we have taken our refreshment, we shall proceed, if you are all amenable," he said with a gaze that took all into account, "to the Kensington Gardens. No parcels or packages are allowed in the gardens so this is why we have planned to have our picnic first. Unless you should prefer to see the gardens and then feast," he added with what Elizabeth felt to be vast consideration for her mother.

"No, I am persuaded we should picnic first and then work up an appetite walking through the gardens. In this way we shall have earned our treat at Gunter's," she replied.

Elizabeth smiled at her mother's logic and continued to sketch, though she ensured that she regarded her subject with enormous caution so he should not suspect her object. A quarter of an hour was spent in this pleasant manner when, without the slightest warning, the carriage pitched to one side in an alarming fashion and, amid a variety of shrieks and screams, Elizabeth was thrown against Mr. Lloyd-Jones in a most unseemly way.

It was for but a moment until she was thrown immediately back into her place, but not before she experienced the sensation of being pressed against a rousing set of rock-hard muscles from shoulder to knee. She was suddenly very much aware of the heady mixture of starch, soap and flushed skin that emanated from his neck as he turned to look down into her upturned face, his eyes wide with an emotion she fancied indicated his anxiety for her safety.

"I am quite all right, Mr. Lloyd-Jones; I believe we all are," she said as she took in the expressions of the others. "What could have been the cause of such an escapade?"

He cleared his throat before he replied in a voice rather huskier than usual. "It might have been anything, a dog or a child not minding where they were going. As we are already on our way, again, it could not have been a serious mishap. Mrs. Armistead, Miss Hale, Analisa, you are all free of injury?"

Upon receiving a chorus of yeses, he replied, "Very good. We shall soon be at the gate of Hyde Park and we may then disembark and enjoy the day." He turned to Elizabeth with one of those smiles that never failed to cause her some shortness of breath. "What have you been working on so industriously as your mother and I conversed?"

"It is nothing, really," she replied as she pulled back the cover to see that she had inadvertently drawn a line through the face. "Oh dear, it is truly nothing, now. It was ruined during the course of that little contretemps."

"Then you shall not object to my looking at it, is that not so? It is ruined not by you but by circumstances and you can feel no vanity with regard to it," he insisted.

Quickly she threw her hand against the cover of the book. "Indeed I can do. But I shall draw you another before the day is out and you may view it all you wish."

"Thank you. I should enjoy that excessively." As he spoke, the carriage jostled such that he was forced to brace himself with his left hand against the bit of seat between the two of them. Elizabeth presumed his action was meant to prevent his colliding into her as she had against him. However, when the moment was past and the fingers of his hand curled around the front of the seat, she realized it was his intention to allow it to linger not an inch from her knee.

She again opened her sketchbook in an attempt to divert her thoughts from that which should prove to discompose her. Turning to a fresh page, she began a drawing of his sister. It was a subject Elizabeth would be best pleased to share with Mr. Lloyd-Jones with no blushes. However, she found she could not dismiss the presence of his hand from her mind. She regarded it from beneath her lashes and noted that it was elegant and graceful while being entirely manly and strong. There was no sign of lace at his wrist, to his credit, for she felt the clean, straight, lines to be more fashionable.

With each sway of the carriage, the near edge of his hand seemed to draw closer until finally it came in contact with her knee. She fancied she could feel the heat of his skin despite the layers of muslin she wore, not to mention the density of his gloves, and she felt her face grow hot.

To her chagrin, it was this very moment that Mr. Lloyd-Jones turned to observe her. "Miss Elizabeth," he inquired, "do you suffer from the heat? Should you prefer to sit by the glass if I roll it down?"

"No," she replied with certainty. She did not wish to take an action that would seat Mr. Lloyd-Jones next to Katherine. "I am quite comfortable, thank you."

He looked down at her with such mirth in his eyes that she knew he silently laughed at her.

"Mr. Lloyd-Jones," she added as a means to persuade him, "I find that I am quite enjoying our ride and am in no hurry for it to end." She realized all too late how her words must have sounded for he lost no time in plucking his hand from its place near her knee and crossing his arms across his chest. To her astonishment, he seemed to blush and she realized that she could hardly argue against his action without raising more misconceptions, as well as a great number of eyebrows. As such, she resolved to remain silent until they had arrived at their destination.

Chapter Eleven

Once the carriage had come to a halt at the gate, Colin wasted no time in quitting his seat. It had been punishment indeed to feel Miss Elizabeth's seeming discomposure for the duration, one so at odds with his delight at her longed for proximity. As he handed Mrs. Armistead and his sister from the carriage, he wondered at Miss Elizabeth's seeming reluctance to disembark and added it to the tally marks of what he imagined to be her displeasure he had accumulated in his head.

Miss Katherine seemed disinclined to quit the carriage, as well, but she eventually did so, to his vast relief.

"Oh, Mr. Lloyd-Jones," she chirped as she stepped down, and continued, without letting go his hand, with: "What a lovely day for a picnic!"

Colin found it difficult to persuade her to transfer her grip on his right hand in order to take his left arm. Once she did, he was never more repentant as she clung so tightly he felt as if the blood in his arm had no course but to pool in his veins like a river at the gate of a dam. However, once Miss Elizabeth appeared at the door of the carriage, her beauty bordered like a portrait in a frame, he forgot his pain. Her eyes glowed with pleasure, her cheeks bloomed with color and her entire ensemble was the precise green required to complement her eyes as well as his imperial green waistcoat upon which she had failed to so much as comment. Even her bonnet did not escape his approval; it was perfectly fetching and perfectly shaped; so unlike Miss Katherine's over-sized affair tied under her chin with an enormous lemon yellow bow.

He handed Miss Elizabeth out of the carriage and adroitly conscripted her arm in one fluid motion that disallowed her capacity to decline. It was his intention to keep her close for the entire day and he felt like a lord with her arm linked in his as they walked. His sister and Mrs. Armistead followed behind, along with the coachman and a footman who had ridden up on the box for the express purpose of aiding in the transport of a prodigious hamper to the first location that proved amenable to dining alfresco.

"Surely this is not your first visit to Hyde Park," he asked Miss Elizabeth but it was Miss Hale who responded.

"But of course it is. I have never been to England. I believed you to be fully aware of that fact," she said with a coy smile.

"Forgive me, I had not recalled," Colin replied. In truth, he had forgotten her existence in spite of the fact that she clung to one of his arms like a leech in want of a meal. He was perplexed, as well, by her words that were so at odds with her manner. He turned to Miss Elizabeth in expectation of her usual remarks in the pursuit of whitewashing her friend's comments. However, she gazed steadfastly ahead as if thoroughly unaware of the exchange.

"Miss Elizabeth, I see you are considering our picnic options with complete absorption. I am persuaded you shall swiftly find us the perfect spot to enjoy the contents of our hamper."

"What about just there?" Miss Hale cried as she pointed to a spot so far in the distance it was impossible to know her intention.

"I fear my eyesight cannot be as sharp as yours," Colin mused, "as I see only trees already spread below with those who, like us," he said with a smile for Miss Elizabeth, "wish to enjoy their meal in dappled shade."

"Oh," Miss Hale replied, "I had not thought shade as important as all that. I have brought along my parasol, you see," she added with an over bright smile. "I had thought to preserve it in silver tissue until my return to India, but I have had the strangest inclination of late to remain in England."

Colin knew a foreboding. Perhaps Analisa had been correct in her estimation of Miss Hale's desire to marry a Londoner. At the moment it seemed that her quarry was him. Not for the first time he wished he had invited another gentleman along to draw off her attentions.

"Miss Elizabeth, you have not shared with us your perception of Miss Hale's words," he said in desperation.

"Pardon me," Miss Elizabeth replied as she turned to bestow on him a dazzling smile. "I was not attending."

"Miss Hale . . "

"I give you leave to refer to me as Miss Katherine," she demanded.

"Very well. Miss Katherine was sharing with us her sentiments as to the usefulness of a parasol on a day such as today."

"Doubtless it is far more useful when it is open," Miss Elizabeth said with a pointed look for the downcast little bundle of fabric as it hung from its owner's arm. "Besides which, I am persuaded we are adequately protected by our bonnets," she added with a second look, this one directed at the immensely wide and sadly out of fashion chapeau Miss Katherine had donned and which threatened to jab Colin in the chin with every step.

"It is true, it is a most efficient bonnet," Miss Katherine explained. "It is modeled after one of Queen Marie Antoinette's shepherdess hats and cannot fail to block every disagreeable ray of sun."

"I do not find the sunshine the least disagreeable, Miss Katherine, though I must insist that we find a spot of ground that shall prove to be kind to the faultless complexions in our company." Once again Colin turned to bestow a smile on Miss Elizabeth with his words and was rewarded with a smile of abashment in return. His heart turned over at the sight and his being filled with joy when he contemplated on how well matched her appearance was to her most excellent character.

"I do believe I spot a tree devoid of occupants," Miss Elizabeth said as she pointed into the near distance.

"I fail to comprehend you," Miss Katherine snapped. "It is not the tree that needs must be free, but the ground below it."

"I am persuaded you are correct," Miss Elizabeth replied in soothing tones wholly undeserved by her friend. "Do you not see that tree just at the top of that knoll? It seems no one has claimed it as of yet."

"Yes, I see it." Colin hastened his step and trusted that the ladies behind and the servants with their cumbersome hamper would keep up. "I defy any to beat us to it!"

"Oh, but look, just there," Miss Elizabeth pointed out. "There is a party about to descend upon our chosen spot. We must be quick."

Colin looked into her face and when she gave him a beaming smile in return, he knew she read his thoughts. With no idea but to be free of all constraints, he threw off Miss Katherine's arm as he and Miss Elizabeth broke into a run. They arrived at the base of the favored tree just moments prior to the other party.

"I say!" said a man in a wig of questionable origins and excessively high points to his cravat. "Dash it all! We have had this spot in our sights since we entered the park."

"How unfortunate for you that we have arrived ahead of you," Colin said with a slight bow. Miss Elizabeth turned towards the tree, a hand to her mouth to stifle her laughter. It was all he could do to refrain from joining in her merriment until, suddenly, the notion to take her in his arms and spin her about consumed him quite thoroughly. The sensation served to quell his laughter even as one of the females of the party, an extraordinarily tall woman accompanied by an equally tall daughter, cut him dead and led her party on to the next suitable locale.

By this time Miss Katherine and Analisa had joined Colin and Miss Elizabeth under the tree while Mrs. Armistead and the men with the hamper still toiled along behind.

"This is precisely the spot I indicated at the outset," Miss Katherine claimed. "Why you could not perceive it then I cannot say."

"Pardon me, Miss Katherine," Colin said, "I do believe I am needed or our meal promises to be food for the birds." He took off at a run, glad that the dangerously wobbling hamper gave him an excuse to entirely ignore Miss Katherine's comment. He gained his objective just in time to rescue the hamper from going down at the footman's end, whom he then reassigned to go in aid of Mrs. Armistead whose entire journey had gone without the arm of any gentleman.

The women helped with the unloading of the hamper and it was Miss Elizabeth who caught the far corners of the cloth as Colin snapped it into the breeze. They smiled at one another over the length of damask before they each took their turns at carrying dishes from the hamper to place them where all could be reached. In spite of the quantity, it was short work and soon the footman and coachman were on their way back to their conveyance where their own meal waited for them in a far smaller basket.

Colin longed to take his seat and stretch his legs, but the ladies all stood about as if in wait of something. He looked to his sister who in turn looked to Miss Katherine, then to Miss Elizabeth, only to return her gaze to her brother with a lift of her eyebrows.

They were saved by Mrs. Armistead. "I am so tired I believe I shall drop. I think that I shall dispose myself right here," she said as she sank to her knees and peeled off her gloves. "Elizabeth, do come and sit beside me."

"Of course, Mama," her daughter replied in tones of perfect contentment as she moved away from Colin and took up her place next to her mother. This left Miss Katherine entirely free to sink to her place just where she stood. Sadly, it was directly adjacent to Colin.

With an enormous effort, he held back a sigh and invited his sister to sit, whereupon he took his place next to Miss Katherine. At least it was the perfect spot from which to admire Miss Elizabeth though her friend's words would be much louder in his ear. It wasn't that he disliked Miss Katherine; it was only that her efforts to attach him were as tiresome as they were unprofitable. At any rate, with her thick, blonde hair, she was much more to Sir Anthony's taste. Perhaps he would introduce the pair once Tony arrived back in town.

"Mr. Lloyd-Jones, may I place some of this blancmange on your plate?" Miss Elizabeth asked, removing her gloves and taking up the serving spoon placed beside the quivering mass.

"I thank you, Miss Elizabeth, and hope that you shall avail yourself of a piece, as well. It is one of my favorite dishes."

"I shall keep that in mind, Mr. Lloyd-Jones," Miss Katherine chimed. "I am persuaded it will be most useful information to be in possession of when I . . ," she said, her voice trailing off into a disagreeable silence.

"When you what, Miss Katherine?" Colin asked in all innocence, but the manner in which the ladies all looked down into their plates led him to the truth of the matter. That Miss Katherine should contemplate her role as his wife with such assiduousness was disconcerting in the extreme and he found he could formulate no suitable reply.

"Miss Analisa, have you a favorite dish?" Miss Elizabeth inquired.

"Why, yes, I do. I find that I actually dream of this *macedoine* of fruits in jelly, and quite incessantly, I might add."

Colin was delighted to see that Miss Elizabeth and her mother laughed along with him, but it would seem that Miss Katherine failed to see this exchange as the very necessary rescue from her indiscretion.

"I only meant that when I am the wife of an Englishman," Katherine stated as if the topic of conversation had not been successfully turned, "I should know better, due to your revelations, what an Englishman should like for his table. For, as I have said only today, I do intend to remain in England and have decided that an English husband is what is required in order for me to do so."

Once again Colin looked to Miss Elizabeth to compensate for the indiscretion of her friend but, instead, she reached across the cloth to help herself to a strawberry right from under his nose. Her hand, white as cream and dainty as a teacup of the finest porcelain, smelled of lilacs. He found he could do naught but watch its progress as she placed the berry between her rosy lips and bit into it. Could it be for the first time he noticed the whiteness of her teeth or was it only the depth of the color in the berry that made her teeth appear so? He could not say.

"Goodness, me, I think I shall be quite spoilt by this bounty." Miss Elizabeth lifted his plate and began to spoon a slice of apple cake thereon. "I am persuaded the peaches are delicious. How many do you wish, Mr. Lloyd-Jones?"

"I .. I can not rightly say," he replied, removing his own gloves in anticipation of his meal. He would have every one if it should please her, but he could not be certain that was her design. She perplexed him every bit as much as did Miss Katherine and yet it did not displease him, nor did he find it the least unsavory. In fact, he found it to be somewhat divine. Soon he would invite her to walk with him along the river and he would speak to her of his feelings if she proved willing to hear them.

"I find that I quite adore peaches," Miss Katherine began but Colin shot to his feet before she could complete her thought, as thoughtless as it would prove to be.

"I find that I tire of sitting. Miss Elizabeth, would you be kind enough to accompany me for a walk along the river?"

Three sets of eyes looked up at him in some consternation, but Miss Elizabeth rose to her feet and took his arm without the slightest sign of trepidation. Miss Katherine made an attempt to rise, as well, but Analisa very sensibly placed the entire blancmange in Miss Katherine's lap, effectively pinning her to the ground. He made another note to procure a fitting gift for his most excellent sister, a resolve he forgot entirely the moment he turned his back.

Determined that they should walk to where they should not be overheard, Colin at first refrained from speaking. He headed for the edge of the river with its masses of greenery and promised privacy. He would not end the day without opening his budget on the state of his heart. Whether or not Miss Elizabeth wished to hear what he had to say was a question he longed to be answered.

So it was that she was the first to break the silence. "Mr. Lloyd-Jones, I must thank you for this outing. What a pleasure it has been! India is either too hot or too rainy to venture out of doors more than rarely. But here .. " She spread wide her free arm and looked into the sky. "It is such a beautiful, mild, sunny day and I find myself quite content."

Colin caught sight of only her dimpled chin and red mouth from under her bonnet, but he was persuaded he had never before seen a more fascinating dimple or a more enticing red. Before he said what he most fervently wished to say, he must arrange matters so that he would be allowed to gaze into her face of an entirety; there was much to learn from her countenance and he would know it all. The fear that she would not like his words and that it might be the last time he would be allowed to gaze upon that face was one he barely allowed himself to feel.

"I have heard it said that it rains in Scotland, every single day." He knew it was a mistake before the words were out, but he could not seem to refrain from adding upon it. "And that is summer only. The other seasons of the year offer far worse."

She turned to look at him, but the shadow made by her infernal bonnet rendered her eyes impossible to read. "Mr. Lloyd-Jones, if I did not know better, I should think you felt it your duty to make apparent the errors in my thinking."

"What errors would those be?" he asked with a bald-faced innocence that rang false in his own ears.

She looked down and he was robbed of all but the sight of her chin. "Mr. Lloyd-Jones, I had believed myself safe in your company; that you comprehended my circumstances; that your honor would not allow you to place me in a position that should compromise my character."

He thought perhaps her voice shook with tears and he wished to tell her how very remorseful he was. He wished to speak words of approbation for the very character of which she spoke. More than anything he wished to pull her behind the nearest privet and rid her face of that abhorrent bonnet.

To his wonder, she did not object and they stood gazing raptly into one another's eyes, the bonnet wedged between them.

"Miss Elizabeth," he breathed. "I cannot ask you to do or say anything that should force you to compromise your integrity. It is that very integrity at which I stand in considerable awe. I should be a fool to mar what is one of your most admirable qualities. And yet I cannot let this opportunity pass without telling you it is far from the only quality in which I most ardently delight."

"Mr. Lloyd-Jones, I must beg you to stop!"

"Why?" he asked as he tossed the hat to the ground and took her hands in his. "Are my attentions so unwelcome?"

"No!" she said so quickly that he felt he had reason to hope. "That is to say, there is naught in your manner or your character that I find in the least unwelcome. If I were but free," she said, shaking her head, her eyes wet with tears, "but it is of no use. I have made my choice and I must abide by it."

"Then it is not that you cannot love me?" he asked, his feelings a painful mixture of hope and resignation.

"It is not a matter of my capacity to love you, nor is it an event to look for in future," she said, gathering his hand to her face. "It is because I cannot stop that I am torn in two."

It was then that he knew the full tragedy of his position. "What sort of madness is this?" he begged as he attempted to consign every aspect of her beloved face to memory. "What madness that I would not wish changed about you the very quality that frustrates my desires? I wish to add to my own your strength, your resolve, your determination to abide by what is right and true. And yet, in so doing, I should destroy your very essence. Is there no way to make you mine without making you somehow . . less?"

To his astonishment, she fell against his chest and began to weep. He put his arms around her and held her tight, far tighter than he ought, and wondered at how perfectly natural it felt to hold her, her cheek against his coat, his own against her hair. He closed his eyes and prayed that she would not soon be shed of all her tears. He prayed that when she proved to be, he should know what it was he ought to say. Lastly, he prayed that she would raise her head to look at him in such a way that he would find it impossible to resist the intense yearning to cover her mouth with his own.

It seemed an eternity, yet sooner than he hoped, when she lifted her face to his, a glossy ringlet pressed to her face like a flower between the pages of a book and her jewel-like eyes sparkling with tears. "How could you make me less?" she murmured. "I have traveled all the way from India only to find that it is you who makes me *whole*."

He could not say how his hands found their way to her face, one to each cheek, his thumbs just brushing the boundaries of her mouth. The cast of her eyes implored him to kiss her even as her hands came up to pull his away, but he was stronger than she. He ran one hand across her face and into her hair and dropped the other to her waist, pulling her against him until he could feel the pounding of her heart in tandem with his own.

As she dropped her arms to her side, she closed her eyes and waited, her long, black lashes swimming in tears. Lowering his face to hers, he drew his nose along her cheek, willing her to grant him one last look into her eyes so he might read in them her desires. Instead, tears beaded under her lashes and ran down the creamy perfection of her skin. He rubbed them away with his cheek against hers and then, when he could resist no longer, he brushed his lips very lightly along hers, undemanding and soft as a whisper.

When she still did not respond he knew that his prayer had not been granted. With a shuddering sigh, he loosened his grip and rested his forehead against hers, her mouth still tantalizingly near. "Say something," he begged. "Please? Will you not say something?"

She did not, but she put her hands around his neck, her fingers twisting in his hair. A tremor went through him at her touch and he marveled that he could have ever thought he loved anyone, wanted anyone, cherished anyone but her. When she pulled her head back, exposing the heated skin of his forehead to the cool breeze, he knew that he had felt her last caress. As such, it came as a shock when she leaned in and placed a lingering kiss upon his cheek, one full of the same longing he had seen in her eyes.

When she pulled away, he saw that she still could not look at him. He bent to retrieve her hat from the grass and placed it on her head to cover the shambles he had made of her coiffure. He tied the bow under her chin and wiped away the last of her tears with trembling hands, and still she would not meet his gaze. Finally, he took her hand, so small in his, and pressed it in his own.

"I have no right. You are soon to be another man's wife," he said, though his throat ached and his tongue stumbled over the agonizing words. "And yet I find I cannot part from you without saying what is in my heart. Miss Armistead . . . my dearest Elizabeth . . . I admire and love you more than I ever imagined possible to love anyone."

She raised her head at the words, but she did not profess her love in return, in spite of the wealth of emotion in her eyes. Thoroughly thwarted, he released her hand and ran his own through his hair. "I know not what you think of love as a predictor of a successful marriage. There are those, rather I should say *many*, if I am honest, who believe the sensibility of love to be of the least use in a marriage. I cannot agree. It is ironic, is it not?" he asked with a rueful laugh. "The tragedy of my life will not be that I was used by a woman who was never worthy of my love, but that I love, with all of my heart, a woman far worthier than I can ever hope to be."

Finally, she opened her mouth to speak but the words that came to his ears were not hers.

"I cannot imagine what the two of you have been about here in these bushes," came the voice of Miss Katherine from somewhere behind him.

Elizabeth's eyes grew very wide. She bit her lip, but she said nothing. It was as if her voice had been stolen away.

"Please," Miss Katherine said as she stepped around him and put her arm through his. "Have no anxiety on my account. It is not as if I suspect you of any wrong-doing; quite the contrary. Elizabeth is well known at home for her prudishness. Even her betrothed has had naught from her but one brief kiss at their parting."

Elizabeth's gaze flew to Colin's with this admission and her face bloomed with color. He wondered at her capacity to feel such shame when it was her very virtue that was among those qualities he most treasured. "Miss Hale, whatever it is you are about, you shall catch cold at it. Miss Armistead and I are only discussing architecture. We find that we agree on how things ought to be built," he said, watching her eyes in hopes that the shadows soon departed. "Foundations are of particular interest to me and she has been so kind as to listen to my theories on the subject."

Miss Katherine made a face. "I cannot conceive of anything more tiresome! Do say you will rejoin us. We ladies on our own have grown quite restless. Elizabeth's mother, in particular, feels the possible loss of our outing to Gunter's quite keenly."

"But of course we shall go to Gunter's," Elizabeth said quietly. "It is a lovely day such that I am not likely to see for years to come. I wish to make the most of it."

"Will you take my arm then, Miss Elizabeth?" Colin asked through his surprise at this return of her equilibrium.

"I think not," she demurred as she untied the ribbons of her bonnet and retied them in what Colin could only assume to be a more expertly placed bow, whereupon she stepped round him, still refusing to meet his gaze, and led the way back to the others.

"How I dislike it so when she gets in one of her moods," Miss Katherine asserted as they followed along. "It is as if she believes herself to be the only one entitled to her own opinion whilst the rest of us must agree or be forever in the wrong."

"Have you ever known her to be mistaken, Miss Katherine?" Colin asked, his heart twisting within his chest with apprehension.

"Why? Do you question her choice of husband?" she asked with another of her coy smiles. "It isn't as if you are the only one to do so. No one is happy about it, least of all she. It was said that her father was enraged when he learned of their betrothal, that Mr. Cruikshank was only after her money, that he had rather see her married to a native than to one such as Mr. Cruikshank."

Colin slowed his pace so as to put more distance between Elizabeth and his words. "Pray tell, what sort of man might Mr. Cruikshank be? I must confess I have been yearning to know this age."

Miss Katherine tilted her head to one side. "For one thing he is a commoner. Then, of course, so is Elizabeth. Only, as I have learned, commoners with money are somehow more acceptable, are they not?"

Colin ignored her question and pressed on with his own. "Then it is not a love match? It is only her money that he is after?"

"She believes him to love her well though who can say? Mr. Cruikshank had offered for me and my considerable dowry not many weeks before Elizabeth found him under the bridge."

"How can that be?" Colin asked with more than a little astonishment. "That is to say, any man would be honored to have you as his wife. And yet, how could Miss Armistead fail to discern his intentions when he had so recently offered for another?"

"By that I am persuaded you mean another young lady with a dowry that could rescue even the Prince Regent from the river tick," Miss Katherine suggested.

"You are not wrong." Colin fastened his gaze to the rapidly receding figure of his beloved and considered his next question. "If there was one fact you might share with me about Mr. Cruikshank, which would be the most illuminating?"

"Oh, no, that I shall not do," Miss Katherine said with a wag of her finger. "I am afraid you shall have to form your opinion of Mr. Cruikshank independently from mine. However, once he has arrived, I believe it shall prove vastly entertaining."

"Vastly entertaining for whom?" Colin demanded.

"For me!" she replied and with a laugh she let go of his arm and danced to Elizabeth's side.

Colin found no pleasure in the remainder of the outing. Not only did Elizabeth refuse to look at him, let alone speak to him, he found that Analisa was singularly quiet, as well. This left him with the task of entertaining Miss Katherine and Mrs. Armistead all on his own. To add insult to injury, the afternoon was not to be salvaged by the promised sweet at Gunter's as the establishment was not supplied with his favorite flavor of ice, that of pistachio.

The drive home was a misery; Elizabeth was once again seated where he could least see her and Miss Katherine was making the most of her place at his side. Somehow he doubted he should be as eager to forestall the physical advances Miss Katherine insisted on making if it had been Elizabeth who attempted to rub her leg against his. At the same time, he could not imagine that it was an activity in which Elizabeth would engage in the first place.

Once they arrived at Lady Augusta's establishment, Colin exited his side of the coach in hopes that he should at least be allowed to escort Elizabeth to her front door. However, by the time he had appeared on the other side of the coach, Elizabeth was already rapping on the door for the butler to admit her. The final blow to his equanimity was that she failed to so much as turn her head to acknowledge either himself or Analisa before she was swallowed up into the house.

Their return journey to Lloyd-Jones House was spent in utter silence. Rather than enter his father's home, he saw his sister safely inside, then waited out front whilst his curricle was brought round. Upon arrival, he went directly to his bedchamber where he stayed for the remainder of the evening.

His butler disturbed him only once, to ascertain when and where he desired his dinner, a meal for which Colin had no appetite, and to leave him a letter on a silver tray. Colin thought he would not bother with it until morning but decided there was no news that could deepen his despair.

In that he was wrong.

Jonesy,

It would seem that I am betrothed to an empty-headed goose who uses me to accomplish some sinister plot of her own. Additionally, I am to fight a duel with Lord Avery over her honor. It is not a duel I can win as I mustn't do away with the only man who has the slightest inclination to take the baggage off of my hands, and yet, I am too fond of my shirt to allow him even a single shot. How I shall come about I know not, but do not despair!

Tony

P.S. How much can change in so short a span!

"How much, indeed," Colin murmured as he balled the letter in his fist and tossed it into the fire.

Chapter Twelve

Elizabeth dragged herself through the front door of her aunt's townhouse and was immediately presented with a piece of correspondence by the butler.

"Here 'tis, Miss," he said, beaming. "I know how very much this has been looked for."

"Thank you, Andrews." She took the small, neatly folded square of vellum and wondered at her utter lack of gladness. She had anticipated this moment since almost before she had boarded ship for England and had yearned for the communication that signaled Mr. Cruikshank's reappearance in her life nearly every day since. However, as she looked down at the neat copperplate, all she could think on was that she did not recognize his handwriting. This reflection was followed by the realization that he must have had someone else write it for him; that she, at any rate, knew nothing of his handwriting, knew nothing of so many things about him. How could she have agreed to marry him?

With trembling fingers, she spread wide the vellum and confirmed the news that his ship had docked, that he was only awaiting her return correspondence before he presented himself at her Aunt's house. How he was to arrive on his own, she could only guess. Certainly it would be more convenient should she send Aunt Augusta's carriage to retrieve him. Elizabeth knew she ought to immediately respond with the news that they would call on him at his lodgings without delay, and yet, she could not bring herself to write.

She told no one of the letter, though she knew they all had guessed based on the expressions of apprehension that ringed the table at the evening meal. After a listless rubber of whist after dinner and a valiant attempt to read *Sense and Sensibility*, a story altogether too discerning for her current tastes, she blew out the candle and tried to sleep. After a number of hours abed spent tossing and turning, she could put off her correspondence no longer. However, the first letter she wrote was not for Mr. Cruikshank.

His ship has docked. I shall put him off until evening.

As ever,

E.

She then wrote to Mr. Cruikshank in care of the concierge at his lodgings and directed him to wait until she and her mother arrived to collect him just before dinner. She prayed that he would prefer waiting for her in favor of making his own arrangements which would prove to be both costly and inconvenient, though what he would do with himself all day as he waited, she knew not. She then returned to bed to sleep the few hours left to her before an early rising in order to have her letters posted at the earliest possible moment.

After a long day that seemed to go on forever, she was in the salon entertaining callers, her nerves stretched to their very limit. As such, she nearly gasped with apprehension when the butler scratched at the door and entered with a silver salver bearing a single card. She dared not hope that it bore the name of Mr. Colin Lloyd-Jones but found that she utterly failed to do otherwise. As the butler strode in her direction, she felt her heart begin to hammer with the certitude that the man she loved waited not at some lodgings but under her very roof. When she saw that the card was indeed meant for her, she was assailed with trepidation.

She wished she knew whether Mr. Lloyd-Jones, as the owner of the card surely must be, had already received her letter or if he came without the knowledge that Mr. Cruikshank had arrived on British soil. She took the card and handed it, without a word, to her mother.

"Oh! Elizabeth," her Mama breathed. "What a delightful surprise. You are most likely astonished to know that Mr. Lloyd-Jones pays us a visit," she revealed to the nosy woman and her daughter who were seated on the sofa across from the Armisteads. "But, you must know, he and his sister are nearly family to us."

"Mama, I fear you overstate the case," Elizabeth said faintly. Though the wide-eyed stares of their current guests were somewhat alarming, it was her anticipation of the guest not yet arrived that so discomposed her. She hoped that the fluttering of her stomach and the pounding of her heart that always occurred whenever she cast her gaze upon him would not be apparent to the tale bearing ladies who would doubtless choose to stay rooted to the spot in anticipation of Mr. Lloyd-Jones' arrival.

When he stepped into the room she saw directly that he had had her letter; the mirth that always lingered in his compelling eyes had fled and he did not smile. "Good day," he said with a bow that took in all of the occupants of the room but the tragic cast of his features when he once again lifted his head was for Elizabeth alone.

"Ladies," her mother started, "I do believe I am meant to be elsewhere."

"No," he said, throwing up a hand to forestall her, "pray do not inconvenience yourself on my account. Miss Armistead doubtless recalls that she is engaged to ride out in my carriage this afternoon."

"Yes, of course," she said as she rose to acquire her bonnet and reticule. She had placed them in a chair in the far corner so that they would be handy should he appear and not on display if he did not. "I have been anticipating it with pleasure."

"You have said nothing of this to me, Elizabeth," her mother insisted but her daughter paid her no heed as she took his arm and quit the room.

As he led her down the stairs and out of the house, she admired his composure nearly as much as her own. Her stomach was in turmoil, her knees weak, and without his arm she would have tumbled down the stairs, thinking as she did on how these would be their last moments together before she became another man's wife.

Once they were safely perched in his curricle and her bonnet carefully tied against the breeze, he lost no time in whipping up the horses and hurtling down the road at a spanking pace. She thought, then, that he might be angry, and her trepidation grew. She found herself too breathless to speak and he spoke only once to ask if she were quite all right. She nodded that she was but wondered for how long it should be the case. The speed with which they moved felt dangerous, indeed, and then there was the question of when they would stop and where.

At last, he veered off onto a deserted lane and they fetched up behind a sadly dilapidated church that faced out onto the other side of the square.

He jumped out and ran round to take her hand and help her down. "There is a bench just the other side of that wall," he said with a nod at what must have once been part of a cloister but was now mostly fallen stone and masonry. To her great astonishment he put his arm around her and held her tight against his side as they walked. The bench looked upon a garden that grew in abundance despite the ruin all around it. As they sat he kept his arm about her and, eventually, she recovered enough from her apprehension to settle her head against his shoulder.

He said nothing for what seemed an age whilst she fretted over what her first words should be. Finally, she dared to ask what she already knew to be true. "You have had my letter?"

He tightened his arm about her and looked off into the distance despite the lack of a view. "I thank you for your kindness in sending it. And yet, its contents," he said, his breath catching in his throat, "conveyed a message I find I cannot like. Am I correct to conclude that our outings together are now at an end?"

Tears sprang to her eyes and closed her throat so that she was only able to render a tiny nod.

"I have thought and thought again *how* to say the words," he said, a bit savagely, "but I cannot. If we are to part, it must be at your word. I shall not bid you goodbye."

"I comprehend that it must be myself," she said, forcing the words from her trembling mouth "to make it clear who I am to be to you from here on out. I have knowingly encouraged your attentions and for that I must beg your pardon, for I mean to marry Mr. Cruikshank. That is something I am every bit as determined to do as I was before we met."

"Say only that you wish it far less than you once did," he said, his breath heaving in his chest. "It shall be the smallest of concessions for you but the greatest of gifts to me. And when you say it," he said as he shifted to face her, "let me see the truth of it in your eyes."

She turned towards him as the tears spilled down her cheeks. She felt his fingers as they ran along her neck until they caught in the ribbons of her bonnet and pulled them loose. Slowly, she pushed the bonnet from her head but she could not bear to meet his gaze. "I wish it far less," she whispered.

He put his hand to her wet cheek and so gently drew her face to meet his that she did not comprehend it. When she lifted her gaze and was met with the sight of him looking down upon her, and with such tenderness, her heart turned over.

"Elizabeth. Say that you will not go through with it. Say that you will marry me."

She attempted to turn her head away, but he had taken her face in both of his hands so she could not. Her only defense was to close her eyes, but his next question brought them fully open with alarm.

"Did Miss Hale speak true when she claimed you have rarely been kissed?"

Her heart took up its hammering again and she found that her gaze had fastened onto his well-shaped lips. To her dismay she was powerless to look away. "Only by Mr. Cruikshank," she whispered, "and only the once."

"In that case, might I ask if it is judicious to state that you have never been kissed by the man you love?"

She looked up, then, into his impossibly light gray eyes, and found it pointless to dissemble. "Yes, most judicious," she said weakly.

"In that case, my adored Miss Armistead, you shall know, before it is too late, what it feels like to be kissed by the man you love nearly as well as he loves you."

Why such a statement should cause her such misgiving, she could not say. "But how shall I know," she asked as she put her hand to his chest to prevent his drawing too near, "that he is not like the others who have professed to love me, and all for the sake of what they feel when they look at me?"

"How can one not love you for the pleasure of gazing upon eyes the color of a field glowing in the sun after a hard rain or the feel of one of your curls as it clings to his skin?" he asked as he lifted a trembling finger from her face and stretched it far enough to touch a ringlet. "And yet, you deserve to be loved so much more for your flawless perception, limitless patience and compassion, lively temperament, faultless integrity and your so cherished virtue. He who perceives these qualities in spite of the sound of your laughter and the perfume of your skin," he breathed as he leaned closer, regardless of her hand to his chest, to brush his nose along her cheek, "deserves to be best loved by you."

Suddenly, she felt faint with an exquisite need to feel his lips against hers but his attention was wholly taken up in rubbing his nose in circles along her cheek. It brought his mouth in and out of tantalizing proximity, causing her lungs to squeeze and her breath to come in fits and starts. When he finally dropped his hands from her face to gather her near, she was so bold as to align her mouth with his. The unanticipated motion sent his bottom lip skimming along the top of hers and it continued on up to hover against her temple for so long she feared he had thought better of kissing her altogether. The notion pained her past bearing and, determined to seize this last means of divulging all she could not say, she turned her face once more in pursuit of his mouth.

She had moved merely a fraction before his lips met her own with a speed and intensity that robbed her of breath and sent her senses spinning so that she found she must put her arms about his neck to steady herself. He tightened his hold on her and his mouth pressed against her such that she experienced wondrous sensations that were entirely new to her. She had not known that a kiss could be so full, last so long, and bring to life so many sensibilities of which she had previously been thoroughly unaware. It occurred to her that, as long as his mouth was pressed to hers, she would have no need of food or drink, rest or sleep. There was nothing that came to mind that mattered in the least compared to the feel of his arms around her, the sound of his ragged breathing, the scent of his skin, and the taste of his lips.

He left off kissing her mouth in order to trail kisses along her jaw and down her neck when, without the slightest warning, he pulled away to gaze at her, his eyes bruised with pain. "I had counted on having a better command of myself than that. I must beg your pardon for taking liberties neither of us intended."

"I did not perceive them as liberties," she murmured even as she acknowledged that the one dry kiss Duncan had bestowed on her now seemed as unwelcome as if he were a stranger who had forced himself upon her.

In reply, Colin drew her close against his chest. "I am the man you love, but you will be his wife. If only I could find a means to be both, one that did not compromise your principles, I would be the happiest of men."

She rubbed her cheek against his coat to distract herself from the desire to cry when suddenly she recalled what she had brought with her. Pulling away, she reached into her reticule and drew out a tiny pair of scissors and two small bags made of silk. She took a lock of his hair in her fingers and looked to him to apprehend if he objected. He gave her a slow, sad smile such that she felt no hesitation in clipping a curly lock from its brothers. She wrapped it round her finger and was about to place it in one of the bags when he stayed her hand and kissed the dusky lock. She gave him a tremulous smile and tucked the curl safely away before passing to him the scissors.

Though his fingers trembled, he took care to find a small ringlet at the nape of her neck that would not be missed and snipped it quickly before she could think to regret it. He gave it to her to kiss, and then he kissed it, as well, before he slid it into the remaining silk bag and secreted it in the inside breast pocket of his coat. "I shall keep this by me always, never doubting."

"And I shall do the same. I shall have it made into a brooch and wear it every moment of the day." It was not as if her husband would see it and take offense and she found that the truth of it caused her to break into earnest tears.

He pulled her once more against his chest and stroked her hair. "Elizabeth, why must you endure this pain? You have the power to end it all forever by crying off. There is not a man or woman in all of England who should blame you."

"Save him," she said, sitting up and drying her tears. "You and I, we would be happy, but he would be heartbroken, bereft and nearly alone." She did not add that he would be unable to support himself through work or even throughout the hours of a single day.

"But you needn't sacrifice your happiness for him. You needn't sacrifice *ours*. There are other women in the world, a fact I have gladly learned. As have I, he is very likely to meet one who truly loves him in ways you do not."

"I think not. It is too romantic a notion for this world. Perhaps that is all it is to me, as well. But I have made a promise and I cannot go back on it. I cannot! I pray, do not press me further."

"I will not, I swear it," he insisted, taking her hands in his. "I wish for your happiness far more than my own. If only I might know that you will indeed be happy."

Elizabeth had no satisfactory reply to this. "I must return," she said as she removed her hands from his, retrieved her bonnet and placed it on her head. "I shall be forever grateful that you have come today," she said, her voice wavering, "but it is time for me to begin my new life."

He stood, with no word at all, and held out his hand to help her to her feet. As they returned to the carriage, he did not put his arm about her as before and stayed far enough distant that she could not link her arm through his. He handed her up into the curricle and when she had taken her seat he gave her the smile that was meant only for her, the one that seemed to melt her bones and that she feared she would never again behold. Then he took his place beside her, taking such care to keep his distance that her heart broke, and drove so sedately that there was no chance that she might jostle against him. It was a far more peaceful ride than the one prior and she was grateful for the time it gave her to cool her face and gain her composure. And yet she could not help but mourn what she had lost.

When they arrived, he held out his hand to help her down from the curricle. She stood and looked down at it, fully aware that it was the last time that they would touch. She felt dizzy with grief but willed herself not to swoon. To her great astonishment, he put his hands to her waist, lifted her from the carriage and slowly lowered her to the ground, all the while his gaze locked with hers. They stood perilously close to one another and just as she decided she would put her hand to his cheek one last time, the front door opened and Katherine came tripping down the steps.

"Mr. Lloyd-Jones!" she cried as if he weren't a mere foot away. "I should be most grateful for a turn in your curricle, as well."

With great reluctance, he tore his gaze away from Elizabeth and backed away in order to sketch a brief bow for the benefit of both ladies. "I regret that I have other matters to which I must attend. Some other afternoon, perhaps." Quickly, he mounted the steps and took up the reins and, with a savage flick of the reins, drove away without a backwards glance.

"Well, that was very lowering, indeed," Katherine insisted. "I only wished to ride in his curricle, not marry him."

"Oh?" Elizabeth said more testily than she wished but far less than she felt. "Do you not? And what of Mr. Cruikshank? I suppose you have no wish to marry him, either!"

"I .. My papa has forbidden it," Katherine replied, her eyes wide.

"Therefore, you now want another man you cannot have," Elizabeth snapped as she marched up the steps to the front door. It was opened by a footman whose expression of alarm widened with the door.

"Who is to say I can't have him?" Katherine demanded. "Do you have the final word as to who is to marry your tossed-aside suitors?"

"Do not be childish, Kate. It doesn't suit you." Elizabeth swept through the door and went directly to the staircase, Katherine just behind her. "Please," Elizabeth begged, "I have the headache and wish to go to my room."

"Then you are not to marry Mr. Lloyd-Jones?" Katherine demanded.

"Why should anyone think I would marry Mr. Lloyd-Jones?" Elizabeth picked up her skirts and hastened her steps up the staircase.

"It is not as if I were the only to notice; the two of you are forever smelling of April and May."

Elizabeth stopped and turned to give Katherine her full attention. "What is it that you wish me to say? That I love him? That he loves me? It is of no consequence. I am to drive out to Mr. Cruikshank's lodgings with Mama to bring him hither, the notice of our engagement is to be posted in the newspaper and the banns read, at which time we shall be married. Is this not why I have come to England?"

"But, if that is how you want it, Elizabeth, why should I not marry Mr. Lloyd-Jones?"

Elizabeth only just refrained from stamping her foot. "Because it is beholden on you to wait for him to offer and he never shall!" she insisted before turning to stomp up the remaining stairs.

"His heart was broken over Miss Ponsonby," Katherine said as she picked up her own skirts and hastened after Elizabeth, "and yet, here he is, madly in love with you. Who is to say that he shan't be quite ready to fall in love with me a fortnight from now, as well?"

Elizabeth felt as if her head would split in two. "I couldn't say, Katherine, I suppose he might." Tears started in her eyes and she ran across the landing to her chamber door. "I intend to lie down for a while before I dress for dinner. I shall see you when we have returned from fetching Duncan." She put her hand to the latch and stood, her lungs heaving, facing the door until Katherine swept by.

The moment Elizabeth was certain Katherine would not turn about and renew the argument Elizabeth entered her room, shut the door and pulled the bolt. Fast falling tears obscured her vision as she stumbled towards the bed and sank down, leaned her head against a post and gave vent to her feelings. She was finally sobered by the realization that she used the little silk bag with the precious lock of hair to stem her tears. Staring at it for some moments, she finally concluded that a proper hiding place must be found for it, one that kept it by her always.

She removed the scissors from her reticule and employed them mercilessly to cut one of the ribbons from her bonnet. Threading the ribbon through the drawstring of the little bag, she tied it around her neck and found that the silken bundle fell just low enough to be concealed in the folds of her stays. With the treasure where she could feel it, she felt somewhat restored and could turn her mind to selecting a gown to celebrate the arrival of her bridegroom. He would not see her choice, however, it would be an indication to everyone at table as to her sentiments and they must be led to believe she was the happiest girl who ever drew breath. As such, she took the red silk gown from the clothespress and rang the bell for the girl to come and freshen it up.

With the little bag tucked next to her heart, Elizabeth was able to close her eyes and sleep until the girl returned to help her mistress don the gown. Though there would be few to appreciate it in days to come, Elizabeth was grateful to have the gown as a tangible memory of the informal dinner and dance at the Lloyd-Jones establishment. Neither Mr. Cruikshank nor his mother need ever know what thoughts were hers when she wore it after her marriage. To her regret, the scent of Mr. Lloyd-Jones' cologne no longer lingered in the red threads but she supposed it was too dangerous to have it otherwise. She noted that the ribbon that held the bag, a distinctive green one with embroidered leaves of gold, was visible around her neck but, that could not be helped.

As she tossed the bereft bonnet into the back of the clothespress, she found one she had yet to wear and tied it under her chin. She collected her reticule, minus the scissors, her long kid gloves and a grass green cloak and quit her room in search of her mother.

"There you are my darling!" her mother sang. "It is time to fetch home your Mr. Cruikshank."

"Yes. Indeed." Elizabeth was careful not to meet her mama's eyes and swept down the stairs ahead of her so as to hide any signs of distress that might remain in Elizabeth's face. "I cannot say how eager I am finally to have him safe beside me. I am ever so glad that we are to have dinner at home, tonight," she chattered cheerfully, "as I am not certain how well he has learned to cope whilst we have been apart. However, I am persuaded he should enjoy an evening entertainment. To where are we invited tonight?"

"I believe it is the Roberts' but it shall depend on Mr. Lloyd-Jones and his sister."

"What have they to say to it?" Elizabeth asked in a low voice. She had obtained the bottom of the stairs and was glad of the need to pull on her gloves as it kept her eyes downcast.

"Why, I have invited them to dinner, tonight. Have I done wrong?"

Elizabeth looked up and gave her mother a bright smile. "Of course not. Why ever say so?"

"Well, I don't know," her Mama said as she pulled the cloak around her daughter's shoulders and tied it shut with the broad, satin ribbons. "I thought perhaps there was a bit of a contretemps when he departed this afternoon."

"No. No contretemps," Elizabeth murmured, "though, it is true, Katherine was most annoyed that he departed without offering to give her a ride."

"Well, I thought that is what I heard. It isn't as if the entire house overheard the exchange, mind you," her mother vowed, "but I was by the window in the sitting room and you know how the sound rises."

Elizabeth acquitted her mother with a smile.

"Well!" her mother exclaimed. "You must see that I felt it only proper to invite him so as to give Katherine her chance at attaching his interest."

"Mama, please don't," Elizabeth begged but her mother did not attend her daughter's words.

"I am persuaded you shall enjoy the company of Miss Analisa, as well. Besides which, you must wish to make them both known to Mr. Cruikshank; the Lloyd-Joneses have been family to us these past weeks."

"Yes, I suppose it would be odd if we did not make them known to one another. It is not as if the Lloyd-Joneses have not been aware that he is to arrive from the outset."

"My point precisely. Now, I do believe the carriage is waiting and so is your Mr. Cruikshank."

Elizabeth offered no reply and the remainder of the journey was made in almost complete silence, leaving her with a generous amount of time to reflect. How she was to carry on during dinner with Colin Lloyd-Jones at table, she could not guess. Despite his blindness, Duncan was not a half-wit and there were sure to be undercurrents he would sense and wonder at. She could hardly explain every obtuse comment that was made in the case he might construe the truth from her protestations.

She hadn't the time to arrive at a satisfactory solution before the carriage drew up outside his lodgings. To her surprise, Duncan waited outside the establishment where she could readily see him, a circumstance for which she was grateful as it obviated the necessity of going inside to inquire after him. With naught else to do but quit the carriage and greet her betrothed, Elizabeth drew a deep breath and opened the door.

It was odd, indeed, to approach the man she was to marry after so long an absence and receive no reaction from him. When he had been abed in hospital, he had known her step as well as her scent and he had always greeted her before she spoke. Matters would be different in London and she wondered what manner of challenges would be presented as a result. She looked into his face and felt her stomach drop and her pace slow.

"Come dear," her mother said as she took Elizabeth's arm and drew her forth. "It will not do to put off the inevitable."

Once she drew near enough, he turned at the sound of her step, a quizzical expression stamped to his features.

"Duncan, it is I," she said, hesitant to step too near before she had identified herself.

"Elizabeth? Can it really be you?" he asked as he put forth his hand.

She took his hand and linked her arm through his. "Yes, it is, and Mama, too."

He bent to sketch Mrs. Armistead a bow and she was forced to take a few quick steps back in order to avoid his chin making contact with her head. "My," she said, "you seem to be making great strides in your independence."

In truth, he looked more than a little shoddy, precisely as one would expect from a blind man who traveled alone.

"Haven't I, though? I believe the time at sea was well spent in that regard."

"Yes, you look exceedingly handsome," Elizabeth insisted. Silently she wondered if there were a way to get him properly shaved and availed of a clean cravat before the Lloyd-Joneses arrived for dinner.

"We must hurry if we are to arrive in time, Duncan. Shall we proceed?" Elizabeth asked as she gave his arm a bit of a tug.

"Aye, I am at *aux anges* to make your aunt's acquaintance. I have ne'er met a Lady afore."

Elizabeth suppressed a desire to wince. His heavy Scottish burr had never troubled her in the past. In fact, she had scarcely noticed it. However, compared to the elegant phrasing of the Lloyd-Joneses, Duncan's accent sounded positively savage. "Aunt Augusta is every bit as eager to meet you as is Miss Hale," Elizabeth added as a means to test the waters; she had known nothing of his offer for Katherine before they left India.

"I shall be verra glad to meet Miss Hale again," he said softly.

His reply left Elizabeth in as much doubt as ever.

Chapter Thirteen

Colin believed he had never seen so disheveled a gentleman, if his use of the term gentleman was an accurate assessment. He had been taught that it was rude to stare but trusted Mr. Cruikshank would remain in ignorance of Colin's manifest consternation. He wondered if he were the only person at table who felt that Mr. Cruikshank looked as if he had shaved, in some cases, with a spoon, and in others, with a carving knife. His cravat resembled nothing more than a dish of Spotted Dick and his waistcoat was buttoned all askew. His cuffs had clearly not been attended to in many a moon and though the scars about his eyes were interesting, they were utterly eclipsed by the fact that Elizabeth had entirely failed to mention that her intended was blind. That she had kept this intelligence from Colin by design was patently obvious. Nevertheless, he refused to behave badly and add to her already undeniable discomfiture.

"Mr. Cruikshank, how was your ocean voyage?" Colin asked.

"Oh, it were a treat, it were. Though I couldna see, I had the feel of the spray to my face and the scent of the water to give me a feel for where I were."

Colin could feel the heat of his sister's gaze on his face but turning to share in her mirth should only serve to further humiliate Elizabeth. "Sea legs are difficult enough to acquire without a loss of vision, Mr. Cruikshank; how did you fare in that regard?"

"It was verra difficult but I came about," he said, turning his head towards the sound of Colin's voice. "I had long enough, didna I?"

"Yes, it is remarkable that you were able to tend to your own needs for the entire voyage. I stand in awe of your considerable finesse."

"There were some dark days, indeed," Mr. Cruikshank replied as he slid his hand across the table in Elizabeth's direction. "Howe'er, I thought about my own Elizabeth and I came round soon enough."

She laid her hand on his and looked down, biting her lip as she usually did when she was not sure she ought to say what had come to her mind.

"Miss Elizabeth," Analisa ventured, "you must be vastly pleased with the improvement Mr. Cruikshank has made in the time you have been apart. I am persuaded I should not do half as well were I unable to see."

"Indeed," Elizabeth replied. "He is a man of great character. His persistence in times of trial and his constant good cheer in spite of troubles are truly admirable."

Colin doubted not that she meant every word of it. Indeed, before making the acquaintance of her intended, Colin would have expected nothing less than the absolute truth to ever fall from her lips. However, the glaring omission in regard to Mr. Cruikshank's circumstances made possible a sliver of doubt. In order to better consider a suitable topic of conversation, Colin pushed aside the panic that assailed him when he wondered what else Elizabeth might not have divulged. He should have liked nothing better than to pepper Mr. Cruikshank with any number of questions but Colin suspected they would not be in the least welcome.

"What are your plans for the future, Mr. Cruikshank?" Colin asked even as he realized his question was far from well considered if the way Elizabeth's gaze flew to his face, her eyes wide with apprehension, was any indication.

"Why, I plan to farm my land and take care o' my family."

Colin doubted there would be any farming of land on a sandy rock such as Sheridan. "And what of Miss Armistead?"

"What o' her? She shall be my wife and bear my children and work alongside me."

Colin allowed a surge of revulsion to wash over him. "Forgive me Mr. Cruikshank but don't you mean to say that she shall work *for* you? Or will her dowry negate the need for either of you to farm anything?" He restrained himself from pointing out that a blind man could hardly be expected to wield so much as a hoe, but only just.

"Mr. Lloyd-Jones," Elizabeth interjected, "you go too far."

"No, leave him be, Elizabeth," Mr. Cruikshank said, blinking rapidly. "If I am not mistaken, I feel that he has stood your friend in my absence and it would not be surprising if he were a might fashed o'er our circumstances."

"Yes, he has been a friend, and Miss Lloyd-Jones, as well," Elizabeth said with a warm smile for Analisa. "However, I do not feel it gives him leave to interrogate you as if you were a criminal on trial."

Colin could only wonder at her choice of words; there was indeed something rather criminal about Mr. Cruikshank and Colin intended to discover exactly what. "Have you not been in service to the crown?" he asked, avoiding Elizabeth's gaze. "How fares the farm in your absence?"

Mr. Cruikshank smiled coldly and, in spite of his lack of vision, seemed to look directly into Colin's eyes. "It fares well enough. We shall need to plant directly upon our return, but I have no doubt Elizabeth is up to the challenge."

Colin's gaze swung to Elizabeth's face just in time for him to note the color that swept up to the roots of her hair. "You mean to put your wife to work on the land? In your stead?" Colin demanded.

"She shall soon grow accustomed to it and I shall soon learn to cope," Mr. Cruikshank said smoothly.

"What is there to farm in Sheridan?" Lady Augusta asked, her voice rising up from her place at the head of the table. "Perhaps you intend to farm mussels or crab? I daresay you should need a brace of good, hearty *men* in aid of such an endeavor."

Mr. Cruikshank sucked in his breath and seemed not to know where to train his sightless eyes.

"Hortense," Lady Augusta said to her sister-in-law, "do you intend to be off again tomorrow to find a suitable caterer for the wedding breakfast? I have said again and again that my cook is up to the task. Of course, he is not as talented as Mr. Lloyd-Jones' cook, of that I am most positively persuaded."

"Yes, indeed," Mrs. Armistead agreed, "every morsel of that splendid meal was divine."

"By all means, Elizabeth," Mr. Cruikshank said, "let us put her to the task if Mr. Lloyd-Jones does not object."

"Oh, no, I am persuaded it should be a terrible inconvenience," Elizabeth insisted.

"She shall prepare your wedding breakfast, Miss Armistead, if you wish it," Colin said, willing her to comprehend his stipulation: that it would depend entirely on the groom. Her obvious distress at his words was as painful as if it were his own, but his curiosity as to a certain ribbon around her neck soon permeated his thoughts. It was the same distinctive ribbon that had adorned the bonnet she had worn that afternoon and he wondered what it could hold. He stared at her until she was forced to meet his gaze, whereupon he put his hand over the breast pocket where lay the little bag containing the lock of her hair.

Her eyes glistened with unshed tears as she ran her finger along the ribbon and he knew that the lock of his hair hung round her neck. He knew, as well, the truth, in startling clarity: Miss Elizabeth Armistead loved Colin, but she would not marry him. That she did not love her intended hardly mattered; she hadn't loved him a day in her life and yet he would be the one with whom she would spend her life. Mr. Cruikshank would possess her beauty, her fortune and her continual presence, but Colin would have her heart.

It was not nearly enough.

Rising to his feet, he sketched a bow to all assembled and made his excuses. "I find that I have forgotten a previous engagement. It is .. imperative. I should be grateful, Lady Augusta, if your carriage was called out for Analisa when the evening has come to an end."

"Oh, but Colin, what could be more imperative than this?" she insisted with a wide-eyed look for her brother coupled with a slight inclination of her head in Elizabeth's direction.

"I really couldn't say," Colin said. It wasn't a lie.

"I shall walk with you to the door, then, shall I?" she asked.

"I shall walk with him," Miss Katherine said and she was out of her seat and taking his arm before anyone could part lips to object.

As she linked her arm in his, he looked to Elizabeth, mute and miserable, for what might be the last time. The thought crossed his mind that if he had only abided by the pact Tony and he had made, his heart would not, even now, be crushed and throbbing, the breakage of which into tiny pieces was imminent. He wished to be far and away from even Analisa when the moment came. The last image of Elizabeth he beheld before he turned away was of her eyes bright with candlelight and tears, her hand at her throat and her fingers caught in the ribbon that adorned it.

"Come, Mr. Lloyd-Jones," Miss Katherine said in a voice so cheerful it grated on his ears. "You shall soon call on us again, I have no doubt."

Colin waited until they had reached the landing and were heading down the stairs to disabuse her of her misconception. "Miss Hale, I shan't be calling here, again, but pray, do not perceive it as a slight."

"What can you possibly mean by that, Mr. Lloyd-Jones?" she asked in a voice full of laughter. "I am persuaded you are merely jesting."

"I assure you, I am not. Miss Hale, certainly it cannot have escaped your notice that I have been courting Miss Armistead?"

"Well, yes," she stammered. "I knew it would come to naught and that soon you would be looking about for a sop to your wounded heart, just as you did after Miss Ponsonby."

Colin paused at the bottom of the stairs and gently extricated his arm from Miss Hale's grasp. "I pray that I have never given you reason to hope, Miss Hale. What I felt for Miss Ponsonby is nothing compared to what I feel for Elizabeth. I ought to have kept my own council and remained home for the duration of the season," he said ruefully.

Miss Hale, visibly shaken, looked down at the ground. "I can hardly credit it. Is there nothing I might say that should lead you to look on me with any favor?"

"I fear that I shall never look on any woman with that sort of favor again. Goodbye, Miss Hale." He crossed the hall, collected his hat and gloves and had the door closed behind him before he changed his mind. As there had been no time to order his carriage brought round, he decided it best to walk. It was early yet and the lamps still lighted but the air was brisk and he recalled that he had forgotten his outer coat. It was one he did not wish to lose but consoled himself with the thought that, if Analisa should not collect it on his behalf, Elizabeth might carry it to her chamber and hold it close.

He arrived home, cold and hungry, and ordered that a fire should immediately be laid in the dining room and food brought forthwith. He paced the floor in the library whilst he waited for the dining room to become habitable and was relieved when he could sit in the room that spoke so much of his beloved. He passed the time in waiting for his meal in staring at the painting that marked the day of their coming together as something more than mere acquaintances. As such, he failed to hear the butler enter.

"Dinner is served, sir." Evans laid a tray on the table in front of his master.

"Thank you. Please let Cook know how very pleased I am with her amenability."

"Very well, sir. Will that be all?"

Colin had need of only one thing but was fairly certain the butler hadn't a cure for an ache in the chest that grew with every passing moment. Appalled at a sudden surge of blinding tears, Colin picked up his fork and took a stab at the closest item on his plate. He had not wept since he was a child and felt that weeping would not help him now. Tossing the fork aside, he pushed back his chair, went to the painting over the fireplace and regarded the colors through the prism of his tears.

"Sir?" Evans inquired.

"Pray, forgive me. There is one more thing," he said, never taking his eyes from the painting. "I would like this taken down and wrapped up before breakfast in the morning. Have it sent to Miss Elizabeth Armistead in care of Lady Augusta, Sommersby House, with a card of congratulations on the young lady's upcoming nuptials."

"Very good, sir."

The butler asked no more questions and immediately departed, to Colin's great relief, as he would have none witness the moment when his heart finally gave way.

Matters were not much improved come morning. If his heart had indeed broken the night prior, it had done nothing to relieve his pain. Either way, the dining room was now a grievous reminder of all he had lost. He should not be surprised were he to open the door and find pieces of his heart scattered like a trail of rubies across the antique rug. As such, he resigned himself to again taking meals on a tray in the library.

Once he had his breakfast diverted and had ensconced himself in his chair by the fire, he noticed that his calendar attested to the fact that he had only known Miss Armistead even existed for a single fortnight, a fact he could hardly credit. It seemed as if he had known her for the better part of his life; all that had occurred prior was merely a prelude to what should prove the seminal moment of his life: the one in which he had fallen in love. Such pitiful thoughts proved damaging to his appetite and he had made little inroads on his breakfast when the door to the library opened and Analisa rushed in.

"Oh, Colin! You look positively dreadful!"

"Why thank you, that was all that was wanted," he said in what were meant to be bantering tones. However, when he saw the stricken look on her face, he pushed aside the tray table, rose to his feet and opened his arms wide.

She surged into his embrace and burst into a bout of weeping so violent as to thoroughly wet his coat in so short a time he could only wonder.

"Oh, Colin," she said between sobs, "she is to wed that . . that . . *man!*"

"Yes. It has been her intention from the beginning. She never led us to believe otherwise."

"But he is blind!"

"I do believe she values that in him above all else," Colin said sadly.

"But to be stuck in the wilds of Scotland! With *him!*"

"It is most tragic, I agree," he said, willing down his own passionate objections on the subject.

"But . . But, she is so beautiful! And he can't even see her!"

"One can only assume he loves her for her internal beauty. There is much of it to love."

"As do I. As do you! Have you not told her, Colin?" she begged.

"Yes," he said, closing his eyes against the throb of pain that invariably rose when he thought of the moments when he had so thoroughly expressed his feelings on the subject. "Her course is set and she is determined. My declaration was not enough. Perhaps it is I, myself, who is not enough."

Analisa pulled away from his shoulder to search his face. "You? Not enough? That is an impossible notion. No, it is something different." She dragged herself out of his arms and fell into a chair. "I believe it must be a matter of trust."

"She has not known me for long." He ran a hand through his hair. "Perhaps that accounts for it."

"No, it has naught to do with you; it is her. I believe she fears that you, or any man she weds, cannot see past her outward beauty in order to love her for how she sees herself, whom she knows herself to be."

The words he had said to Elizabeth on that very subject only the day prior came to mind. "She should have no misgivings on that score," he said as he sat in hopes it would disguise the trembling in his limbs. "I am persuaded you are correct in that this could be the reason she first agreed to marry him. However, I have left her in no doubt as to my feelings in regard to her inner beauty. I am persuaded she took me at my word."

"Very well, then, it is something else. What could it be?" Analisa asked as she looked to him with anguish in her eyes.

"She has made a promise and she cannot break it," he said, rising again to his feet to pace the room. "At least, those were the words she spoke. At the time, I had been willing to accept it as the truth but now that I have met him . . " He threw his hands into the air in despair. "It is not only his circumstances that are of concern; there is something repulsive about him. How she could have failed to ascertain it, I am at a loss to say."

"Perhaps it is a romantical notion that has blinded her to the truth. What could be more appealing to a young girl than an injured soldier who, near death, has rallied purely through her attentions to him? Why, it could almost be a novel along the lines of Mrs. Radcliffe!"

Colin gave a harsh laugh. "Now you go too far!"

"Perhaps, but not by much. Oh, Colin! What are we to do?"

"We? Where is the 'we' in this?" He turned to see the tears start again in her eyes and went to take her hand. "I am ever so grateful you are here. You are the best of sisters and I shall be devastated when you are too much occupied to spare time for your lonely brother."

"Colin! Never!" she admonished.

"Yes, for that is the order of things, which brings me to the subject of my lack of persistence. I shall return my attentions to finding you a husband, just as I ought to have done in the first place, and you shall carry on as if we had never met Miss Elizabeth Armistead."

"But, how can I?" she cried, pulling her hand from his. "I was persuaded she was to be the sister I never had. I should have loved her nearly as well as you, if not better; you can be so vexing at times! And what of you? A second heartbreak in the course of a month is insupportable!"

Colin walked to the mantle and absently flipped through a stack of invitations. "Where do we go tonight?"

"You don't mean to say that you intend to go out?"

"I must if I am to find you a husband I shan't dislike excessively."

Analisa sprang to her feet and took the stack of invitations from his hands. "It's the Scott-Montgomery musicale tonight but I am persuaded you are not up to it. Your eyes are red-rimmed and haggard, your hair is standing on end all over your head and your mouth appears as if it has forgotten how to smile."

Colin smiled. "I have already rectified the last and the others can be cured by cool water and some judicious combing."

"Well. I suppose it could be managed. A musical evening is far less taxing than a ball or a rout as you shan't be expected to converse overmuch."

"Indeed. I shall sit in the corner and search the audience for a suitable prospect through a looking glass," Colin said with as much cheer as he could muster.

"Looking glass? Next you shall tell me that you have become Sir Anthony!"

"Ah, yes, I knew there was something I ought to tell you. Tony was meant to have fought a duel over the honor of a girl he does not admire but to whom he has unaccountably become engaged."

Analisa's mouth dropped open and they stared at each other in abject horror until, suddenly they broke into insuppressible laughter. "How ironical that the always proper and so refined Sir Anthony should find himself in such a ridiculous fix!" she managed to say amidst her tears of merriment.

"It is certainly not the manner in which I thought his bachelorhood should come to an end," Colin riposted. "He shall never live this down!"

Analisa fell back into a chair and dabbed at her tears with a lace handkerchief. "It is a mystery how closely related is tragedy and hilarity," she said with a chuckle. "I could not say if these are tears of joy or sadness."

Colin heaved a sigh and hastily turned away lest the quickly returned sorrow had made itself apparent on his face. "Doubtless Tony finds nothing joyful in it. He, however, is on his own. It is with you I needs must be most concerned."

"Then you shall escort me to the musicale?" Analisa rose and laid her hand on his arm. "Do say that you shall arrive in time for dinner. Mama and Papa shall be most pleased to see you."

"I think not," he said, putting his hand over hers. "I am not yet prepared to be peppered with questions or their disappointment when they receive woefully inadequate replies. But soon, I swear it," he added. "But see here, do be ready in time; I abhor being late."

"Yes, yes!" Analisa insisted as she headed for the door. "Don't I know it?"

It wasn't until he was certain she was gone that he dropped into his chair by the fire and sank his head into his hands. She had spoken so many of the words he hadn't allowed himself to so much as consider. As painful as the interlude had been, he loved her for it.

He had so often in the past weeks thought to show his appreciation for her with a little gift and decided that this was the day.

Within the hour, he had combed the offensive hair and was making his way down Bond Street in search of an appropriate token for his sister. As he turned into his favored jewelers, he thought perhaps a pendant or a hoop ring of dainty pearls would be just the ticket. He was about to hail the proprietor when he realized the identity of the customers upon which he waited; Elizabeth and Mr. Cruikshank.

Quickly, Colin returned to the street and berated himself for his wish to return to the shop and shamelessly eavesdrop. Finally, he decided that it was unlikely that he should be called to account by a blind man and a woman who wished to keep his interest a secret. Seduced by the ease of it, Colin entered the shop as quietly as possible and made certain that he was not in Elizabeth's line of vision.

"I intend to buy you the finest ring in the establishment," Mr. Cruikshank insisted. "Have the man show you whate'er you wish."

Colin could not help but notice that someone had given Mr. Cruikshank a clean shave and set of linens. He had to admit that the improvement was notable. It did little, however, to improve Colin's mood.

Of course, the money used to buy the ring would come from the funds her father gifted her upon her departure, but no matter; Colin was in agreement that Elizabeth should have the finest jewels money could buy.

"I should be happy with a simple, gold band," Elizabeth demurred.

"Nay, that shouldna do! At least have a row of diamonds or rubies!"

"I should like that, Duncan. Thank you! However, I would feel better if it were pearls rather than diamonds. They are so very dear!"

Colin could not believe what he was hearing. A hoop of pearls was what he aimed to purchase as a mere token of appreciation for

HEIDI ASHWORTH

his sister. Certainly Elizabeth deserved something far grander as a wedding ring. If it were he, he should choose nothing less than a rose-cut cluster of diamonds or, far better, emeralds. No! Both!

"Well, none can claim that I didna try," Mr. Cruikshank said cheerfully. "What is that you are writing, m'dear?"

Colin dared to step a shade closer, determined to see what Mr. Cruikshank could not and learned that Elizabeth was, indeed, writing on a piece of paper that lay on the counter.

"I am only giving the proprietor the address to which to deliver the ring," she said as she left off writing and pointed through the glass case to an object Colin could not perceive. "I am persuaded whatever I choose it shall need sizing and rather than returning to pick it up later, we might have it delivered."

"Very clever of you, lass!" Mr. Cruikshank crooned.

"Then it shall be the ring and the brooch," the proprietor announced.

"No, just the lovely pearl ring," Elizabeth said but she nodded her head very clearly in the affirmative. She then drew from her neck the ribbon from which dangled the little silk bag that Colin knew contained a lock of his hair. "Should you have any questions or difficulties, I have written my direction on the paper." She proffered to him the bag with two hands.

The shop owner took it from her with a wink of his eye and a finger to his nose. "I shall do just as you have asked, Miss. And, sir, I congratulate you on your upcoming nuptials!"

"Thank you," Mr. Cruikshank said with a slight bow over the stick he leaned upon. "I am persuaded I shall be the happiest of men."

Colin was so absorbed in the scene that he did not think to step out of the shop ahead of them and was struck by the expression on Elizabeth's face when she turned to see him standing nearly in her path. He admired her fortitude in holding her tongue, but the tears that sprang to her eyes spoke volumes.

188

"Come, Mr. Cruikshank," she said as she took his arm. "I shall lead you back to the carriage if you are done with your shopping for today."

Colin stepped aside, swept his hat from his head, and executed a deep bow. When he looked up, the pair had vanished. He had not expected to see her out and about with a blind man, had thought himself safe from seeing her again. Shaken by the encounter, he made his way slowly to the counter and attempted to remember why he had ventured out of the house that morning.

"Ah, Mr. Lloyd-Jones?" the shop owner, from whom Colin had purchased Cecily's wedding ring in addition to a few other sundries, greeted him. "How might I help you today?"

"It is ironic, is it not, that I came for a ring very much like the one you have just sold. Suddenly, however, it seems thoroughly undesirable. I think I should like a hoop of garnets, instead."

As the shop owner moved to another case to find an example of what Colin requested, he scrutinized the case that contained the object Elizabeth had pointed to through the glass. It couldn't have been a ring since that had been already selected and placed on the counter for her inspection. His search produced a tray of brooches, all suitable for the preservation of a lock of hair curled inside the setting in place of jewels.

"Might I also inspect this tray of brooches?" Colin asked.

"Yes, indeed," the proprietor said as he produced the tray requested. "Oh, pardon me, this one," he explained as he drew the largest one from the tray, "has been sold."

"Might I ask if it was to the young lady who was just in the shop."

"Yes! Are you acquainted with her? Well! She was forced to write me a note as her intended is quite, quite blind. She wishes to have a lock of her hair set in the brooch that I assume she intends to present to him as a wedding gift. I should think a brooch a bit inappropriate for a man to sport on his coat but perhaps it is only intended for a keepsake."

"Yes, I am persuaded you are correct," Colin said with a frozen smile. "Thank you. As for the ring, I have thought better of it." He could only imagine how Elizabeth's sensibilities might be injured if Analisa were to sport such a ring, one grander than a wedding ring and presented to her by her brother. It would not do. With a tip of his hat, he quit the shop and made his weary way home again.

Chapter Fourteen

"Elizabeth, my love," her mother crooned from the passage outside her daughter's chamber door. "A package has arrived for you."

"So soon?" she cried as she drew open the door and looked about for the expected parcel from the jeweler's. "But, where is it?"

"In the front hall, of course," her mother said, her eyes bright with curiosity. "It is far too large to traipse it up the stairs."

"I am astonished!" Elizabeth replied as they moved down the stairs as quickly as their skirts allowed. "I hadn't expected anything to arrive today but my wedding ring from the jeweler's." The additional purchase of the brooch she abstained from mentioning.

The contents of the package were made immediately known to her the moment she saw it. "It is the painting that hung in Mr. Lloyd-Jones' dining room," she explained, her heart sinking. Though she would treasure the painting for the rest of her life, she had cherished the notion that it would be treasured, instead, by Mr. Lloyd-Jones. Perhaps he did not wish to be put in mind of her; the thought make her heart sink even lower.

"How marvelous!" her mother exclaimed as she read the accompanying card. "And how thoughtful! He could not fail to note how much you admired it and now he has sent it to you as a wedding gift."

"Yes, I suppose that must be true." Elizabeth pulled enough brown paper from the frame to verify that it was, indeed, the same painting and restrained a sob.

"Elizabeth, my dear, are you quite all right?" her mother asked.

"Yes, of course. It's only that I suppose I felt that Mr. Lloyd-Jones held me in higher regard."

"Foolish girl! This is a most generous gift, so generous as to be nearly exceptional."

"I daresay you are most correct, Mama. It's only that I had hoped he would keep it, as a remembrance of me."

Mrs. Armistead cocked her head and gave her daughter a piercing look. "I do believe there is more to this painting than I can know. However, it seems to me a selfish notion to wish him to pine after you. Is that what you truly want, my dear?"

"Why should he pine after me, Mama? We are only friends, just as are I and Miss Analisa."

"Elizabeth! You know I do not believe a word of that! I should be surprised if any but Mr. Cruikshank did. It is a blessing he is blind or he should see the truth, as well."

"Mother, what a thing to say!" Elizabeth admonished as she dropped her face into her hands and began to weep. "I suppose it is true that I love him, just a little," she said tearfully. "And I suppose he loves me, just a little, as well."

"Just a little? If it is true that it rains just a little in India during the monsoon season, well then of course the two of you love one another 'just a little'!"

"Oh, Mama!" Elizabeth cried. "You make it sound as if we meant to fall in love!"

Her mother draped an arm across her daughter's shoulders and held her close. "There, there, my darling, it shall all come out all right in the end, you shall see."

"But I don't see! I have made a promise, one which I must keep or Mr. Cruikshank shall suffer. I cannot be held accountable for such an evil."

Elizabeth was shaken from her tears with the ringing of the front bell. She stepped back into the shadows of the hall in the case it was Mr. Lloyd-Jones; she had no wish to see him at the moment. Andrews opened the door and closed it again almost immediately, a small parcel in his hand.

"That should be your delivery from the jeweler's!" her mother exclaimed.

"I will share its contents, Mama, but not just yet," Elizabeth instructed as she took the parcel and headed up the stairs. "It is only a simple wedding ring, nothing overly-exciting."

"Very well, then, dear, I shall wait," her mother said on a rising sigh.

Elizabeth, all of her attention trained on the parcel in her hand, did not reply. She had not expected the brooch to have been completed nearly so soon and was anxious to ascertain whether or not it had arrived with the ring. The moment she had shut the door behind her, she tore away the paper with shaking hands to reveal a small blue box. Inside were two smaller boxes, the smallest of which she placed on her dressing table. She opened the other to reveal the longed-for brooch, the lock of her beloved's hair curled tight and affixed into the setting.

With trembling fingers, she pinned the brooch to the silk bag that once contained the lock and placed it on the dressing table where she might admire it from a distance. She had not intended to don it until the time came when the only other eyes to fall upon it were too weak or sightless to divine its presence. Now that she gazed upon it, however, she could not bear to be parted from it.

Deciding that she might always claim the lock of hair to be the relic of a dear departed loved one, she set about finding a means to wear it that very night. She was to attend the Scott-Montgomery's musicale so it was quite unexceptionable to choose a gown that boasted a bit more bodice than most of her ball gowns. She chose a bronze silk gown with a gold underdress adorned with ruched bishop sleeves and affixed the brooch to it. In this manner, she hoped to avoid unwelcome questions as to its origins from the maid when she came to help her mistress dress for the evening.

Next was the question of the nosegay of white roses Duncan had insisted on purchasing for her after they had left the jewelry shop. It also waited on her dressing table in anticipation of making up some part of her ensemble and she decided that they would do best in her hair. It would never do for Duncan to mistakenly tumble into her decolletage whilst attempting to smell the roses.

Of course, going out meant they might possibly encounter the Lloyd-Joneses but Elizabeth presumed they would choose a ball, an entertainment she was not likely to ever again attend, rather than a restrained musical evening. In that assumption, however, she was disappointed.

Her first inkling of danger was when their carriage, containing herself, Duncan, her mama, Katherine and Aunt Augusta, entered the gates of Scott-Montgomery House. Rather than a townhouse that sat in close proximity to its neighbors, this was an enormous Georgian estate that stood quite alone at the end of a long drive. The front garden was ablaze with a plethora of full length torches set alongside a variety of water features that magnified the firelight to great effect. Amongst it all, people promenaded in surprising numbers. There seemed to be more people outside than Elizabeth had anticipated would attend in total and she was assailed with a frisson of apprehension. It looked to be the event of the season and she suspected that the Lloyd-Joneses would be expected to put in an appearance at the very least.

"What is the matter with you, lass?" Duncan asked as they walked through the gardens to the house. "You seem to be in a bit of a dither."

"It is nothing, really," she replied as she looked about her for any sign of Mr. Lloyd-Jones or his sister. "It is just that there are so many torches; I needs must be wary on my own account as well as yours."

"I am indebted to you, as always," he said smoothly.

The notion of 'always' was one with which Elizabeth was having difficulty coming to terms and she felt herself frown. She was grateful he could not read the expression on her face and not for the first time. He expressed a great number of opinions with which she did not concur and did so in so grating a manner that she found it difficult to remember what the two of them held in common. How she had ever thought she loved this man enough to marry him was beyond her, but she had made her bed and now she must lie in it.

"Is it a very large gathering?" he asked as they entered the house and were met with the low hum of distant conversation. "It sounds as if there is a great deal of people in attendance."

"I am persuaded you are correct but I could not say how accurate until we have entered the room where the guests have been gathered."

"'Tis a pity there are so many guests," her mother remarked. "They have doubtless been forced to set up the musicians in the ballroom. It is such a shame as this house contains the loveliest music room. I had been greatly anticipating spending the evening there."

"Never fear," Aunt Augusta replied. "The Scott-Montgomerys are possessed of the most exquisite taste. I daresay they have fitted out the ballroom with every comfort."

"Well, I find I don't give a pin as to what room we are in or even to what music we are treated," Katherine remarked. "I find it is the prospect of encountering Mr. Lloyd-Jones that has me in a state of sweet trepidity."

Elizabeth should have liked to agree and was overcome with the knowledge that it would ever be thus for as long as she and

Mr. Lloyd-Jones were in the same vicinity. Promptly she decided that the yearly visits to London Duncan had promised her upon their engagement needs must be sacrificed if she were to have any peace of mind. And yet, she strained her neck as she turned her head this way and that in hopes of discovering Mr. Lloyd-Jones and with every bit as much anticipation as Katherine.

"What is it, love?" Duncan asked. "It seems as if your head is bobbin' up and down like a cork in the water."

"I am merely curious to see what I might of the house. It is excessively beautiful; there are paintings and statues and any manner of sights to see everywhere one looks."

"It canna be as beautiful as the views from our cottage in Scotland."

"Don't be ridiculous, Mr. Cruikshank," Aunt Augusta huffed. "The ocean is blue, the sky is blue, or rather, most days they will both be gray. The mind requires variety, color, does it not, Hortense?"

"I should like to comply, Augusta, but I do not wish to disparage my daughter's future home."

"Lady Augusta," Duncan said, "you might find your opinion has undergone a change once you have seen it for yourself. We hope that you shall often come to visit us."

Aunt Augusta rolled her eyes but grunted her assent.

"Well, I say it hardly matters," Katherine remarked. "We are here, now, and it is quite, quite beautiful and I am positively decided that I shall not go back to India!"

"Your mother shall miss you sadly if you do not," Elizabeth's mother said mournfully.

Elizabeth swallowed the sudden lump in her throat and considered what her mother had said. Whilst still in Bengal, Elizabeth and Duncan had discussed the fact that his mother would be in the house to give her company. At the time, it seemed a lovely notion but Elizabeth's mother now seemed irreplaceable. She could not think how she should manage without her.

When they finally made their way up the stairs and into the vast ballroom, Elizabeth was astonished by its grandeur. The room was positively brilliant with more chandeliers than she could hope to count over the heads of an enormous throng of people. If the Lloyd-Joneses were indeed in attendance, it would require a miracle simply to spot them.

Suddenly a chord was struck by the hand of an unseen musician and a hush fell over the crowd.

"I do believe it is best if we were to take up a seat for the duration," Aunt Augusta directed in a low voice. Wordlessly, the party of five took up the closest unoccupied chairs they could find. Others all around were doing the same and within a matter of moments, the milling throng had become a seated audience.

"It is astonishing that anyone should be possessed of so many chairs," Elizabeth's mama murmured. "Though, as I can see, there are a number of sofas close to the front, as well. I suppose those went to whosoever arrived on time," she added with a lift of her brow for her daughter who had insisted that they arrive fashionably late.

Curious as to who had demonstrated such bad ton as to arrive early, Elizabeth scanned the back of the heads of those fortunate souls who were not made to endure a hard chair at the back of the ballroom. However, the little she could see was not very illuminating and she transferred her attention to the actions of the musicians who were warming up.

"I have not long been away," Duncan said, "but this is not what passed for music before I left."

"It is only that they are testing their instruments before they begin to play in earnest." Elizabeth was ashamed of him for his ignorance on the matter, however, she disliked more his need to make such a remark in company. Not that his lack of polished manners would matter once they married and repaired to Scotland as there would be none to hear him. No one to hear her, as well. Or see her. Or her children. Indeed, the circumstances of her future threatened to cut up her peace more and more with every passing hour.

She lifted her hand to touch the silky lock that curled within its brooch and wondered if it could possibly endure many weeks with her stroking it with as much frequency as she had since its arrival that afternoon. She felt it to be inconceivable for Duncan to know about the brooch, and yet, she could not help but turn her head to search his face for any indication that he suspected her perfidy. Instead, her gaze flew, seemingly of its own accord, to the face of the man standing against the wall directly across from her. He was taller than most, impossibly handsome, and the way that he stared at her, the expression in his eyes so weighted with love and grief, threatened to crush her.

Suppressing a gasp of dismay, she dropped her hand from the brooch pinned against her heart and hastily turned to face the musicians.

"What is it?" Duncan asked, his lips next to her ear. It was a sensation most unwelcome. "I feel your agitation from here."

"I am merely exhilarated by the music," she equivocated, hiding their tete a tete behind her fan. She did not wish Colin to see how discomposed she felt with Duncan's face in such proximity to the very places Colin had so recently favored with his kisses.

"I believe it is more than that," Duncan urged but Elizabeth refused to respond to such a baiting.

She forced herself to stare straight ahead and felt it to be quite dull save the moments when the violin bows seemed to be sprouting out of the heads of those seated in front of her. She wished she had taken a moment to inspect the instruments before sitting; she would have liked to know how many violins there were and what other instruments were at play. She clearly heard the tones of a pianoforte as well as at least one cello, and various wind instruments. She spent a goodly ten minutes in the deciphering of what she was hearing before the first selection came to an end.

"Well, is that all there is to be?" Duncan asked.

"Not in the least," she whispered, stealing a glance at the wall. However, Colin had moved away and she could no longer see him. When she heard his voice coming from the front of the room, she felt no small amount of alarm, and found it necessary to fight the impulse to rise to her feet so that she might behold him.

"I shall now play for you Bach's Prelude and Fugue No. 1 in C Major on the pianoforte," he said in a commanding tone she had never had occasion to hear, but which she knew could originate only from him. "A prelude introduces a melody that the fugue then builds upon in two or more instrumental voices, each in its turn, and round and round it goes. I have, again and again, felt that this particular piece very much resembles love; as often simple as it is complex, with a tendency to land us right back where we started and over all too soon. Its very divinity depends entirely on its ephemeral nature."

There came a ripple of laughter from the audience that Elizabeth could only assume was in light of his doomed betrothal to Miss Ponsonby. And yet, Elizabeth knew it was on account of her rejection of him that he spoke as he did. She felt his words to be a harsh assessment and not in the least apt; she knew her love for him would never perish. However, his love for Miss Ponsonby had, by all accounts, melted away the moment he had met another.

Perhaps he should fall as deeply in love with the next young lady as he had with Elizabeth. Perhaps he never truly loved her at all. Tears sprang to her eyes at the notion and she was careful to wipe them away with her left hand as Duncan was unaccountably alive to her every action. She was as moved by the music itself and found that she must employ her handkerchief much too frequently for her tranquility.

"Is it the ague that makes you sniff so?" Duncan demanded.

Elizabeth managed a watery laugh. "I don't believe I have heard a case of the sniffles referred to as such."

"Be that as it may, I still wish to hear your answer to my question," he said in a hard voice to which she had never before been treated.

"I find the music deeply affecting, that is all. Of what consequence might it possibly be?"

"It matters because I canna see you, lass," he said in kindlier tones that set her to doubting her doubts. "How can I comfort you if I don't know what ails you?"

"It is nothing, really; just the music," she said, placing her hand on his arm in an attempt to reassure him of what, if she were honest, was an utter falsehood.

"So long as you are happy, m 'dear," he murmured.

"Yes, why should I not be?" she asked, plying her fan to cool the heat rising on her cheeks. To her relief, he made no response and she was free to listen to the rest of the piece. She was a bit taken aback at Colin's musical dexterity and somewhat hurt that he had never offered to play other than the duet with Katherine. It was a circumstance that could hardly matter, now, but she felt the loss keenly. They might have played together, even, that night when they danced in his sitting room. However, all thoughts were soon held at bay by virtue of the beautiful music.

It wasn't until the last note trembled on the air that her mother turned to her. "Elizabeth, how could you possibly let that man get away?" she hissed. "I am persuaded he would offer for you if you would encourage him in the slightest."

"Mama!" Elizabeth urged. Mortified by her certainty that Duncan had heard her mother's words she rose quickly to her feet and made her way past the guests to the end of the row of chairs. She felt Duncan grasp at her skirts as she moved past him but whether or not he was in need of anything she could not find it within herself to care.

Hurrying through the house, she found her way to the front garden and paused to regain her composure and cool her cheeks. She wished for nothing more than for Mr. Lloyd-Jones to appear at her side and take her in his arms, then took herself to task for entertaining such a self-indulgent thought. She took a few deep breaths to ward off the tears that had started in her eyes and looked about her. Guests wove in and out of the garden and moved past her on every side so it was not until she felt someone take her hand that she knew he was there. She looked up to see him raise her hand to his lips and kiss it.

"Mr. Lloyd-Jones," she said, turning to look into his face. His usually bright and mirthful eyes were yet weighed down with misery and her heart constricted with the knowledge that she was the cause of his pain. And yet, she could not help but feel overjoyed that he had come. "I find I cannot agree with your words in regard to love being over all too soon. It has not been so for me." She did not add how she feared it never would be.

To her dismay, the sorrow in his face deepened and he bent his head, his gaze catching on the brooch she wore as it gleamed in the torchlight. Smiling, he gently touched it with the tip of his finger. "Come," he said, taking a step back towards the garden and tugging on her hand.

She went with him willingly as they traipsed over the grass to the high-hedged maze that stood at the center of the garden. The moment they stepped into its paths of concealment, she heard the music of a fountain, one that was doubtless to be found in the center. In wordless agreement, they moved towards the sound but were forced to hide in a heavily shadowed enclave with the approach of voices.

She had thought only to mask their presence from any who might discover them, so was taken by surprise when she found herself tightly clasped in his arms, his lips fastened to hers. Having supposed that the kisses they had previously shared were the very embodiment of physical affection, she was astonished to find she was woefully mistaken. These that descended upon her now were even more insistent and demanding than the last, and she burned with an inner fire that seemed to set her skin aflame. Knowing she should turn and flee, she instead wound her arms around his neck and pulled him closer. She heard the breath catch in his throat at her touch and it suffused her being with an elation she had never known.

Her bliss turned to a daze of confusion when he suddenly released her, the air heaving through his lungs as he backed away deeper into the shadows of the maze. She took a step towards him and once again she was in his embrace. To her vexation he did not kiss her and instead slid his arm up her back to press her head to his chest. They stood thus for several minutes as she listened to the thunderous pounding of his heart in perfect unison with the rise and fall of his chest under her cheek.

"Elizabeth." Her name fell from his lips like music. "How you feel when he kisses you . . you will always feel thus. How you feel when I kiss you, how I feel . ." He heaved a great sigh and rubbed his thumb along her cheek. "There is so much more to these matters than you might possibly guess. I would pay any price, move any mountain, fight any foe, if only it were I who showed you what it means to be truly loved, body and soul."

She listened as his voice fell away and the beat of his heart resounded under her ear; how it pounded faster when she tightened her arms around his waist, pressing so close that the brooch with its treasured lock of hair was nearly crushed between them. The realization that she had never felt happier unfolded in her mind like a flower in the sun. Suddenly, and quite clearly she knew that the yearning she had felt since she had first met him was an unassailable longing to spend her life with Mr. Colin Lloyd-Jones.

Putting her hands to his chest, she pushed away so that she could gaze upon the little of him she could discern in the dark of the night. "There is something that I would say to you."

"If I spoke too freely," he said with a groan, "pray forgive me. I had not meant to press you further but when I saw you leave the room . . To have one more opportunity to speak with you, to ask you to be mine, I had not the courage to let it pass me by."

"And how fortunate am I that you did not!" she cried, smiling up at him. "It all seems so clear to me now and yet I have been so hopelessly befuddled. I had not presumed, until I had met Mr. Lloyd-Jones with his so comely face, pleasing temperament and exceptional character, that one could love a person's nature every bit as much as one's exquisite exterior. In point of fact, I had not thought it possible to be loved for anything but my outward appearance; such was my experience. And so I seized upon an artificial love in as much as I believed that its lack of capacity to be diverted by my appearance was comparable to being loved wholly for my nature."

"And now that this paragon of virtue has led you to this so avidly wished for conclusion," he said, his voice thick with emotion, "may I dare to hope that you will formally reject this spurious love for one that is so very true?"

"My only regret is that I have left it for so long," she confessed as she allowed her hands to be gathered in his and ardently kissed. "I do so fear that I shall make Mr. Cruikshank miserable but I cannot trade my .. *our* happiness for his. And yet, you perceive how he depends upon me. I cannot bear to face him. I have not had the time to think what I should do."

"Perhaps not, but I have been thinking on it rather incessantly," he said through what sounded to her like a wide smile. "I am aware of how scandalous it is to so much as say the words, however, if we were to elope to Gretna Green, you needn't deal with any unpleasantness. You need only leave a note for your mother and beg her to remain in England until we return from our honeymoon."

Stunned by the ease of his proposition, she was at first bereft of words. Finally, she pulled her hands free from his grasp, threw herself into his arms and cried, "How utterly brilliant!"

To her delight, he lifted her off her feet and into the air, spinning her about until she was giddy and faint. Slowly, he loosened his grasp and allowed her to slide back to earth. "Miss Armistead,

I ask you, and for the last time," he said in charmingly threatening tones, "will you marry me?"

"Mr. Colin Lloyd-Jones, I find I cannot do otherwise!"

He bent his head and kissed her so thoroughly that she could only wonder what new pleasures their wedding night might hold. "Soon you shall be Mrs. Colin Lloyd-Jones," he murmured as his kisses traveled from her mouth to her neck.

"Yes, but when?" she dared to ask. "For Mr. Cruikshank's sake, I cannot think of anything so cruel as to delay the inevitable. Besides which, I fear that if we wait too long, you might be tempted to anticipate our marriage vows."

"As for temptation," he murmured as he moved his kisses back to her jaw, "isn't that a bit like shutting the stable door after the horse has bolted?"

As she submitted herself to another incursion of kisses, she thought that she rather agreed. Eventually, she remembered where they were and that there were those who doubtless wondered what had become of her. "I must go back."

"Yes, but I swear we shall not be long parted. When you arrive home, pack only what you think you will need for two or three days. We shall be free to purchase anything else you wish when it suits us. Be sure to write your mother a note; when you are certain all are sleeping, meet me at the area steps."

"Tonight?" she gasped.

"Yes, but only if you wish; it is an answer to all your troubles. And yet, if it seems to you that I am overhasty and you fear the worst, you have my word that you shall be married a maid."

"It is not that I fear," she insisted. "You have over and over again proved yourself worthy of my trust, though I must confess to being full of apprehension. It is only because of how it will pain those we leave behind. And yet, I feel it to be the scheme that best suits the purpose."

He took her hands and again kissed them. "Go to your mother and make some plausible excuse to depart at the first possible moment. I shall wait until you have entered the house; it would not do to be seen emerging from the shadows together. The small-minded will condemn you for our hasty marriage, but I shall not provide them with what they might see as proof of its needfulness."

With a last squeeze of his hands, she did as he said. They had not entered so far into the maze that she could not easily find her way out on her own and she had no trouble in finding the ballroom where it seemed light as day after time spent out in the night. As she moved along the row of chairs to join her mother, she realized that Mr. Cruikshank was nowhere to be seen.

"Mama, where is Mr. Cruikshank?" she asked, fearful that he had met with some accident.

"A better question might be to ask where you have been," her mother hissed.

"It is very hot in here," she demurred as she took her seat, "and I was in need of some air. It is a lovely night. However, we needs must find Mr. Cruikshank without delay. In which direction did he go?"

"You needn't be worried on that score; he has Katherine to guide him."

"But Mama, Katherine is seated just to the other side of Aunt Augusta."

Mrs. Armistead lifted her lorgnette to her spectacles and peered through them at Katherine. "I was persuaded you went with him, Kate."

"But of course I did, how else should he have found his way about? However, we ran into a gentleman of Mr. Cruikshank's acquaintance. They wished to converse and I did not, so I returned."

"Was it so very long ago, Kate, or have you just arrived?" Elizabeth asked as she twisted about in search of her betrothed.

"I have been here, in my seat, the better part of a quarter hour, I should think," Katherine mused.

"Very well, then, as long as he is with someone who can see to his welfare," Elizabeth replied. "Doubtless he shall be returned to us before long. However, Mama, once he arrives, I do believe it would be best if we return home. I find that going out with Mr. Cruikshank is rather trying and I am spent. Do you suppose the Scott-Montgomery's will be very offended?"

"I daresay they shan't notice we have gone," Aunt Augusta said. "It is such a squeeze here, tonight, I don't know if I can bear the heat, myself."

"And yet I am so enjoying myself," Mrs. Armistead said with a sigh.

"As none have thought to inquire of me, I shall leave you all in no doubt as to my feelings," Katherine expostulated. "Aside from Mr. Cruikshank and his friend, a man old enough to be my grandfather in spite of his leers, I haven't spoken to a single man. I am determined to stay and meet my future husband tonight!"

Elizabeth took a deep breath and considered her options. She might pretend to be overcome by the heat but rather doubted that the others would believe she had genuinely fainted for the second time in as many weeks. She felt that every passing minute was one that put her plans in jeopardy and she cast about for a compelling reason to quit the premises immediately. She turned around in her chair to ascertain whether or not Colin had returned to the room and was approached by a man who leaned over to whisper in her ear.

"Mr. Cruikshank is in need of assistance. Shall I lead you to him?"

"Yes, of course," Elizabeth replied. "Mama, I shan't be a moment. Mr. Cruikshank has been found and I am needed."

If only she were not.

Chapter Fifteen

olin watched Elizabeth move away through the shadows of the maze and quelled the desire to run after her. It was best that their flight was delayed for a few hours as there was much to be done in the meantime. He endured the time spent waiting in the maze by totting up a list of what he would need and what he must do before collecting his bride. First, he would need to find a footman to have his carriage brought round and then he would have the delightful task of informing his sister of his plans. The only prospect more ambrosial than marrying Elizabeth promised to be witnessing Analisa's joy when she heard the news.

When he finally stepped out of the hedges into the torch-lit garden, he was taken aback to find Mr. Cruikshank standing, quite alone, at the entrance to the maze. "May I help you find your way?" Colin asked.

"Who is that?" Mr. Cruikshank shifted from one foot to the other, his eyes dark and unreadable.

"It is Colin Lloyd-Jones. We met last night at Lady Augusta's dinner party."

"Ah, yes, I had hoped I might run into you. There are one or two things I should like to say to you without the ladies listening in."

Colin stifled his impatience and prepared to listen; it was the least he could do in light of his plans to run off with the man's intended wife. "I am at your disposal."

"I would thank you to take me arm and lead me to a more private locale. I shouldna like anyone to hear what I have to say and methinks you shall feel likewise."

"Very well," Colin said as he took the man's arm and led him into the maze. He suspected he would not like what the man had to say and agreed that it was best to hold their conversation where they were not likely to be overheard.

"I have only been returned to the presence of my beloved for a mere day," Mr. Cruikshank whined, "but already I have the impression that her love for me has waned. I canna tell you how it breaks my heart. Now, I could be wrong but I feel that you—along with your sister, o'course—have spent a good deal of time with Miss Armistead. I says to myself, if there is another man who has taken my place, Mr. Lloyd-Jones ought to know who he be."

"I daresay you are correct," Colin replied as he hastened his pace. Doubtless there would be a bench or two by the fountain in the center of the maze; the sooner they arrived the sooner he could safely abandon Mr. Cruikshank and send someone else to fetch him. "My sister and I have enjoyed a warm friendship with Miss Armistead. As for another man, I have seen no sign of one."

"With the exception of yourself, o'course."

"Of course. I believe she felt me to be harmless. The very day we met she learned that a friend and I had entered into a pact to avoid female entanglements for the season. As she was engaged to be married, I and my sister, for whom Miss Armistead felt an immediate affinity, took it upon ourselves to entertain her until you arrived."

"It sounds harmless enough and yet I canna like it. And then there is the fact of how it *felt*. How does it feel now?" he asked, coming to a halt and turning as if to look into Colin's eyes.

Colin supposed a lifetime of habits did not die simply through the loss of one's sight, but the unnerving stare to which he was treated was suspicious to say the least. Grateful that they had somehow stumbled upon the center of the maze, he led Mr. Cruikshank to the anticipated bench and settled him on the one to the far side of the fountain. "How I feel is of no consequence," Colin remarked as he moved away in preparation to make his escape into the maze.

"Why is that, Mr. Lloyd-Jones?" Mr. Cruikshank asked with a cock of his head.

"It is only Miss Armistead's feelings that you should take into account. I have nothing to say to the matter."

"But I think you do," Mr. Cruikshank said, rising to his feet. "Case in point: what is the meaning of the brooch that she wears? It contains a lock of hair that I am persuaded canna be mine."

"She wears a brooch, yes," Colin riposted, "but I daresay she would not have spoken of it to you. How can you know of it?" The solution that came to Colin's mind filled him with such rage that his hands balled into fists at his sides. "I cannot perceive why Miss Armistead should allow you a search of her person, sir!"

Mr. Cruikshank did not respond and Colin was forced to believe the worst. "I leave you now but I will send another to aid you in your return." He whirled around to re-enter the maze and had only taken a few steps when, to his great astonishment, he received a blow to the back of his head. It was not as injurious as it was painful and excessively perplexing.

He turned about to see Cruikshank prepared to strike him another blow with his cane. Colin felt his assailant to have been fortunate to land one blow, but he would be a pitiful specimen if he allowed Cruikshank to land a second. Dodging the blow that came, Colin moved round to place the fountain between him and the blind man. "Cruikshank, this is not a fight you can win."

"But I must, Mr. Lloyd-Jones for I cannot afford to lose," Cruikshank cried as he turned, his cane held aloft, and shambled in Colin's direction. "There are those who seek my life unless I make reparation. Who better to marry but the deeply feeling and enormously wealthy Miss Elizabeth Armistead?"

Colin was prepared for the blow from the cane but not the jab from Cruikshank's left hand. It caught Colin squarely under the jaw and sent him reeling from astonishment as much as pain. "Why is it that I begin to doubt you are as sightless as you let on to be?" Colin baited as he studied his options for escape.

"What is it that makes me think you are the man I've been lookin' for?" Cruikshank retorted.

Colin ignored the question. "She won't marry you, even if you do manage to best me in a bout of fisticuffs. I suggest you toss your cane away, however. It hardly seems sporting."

"And how sportin' shall it seem to Miss Armistead when she learns you have struck a blind man? Oh, no, I shall be needin' this cane to continue my deception. That is, directly after I darken your daylights."

"I implore you to make your best attempt," Colin said, edging his way around the fountain and back towards the exit. "She still will not marry you."

"You think not? Do you not yet perceive? I'll let nothing stop me from getting my hands on that money. It wasn't the rain that landed me under that bridge; it were those to whom I owe my debts. They dared not get near me whilst I was in hospital; feigning blindness was a useful ploy and for more than one reason. But I never did claim to be deaf. It is amazing what you can manage to overhear when everyone pays you no heed. Later tonight, when the lovely miss meets you at the area steps, it shall be me who waits for her and the matter will be settled, once and for all."

Colin could hardly credit the meaning of Cruikshank's words. That he had stood by and listened to their private tete a tete made Colin sick to his stomach. That Cruikshank intended to fetch Elizabeth in Colin's place infuriated him. He was upon Cruikshank in a flash and had landed a punch to his nose before he had a chance to react. The torches that blazed at each corner of the area illuminated the dark stream that issued forth from Cruikshank's nostrils. He swung, but Colin evaded it and landed another blow to the side of Cruikshank's eye. He retreated; Colin supposed Cruikshank had gotten the measure of the situation and found himself wanting. The two of them glowered at one another, each equidistant to the exit closest to the house.

Suddenly, Mr. Cruikshank pulled a flaming torch from the ground and with a mighty roar charged Colin. There was nothing for Colin to do but fall back, back against the stone that formed the fountain itself. The last his eyes beheld was the face of his adversary glowing with rage in the light of the torch. And then it all went black.

Colin noted that the night was very cold. And wet. He must have gone walking out in the rain without his hat and coat. His hands were freezing, as well. He wondered why he had gone to bed without first drying out by the fire. He was sure to acquire a nasty cold. Perhaps he had already; his head hurt like the devil and he was stiff all over. A light penetrated through his closed lids and he thought it odd that he would not have blown out the bedside candle.

Opening his eyes, he attempted to make sense of the flame that hovered close to his face; too close. He moved to sit up and realized that he was not lying down so much as sprawling, half in and half out, of a fountain of water. With a jerk of surprise, he rolled off it onto the grass and contemplated the stars in the sky. He couldn't, for the life of him, remember how he had gotten outside. He had been in his bed only moments ago. His gaze shifted to the flame of light and he realized it was much too large to belong to any bedside candle. To his surprise, there were more of them, one in each corner of the area around the fountain. And then he remembered: Elizabeth was in danger!

He shot up from the ground in a move that would have impressed even Tony though it left Colin dizzy and faint. He would be sure not to allow Tony to perceive such weakness, only, he was not the enemy. Colin rubbed the knot on the back of his head whilst he cudgeled his brain for a thought that made sense. The only potential action that was immediately apparent was that he must find his way out of the hedges. He stumbled about, his footing becoming surer as the fog cleared from his mind, and found his way out of the shadows. When he beheld the dark house and the moonlit garden, he remembered all.

He surmised that his carriage should yet stand somewhere on the premises, however, he hadn't time to hunt round the back of the house for it, nor to hitch up the horses. It was clear that the guests had dispersed and the night well gone. If he were to apprehend Elizabeth and her abductor, he must find a fresh horse. He ran past the house to the back and found a likely looking building sure to contain a horse, perhaps even one of his own, and could not believe his eyes when a saddled horse cantered into view. It was followed by a man, hugely drunk and objecting vociferously, stuck in the reins by the ankle and being dragged along the ground.

"Pardon me, Sir, but I have a most pressing need for this horse," Colin explained as he freed the man and swung himself up into the saddle. "I cannot promise it shall be returned but if you present yourself at Lloyd-Jones House on Berkeley Square, my father will reimburse you." He rather doubted the man followed a word of what Colin said, but that could not be helped; an innocent maid was about to suffer at the hands of a scoundrel of the worst kind and Colin was having none of it.

Having little idea of the actual hour, he rode at breakneck speed for Lady Augusta's townhouse in hopes that he would arrive before Cruikshank. However, once he had attained his goal, he hadn't any more idea if Elizabeth were still in the house or if she had been deceived by her would-be captor. Colin ran down the area steps and made certain that she was not waiting in the shadows with her bags. When he saw that she was not, he banged on the kitchen door in hopes that the boot boy would not be too frightened to answer.

Once again, Colin was blessed with good fortune.

"What is it, Gov'?" the drowsy boot boy asked. "Is London burnin' or wot?"

"No, child, something far worse. Go and fetch the butler and then wake the groom and have him hitch up the freshest horses, mind you, to the speediest carriage and be quick about it!"

The boy was off with gratifying speed and Colin sank onto the bench by the low-banked fire to wait. He thought on the irony of his situation; Miss Ponsonby had been deceived just the same by the man who ruined her; Julian, Lord Trevelin. Colin had been unwilling to marry the unfortunate young lady when he learned of her plight. Surely the abduction of Elizabeth might be perceived as a punishment from above for his lack of devotion to Miss Ponsonby.

With firm resolve, he took himself in hand; the first order of business was to determine whether or not Elizabeth was still in the house. There came a clatter from the passage and he sprang to his feet as the boot boy and a man in a nightcap barreled into the room.

"Sir, what is the meaning of this?" the man demanded.

"Is Miss Armistead above stairs?" Colin asked as patiently as he could. "Hold, boy," he called as the boot boy streaked past on his way out to the mews. "Did you see Miss Armistead leave the house by way of the kitchen door tonight?"

"No, Gov'!"

"Do be certain! She might have sworn you to secrecy, I know, but it was me she was to meet outside, only, she is not there. I fear someone means her harm," he said, turning to the butler. "I must know if she is yet in her room!"

The butler's eyes grew round, doubtless appalled at whom her rescuer should be. Colin imagined he made a fearsome picture, bruised and bleeding as he suspected he must be, his clothing wet and the knees of his trousers stained with grass. And, yet, to Colin's vast relief, the butler chose to put his faith in him.

"Go and have the carriage readied!" the butler shouted to the boot boy and hastened out to the passage with his candle held high. Colin took a lighted lantern from the table and ran after the butler who ascended two flights of stairs at impressive speed. When he threw open Elizabeth's chamber door, Colin thrust the butler aside and held the lantern up to shine on the bed. It was empty. The room had been turned out, clothes and belongings draped across every surface. There on her pillow was the note addressed to 'Mama'.

She was gone. He could hardly believe it was true and was grateful that he had already determined what was to be done next. "Unless they have already been wakened by the noise," he instructed the butler, "let the ladies sleep. They can find the note in the morning; it contains better news than the truth. I shall go and fetch her back before they know anything is amiss."

"Yes, sir," the butler said with a bow that sent his nightcap askew and was all the more ridiculous in that it was performed with precision in a nightshirt and slippers.

Colin raced through the house and prayed that the carriage had been brought round. To his joy, it appeared at the corner of the square and he ran to meet it. "Are you up for a wild ride?" he inquired of the groom. "There is a great deal of money in it for you."

"Yes, Gov'! Where are we off to?"

"Gretna Green!" Colin shouted. He vaulted into the carriage as it clattered off and fell to pondering on his choices. He knew a single rider would have been faster, but Elizabeth could hardly be brought home on the back of a horse. With luck, Cruikshank would assume he was safe from pursuit and would be taking his time. The thought brought fresh horrors to mind, however, and Colin decided it was best to dwell on other matters.

The subject of his wedding seemed a suitable alternative. Now that Elizabeth need no longer consider Mr. Cruikshank's feelings, an elopement seemed too far beyond the pale. They would be married in church and Elizabeth would have the wedding of which she had always dreamed. His thoughts took a new direction when he heard the crack of the whip. As the carriage lurched and surged ahead, he recalled that he had allowed himself to become lost in contemplation.

Putting his head out of the window, he surveyed the landscape in hopes of spotting a carriage on the road ahead and was appalled to see a tiny figure as it toiled along the verge. The child was loaded down with baggage and he wondered what sort of devil would turn anyone out onto the road in the dead of night. It wasn't until the carriage pulled closer that the truth dawned on him; the devil was Cruikshank.

"Faster!" he shouted to the driver as he banged on the side of the carriage. Whether or not the driver heard him Colin could not say, but the groom cracked the whip and the horses quickened their pace. Colin returned his attention to whom he prayed was Elizabeth and perceived how she struggled with her bags. At last she abandoned them and began to run.

"Elizabeth, stop, I am coming for you!" he shouted but the air as it rushed past the carriage tore his words away. He fretted as to whether or not she was able to ascertain his identity and decided it hardly mattered; she would know soon enough.

When they had drawn near enough to her that the groom found it needful to rein in the horses, Colin jumped out of the carriage and ran to meet her. "Elizabeth!" he cried and she dashed into his arms, laughing and crying all at once.

"Oh, Colin! I believed him to be you! How he knew to be there, I don't know, it doesn't matter," she said, shaking her head, "as long as you believe that I would never have willingly gone with him!"

"Shush, my darling, it's quite all right," he soothed, torn by the desire to laugh at her artlessness and his wish to ease her fears. "Of course you thought it was me. The groom is collecting your things and then we shall go home."

She melted against him and he cradled her close until her trembling ceased, whereupon he lifted her in his arms and carried her to the safety of the carriage. Once inside, he thought to lay her on the opposite bench but she clung to him so that he could not separate her from his grasp. It was just as well; he would enjoy the return journey far more with her in his lap.

Gradually, she began to stir and he found he was full of questions. "You need fear no reprisals from me, Elizabeth, however, I find I am all agog to learn how it was that I found you trudging down the road."

"Why, because I wanted to get away from him, that is why!" she huffed. "I had thought you would heartily approve."

"Oh, I do, have no doubt on that score. Only, it seems an odd sort of abduction when the villain allows his booty to go free."

"Yes, well," she said in a small voice, "he was not any more eager to be in my company as I was to be in his."

"Now, there is a statement that might give me cause to doubt," he said lightly in spite of the darker questions that had begun to crowd his mind.

"Oh, but if you had seen him with that leer on his face, you would know how very determined I was to get away from him. When he attempted to kiss me, I pulled at his hair and thrashed about so that he released me."

Colin willed himself to be very still as he asked, in a voice far calmer than he felt, "So, he did *not* kiss you?"

"He did, in the beginning. He wore a cape with a hood which is how I failed to realize it was not you from the start. But when he kissed me, I knew it could not be you. As you promised, it was not the same, not in the least! I pulled back the hood and when I saw his face, I screamed loud enough to wake the dead. They would have been more welcome," she added wryly. "He then insisted that his life was in danger and that he was in great need of money. It was when I threw my jewel box at his head that he had the carriage stopped and I wasted no time in getting out with all that I could carry."

"Then you are . . unharmed?" Colin asked, hardly believing it could be true.

"Of course I am. Can you not see for yourself? Oh, but I see that *you* have had some sort of accident," she murmured as she ran her fingers over his bruised jaw.

Resisting the sudden urge to order the coachman back to Gretna Green and a speedy marriage, Colin emptied his budget on the altercation by the fountain.

"Then you knew before I did that Mr. Cruikshank is not blind. Oh, and there is no farm. His mother is hale and hearty and lives in Dundee."

"I must confess I had my suspicions as to the farm. How I wish that you had learned the truth from my own lips. But you are safe, now, and in my arms, and that is more than I had a mere twenty four hours ago."

Rather than reply, she closed her eyes and was so silent for so long that he thought she must have again fallen asleep. The glow of the carriage lanterns lent enough light to allow him to feast on her almond shaped eyes, cream and peaches complexion and cherry red lips. The longing to kiss her grew into a nearly intolerable need, but he dared not take any action that might remind her of the trauma she had endured.

Suddenly, she opened her eyes and looked directly up into his. "You have not yet kissed me. I walked miles in the dark of night with one thing to bear me up, the thought of your kiss when you found me," she said in a low voice as she stroked his face with her fingers. "I pray that you are not repulsed by the thought of his lips on mine."

Colin, refusing to be tempted by her caress, gently pulled her hand away. "I confess I ardently wish he hadn't touched you, but it is a small concern compared to what might have been."

"And yet, we are headed back to town. I had thought you meant to marry me as soon as may be."

"Is that what you believe? That I no longer wish to marry you?" he asked, aghast.

"I have heard it bruited about that Miss Ponsonby was abducted and ruined during the course of a carriage ride. Is that not why you refused to marry her and cried off?"

"Well, yes," he said, nonplussed, "but her story hardly compares to yours."

"Why not? Because he merely kissed me?"

"No, because I love you! Elizabeth, you don't truly believe that if he had taken more from you than a kiss, I should no longer wish you to be my wife?"

She looked away and the long sweep of her lashes against her cheek was like a poem. "I thought I was certain when I saw that it was you who had come after me."

He kissed her then, not because he wanted to—most desperately—but to reassure her that there would never come a day when he didn't wish to—most desperately. Her lips clung to his with a sense of urgency she had never before made evident, until, at last, she lay back her head. "Oh, Colin," she said on a sigh, "do tell the groom to turn about for Gretna."

"How can I?" he asked even as he wondered at his determination. "Now that you are to be my wife, I must look to your reputation. You are a virtuous young woman and I will not allow any gossip that says otherwise. The banns shall be read, the invitations shall go out, and a new wedding gown ordered, one as different from the last as you can conceive of. We shall then be married in church with the proper witnesses including your dearest friend, your aunt and your mother, and Cook shall prepare our wedding breakfast."

"And the painting?" She looked up at him in mock severity, but the stars in her eyes told the truth as to her actual feelings.

"It shall hang in its place of honor for the rest of our days," he insisted, smiling at her in that way he suspected caused her palpitations of the heart.

She smiled and, sighing deeply, closed her eyes. "Is that all?"

"No; we shall honeymoon at my family's estate in Shropshire for a long as you wish. It is set in a little valley of green hills and is full to bursting with windows that look out onto spectacular gardens, the likes of which you have never seen."

She opened her eyes wide. "Is there a maze of hedges?"

"Indeed, there is," he said as he stroked her cheek. "If you like, we shall find the center of it the moment we arrive. At length, when you have become restless, we shall board ship for a land shrouded in mystery. Something tells me you should like to introduce your father to that paragon of virtue you spoke of earlier tonight."

"Truly? You would take me to India?" she cried, her eyes misty with tears of joy.

"Yes, my darling, I would."

"Oh, can it be? You can't possibly know how I have longed to introduce you to all of its beauties!"

"Yes, but only once you," he murmured, lowering his lips to hers, "have introduced me to all of yours."

Made in the USA
Coppell, TX
12 December 2022

88981237R00128